DISNEY

FROZEN

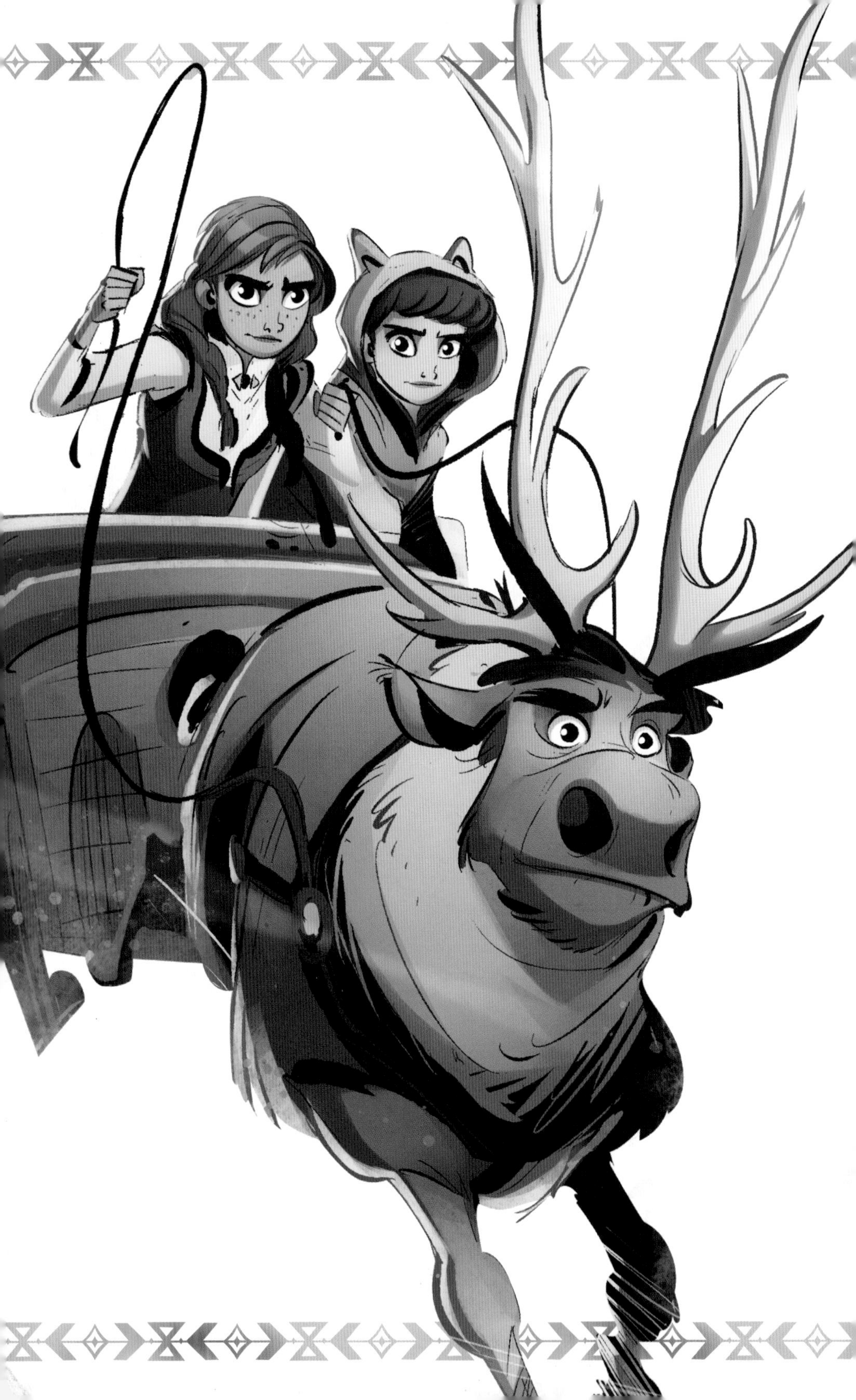

DISNEY FROZEN

BREAKING BOUNDARIES

STORY & SCRIPT BY
JOE CARAMAGNA

ART BY
KAWAII CREATIVE STUDIOS

LETTERING BY
RICHARD STARKINGS AND
COMICRAFT'S JIMMY BETANCOURT

COVER ART BY
KAWAII CREATIVE STUDIOS

DARK HORSE BOOKS

DARK HORSE BOOKS

PRESIDENT AND PUBLISHER
MIKE RICHARDSON

EDITOR
FREDDYE MILLER

DESIGNER
SARAH TERRY

ASSISTANT EDITORS
JUDY KHUU, JENNY BLENK, KEVIN BURKHALTER

DIGITAL ART TECHNICIAN
CHRISTIANNE GILLENARDO-GOUDREAU

Neil Hankerson Executive Vice President **Tom Weddle** Chief Financial Officer **Randy Stradley** Vice President of Publishing **Nick McWhorter** Chief Business Development Officer **Dale LaFountain** Chief Information Officer **Matt Parkinson** Vice President of Marketing **Cara Niece** Vice President of Production and Scheduling **Mark Bernardi** Vice President of Book Trade and Digital Sales **Ken Lizzi** General Counsel **Dave Marshall** Editor in Chief **Davey Estrada** Editorial Director **Chris Warner** Senior Books Editor **Cary Grazzini** Director of Specialty Projects **Lia Ribacchi** Art Director **Vanessa Todd-Holmes** Director of Print Purchasing **Matt Dryer** Director of Digital Art and Prepress **Michael Gombos** Director of International Publishing and Licensing **Kari Yadro** Director of Custom Programs **Kari Torson** Director of International Licensing

DISNEY PUBLISHING WORLDWIDE GLOBAL MAGAZINES, COMICS AND PARTWORKS

PUBLISHER Lynn Waggoner • EDITORIAL TEAM Bianca Coletti (Director, Magazines), Guido Frazzini (Director, Comics), Carlotta Quattrocolo (Executive Editor), Stefano Ambrosio (Executive Editor, New IP), Camilla Vedove (Senior Manager, Editorial Development), Behnoosh Khalili (Senior Editor), Julie Dorris (Senior Editor), Mina Riazi (Assistant Editor), Jonathan Manning (Assistant Editor) • DESIGN Enrico Soave (Senior Designer) • ART Ken Shue (VP, Global Art), Manny Mederos (Senior Illustration Manager, Comics and Magazines), Roberto Santillo (Creative Director), Marco Ghiglione (Creative Manager), Stefano Attardi (Computer Art Designer) • PORTFOLIO MANAGEMENT Olivia Ciancarelli (Director) • BUSINESS & MARKETING Mariantonietta Galla (Marketing Manager), Virpi Korhonen (Editorial Manager)

DISNEY FROZEN: BREAKING BOUNDARIES

Published by Dark Horse Books
A division of Dark Horse Comics, Inc.
10956 SE Main Street, Milwaukie, OR 97222

DarkHorse.com

To find a comics shop in your area, visit comicshoplocator.com

First edition: January 2019 | ISBN 978-1-50671-051-8
Digital ISBN 978-1-50671-058-7

1 3 5 7 9 10 8 6 4 2
Printed in China

WELCOME TO ARENDELLE!

ELSA

The queen of the kingdom of Arendelle and Anna's older sister. Elsa has the ability to create snow and ice. She is confident, composed, creative, and warmhearted.

ANNA

The princess of Arendelle and Elsa's younger sister. Anna has faith in others and puts a positive spin on every situation. She is compassionate, fearless, and doesn't shy away from following her heart—no matter what.

OLAF

A snowman that Elsa brought to life. Olaf is a friend to all! He likes warm hugs and he is full of wonder and optimism—nothing can bring him down.

KRISTOFF

An ice harvester and the official ice master and deliverer of Arendelle. Raised by trolls in the mountains, he understands the importance of friends, family, and being true to yourself. He lives with his reindeer Sven.

SVEN

A reindeer and loyal best friend to Kristoff. They have regular conversations, and though Sven cannot communicate in words, sometimes Kristoff speaks for him. He enjoys carrots and lichen.

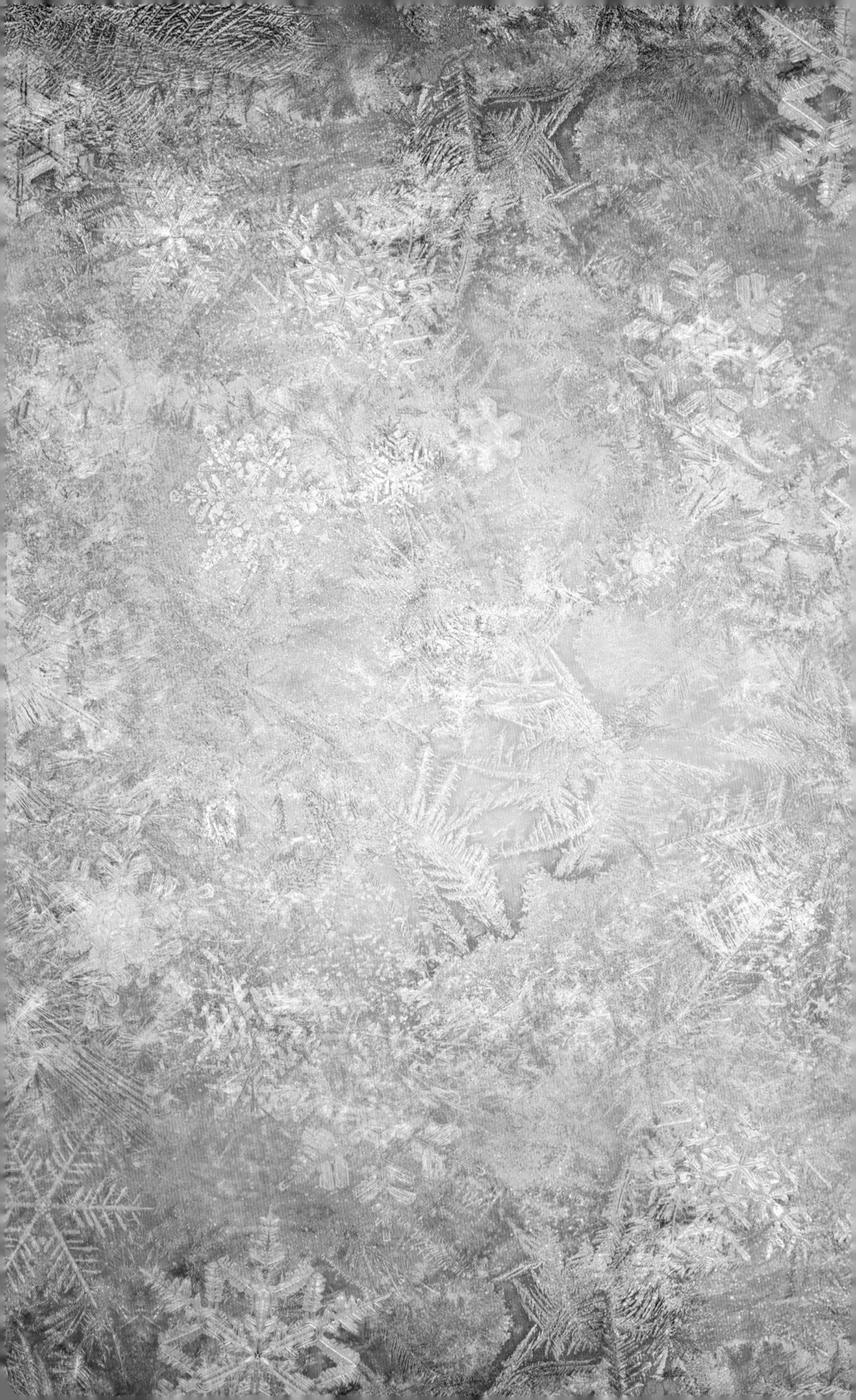

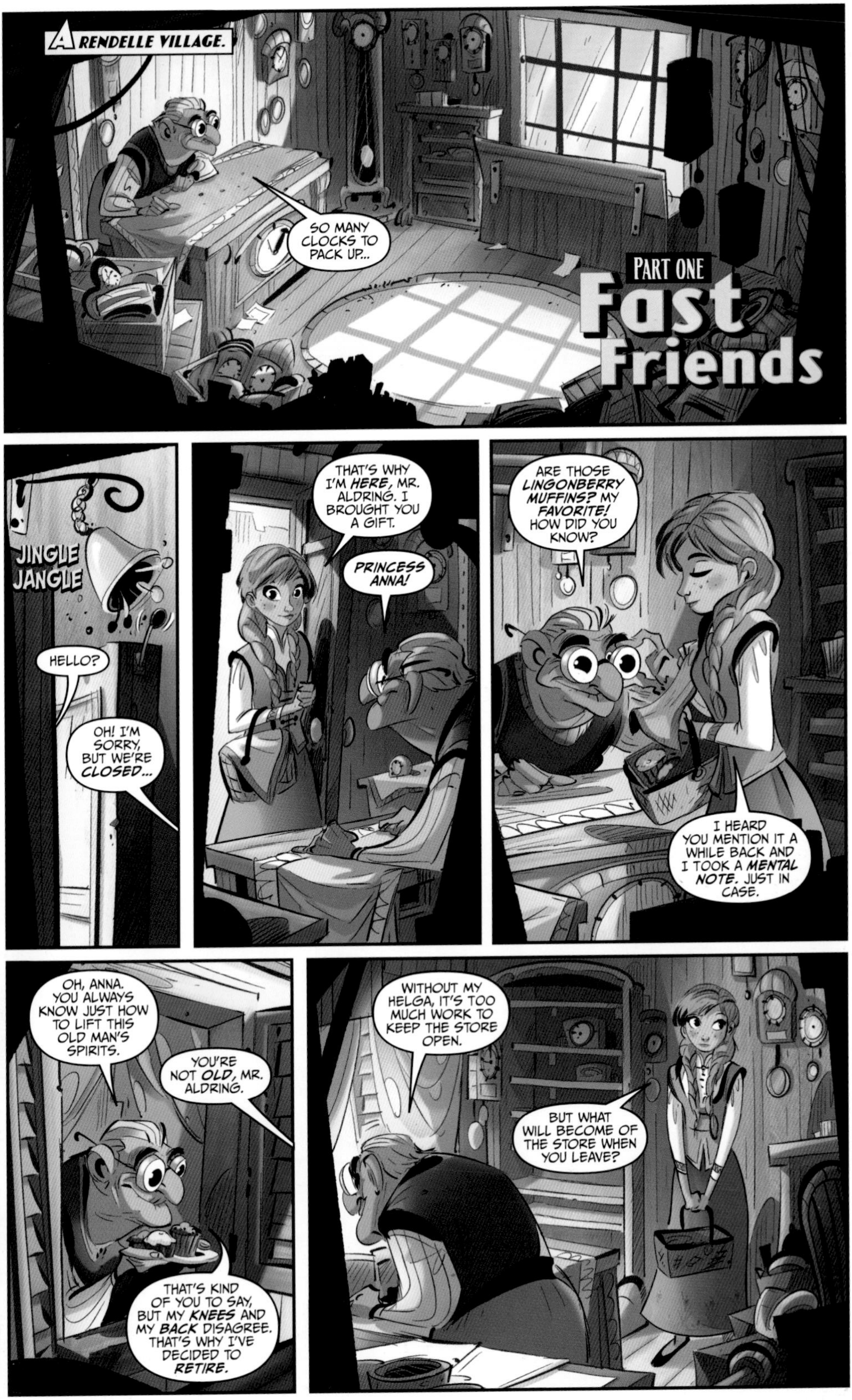
ARENDELLE VILLAGE.
SO MANY CLOCKS TO PACK UP...
PART ONE
Fast Friends
JINGLE JANGLE
HELLO?
OH! I'M SORRY, BUT WE'RE CLOSED...
THAT'S WHY I'M HERE, MR. ALDRING. I BROUGHT YOU A GIFT.
PRINCESS ANNA!
ARE THOSE LINGONBERRY MUFFINS? MY FAVORITE! HOW DID YOU KNOW?
I HEARD YOU MENTION IT A WHILE BACK AND I TOOK A MENTAL NOTE. JUST IN CASE.
OH, ANNA. YOU ALWAYS KNOW JUST HOW TO LIFT THIS OLD MAN'S SPIRITS.
YOU'RE NOT OLD, MR. ALDRING.
THAT'S KIND OF YOU TO SAY, BUT MY KNEES AND MY BACK DISAGREE. THAT'S WHY I'VE DECIDED TO RETIRE.
WITHOUT MY HELGA, IT'S TOO MUCH WORK TO KEEP THE STORE OPEN.
BUT WHAT WILL BECOME OF THE STORE WHEN YOU LEAVE?

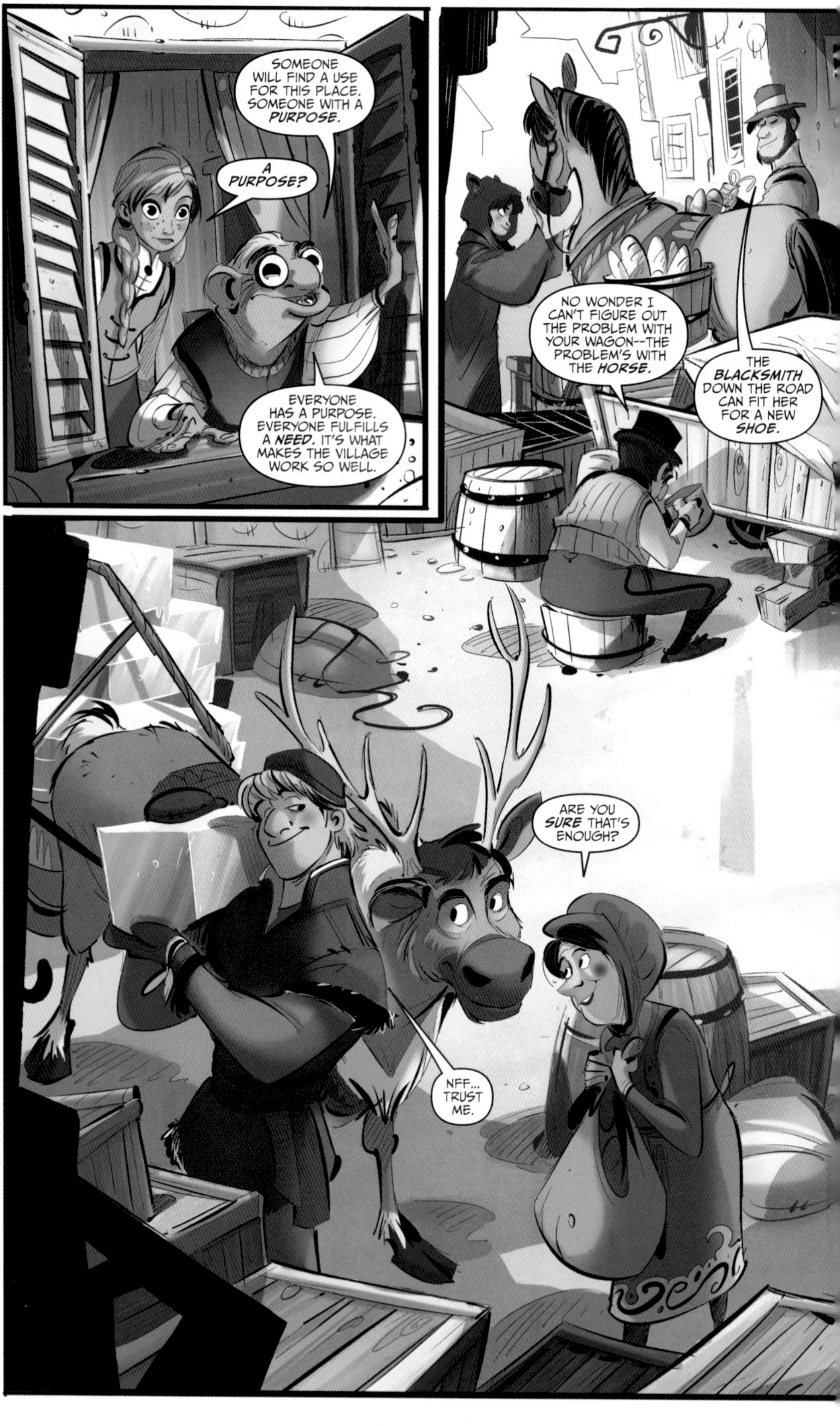

SOMEONE WILL FIND A USE FOR THIS PLACE. SOMEONE WITH A *PURPOSE.*
A *PURPOSE?*
EVERYONE HAS A PURPOSE. EVERYONE FULFILLS A *NEED.* IT'S WHAT MAKES THE VILLAGE WORK SO WELL.
NO WONDER I CAN'T FIGURE OUT THE PROBLEM WITH YOUR WAGON--THE PROBLEM'S WITH THE *HORSE.*
THE *BLACKSMITH* DOWN THE ROAD CAN FIT HER FOR A NEW *SHOE.*
ARE YOU *SURE* THAT'S ENOUGH?
NFF... TRUST ME.

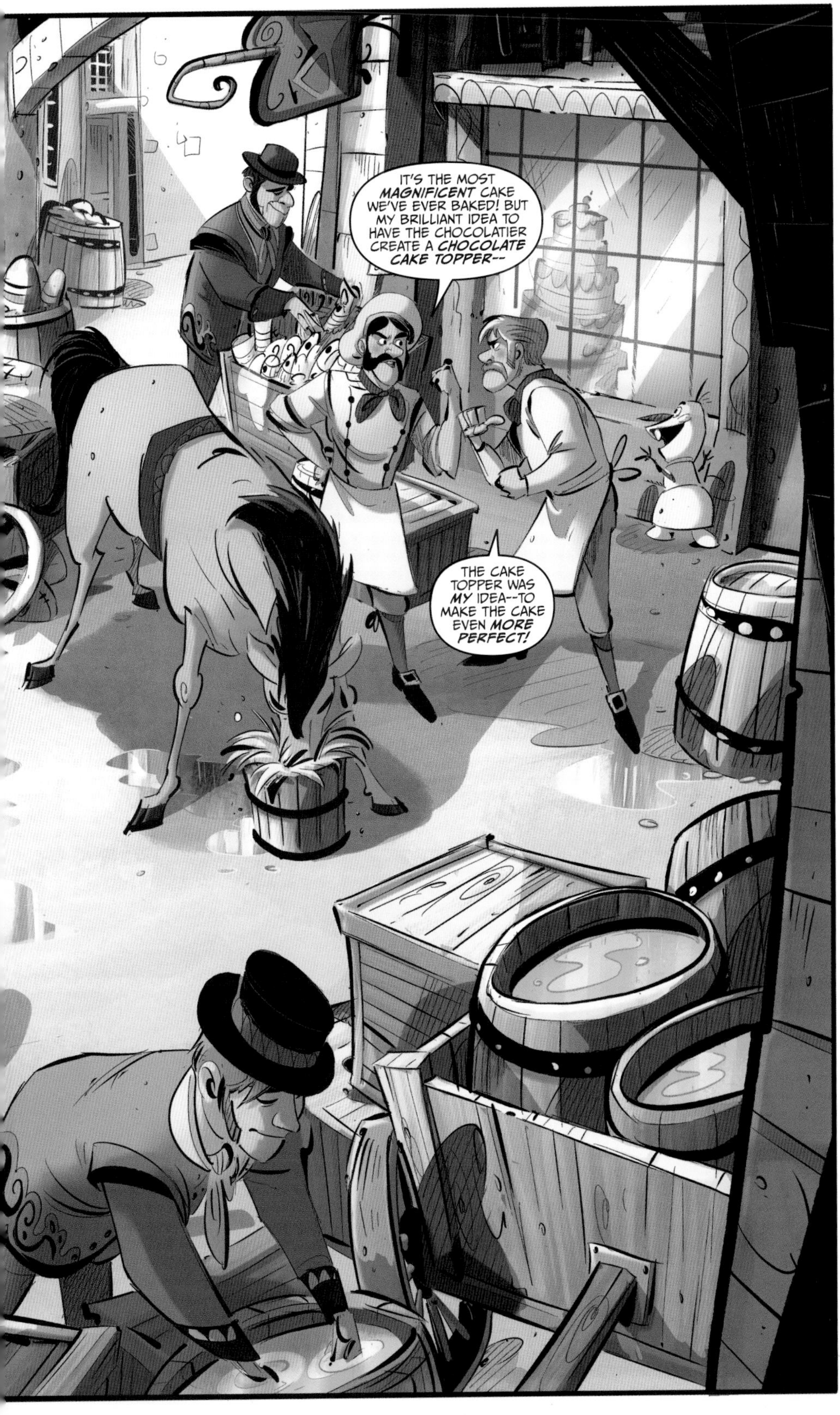

IT'S THE MOST MAGNIFICENT CAKE WE'VE EVER BAKED! BUT MY BRILLIANT IDEA TO HAVE THE CHOCOLATIER CREATE A CHOCOLATE CAKE TOPPER--
THE CAKE TOPPER WAS MY IDEA--TO MAKE THE CAKE EVEN MORE PERFECT!

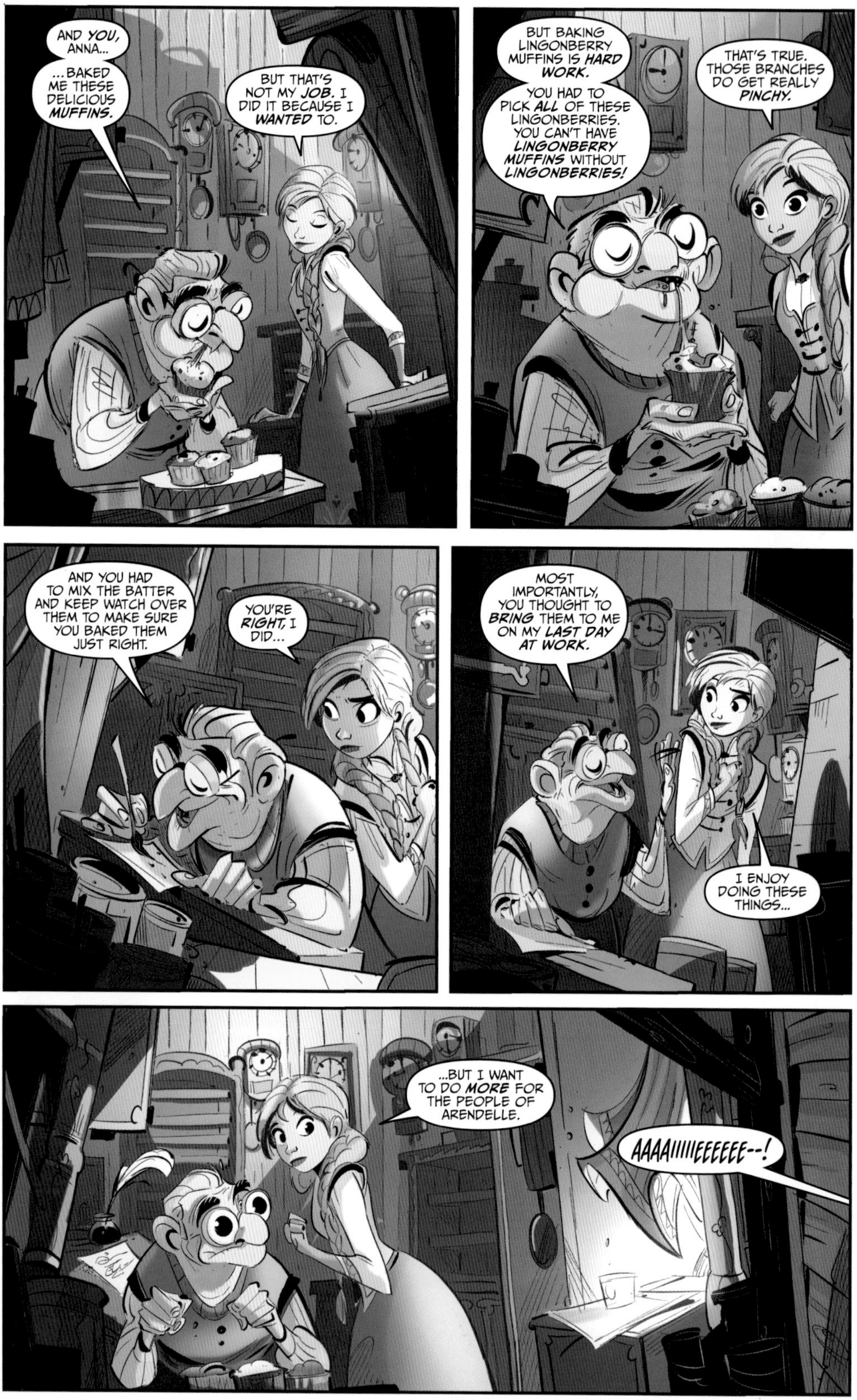
AND *YOU,* ANNA...
...BAKED ME THESE DELICIOUS *MUFFINS.*
BUT THAT'S NOT MY *JOB.* I DID IT BECAUSE I *WANTED* TO.
BUT BAKING LINGONBERRY MUFFINS IS *HARD WORK.*
YOU HAD TO PICK *ALL* OF THESE LINGONBERRIES. YOU CAN'T HAVE *LINGONBERRY MUFFINS* WITHOUT *LINGONBERRIES!*
THAT'S TRUE. THOSE BRANCHES DO GET REALLY *PINCHY.*
AND YOU HAD TO MIX THE BATTER AND KEEP WATCH OVER THEM TO MAKE SURE YOU BAKED THEM JUST RIGHT.
YOU'RE *RIGHT,* I DID...
MOST IMPORTANTLY, YOU THOUGHT TO *BRING* THEM TO ME ON MY *LAST DAY AT WORK.*
I ENJOY DOING THESE THINGS...
...BUT I WANT TO DO *MORE* FOR THE PEOPLE OF ARENDELLE.
AAAAIIIIIEEEEEE--!

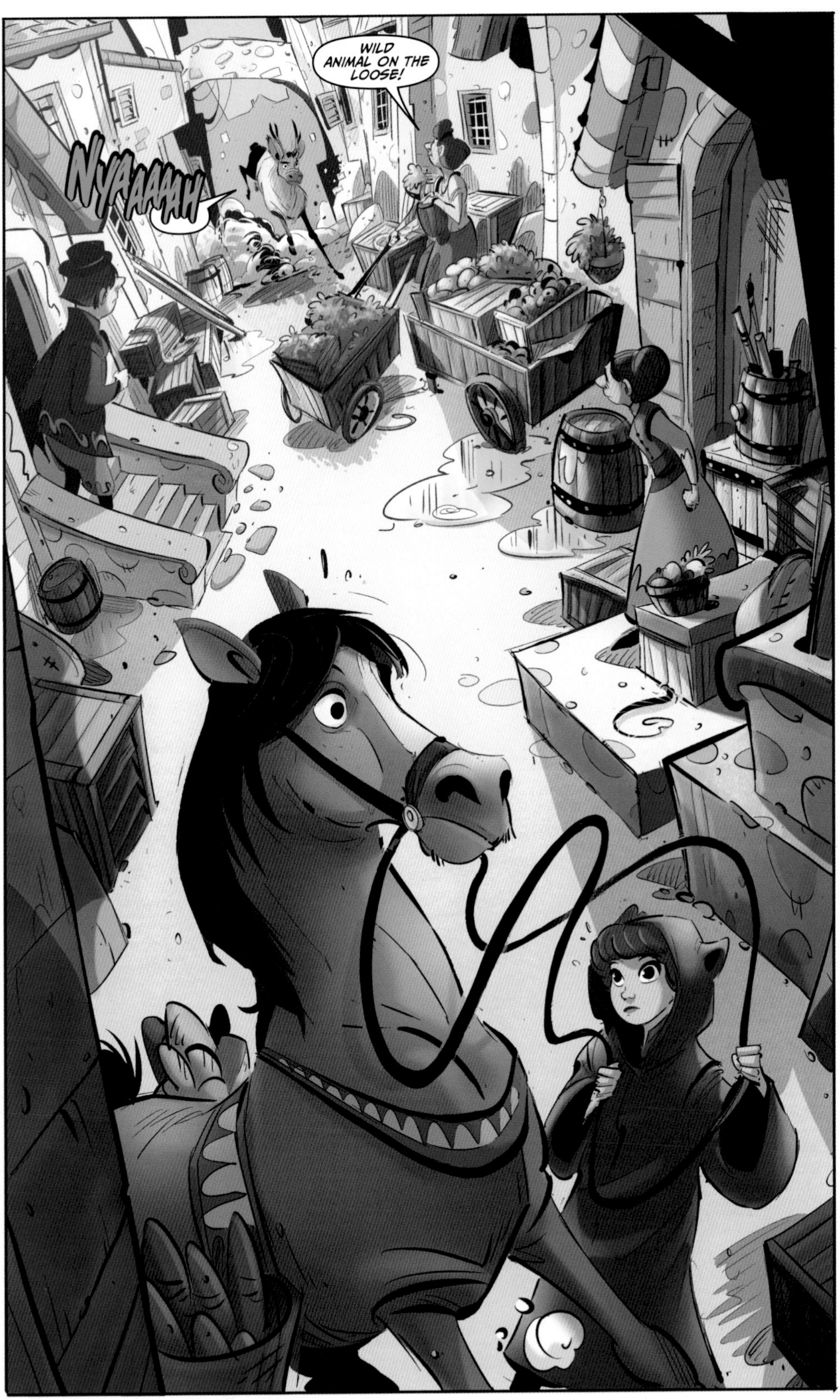
NYAAAAH
WILD ANIMAL ON THE LOOSE!

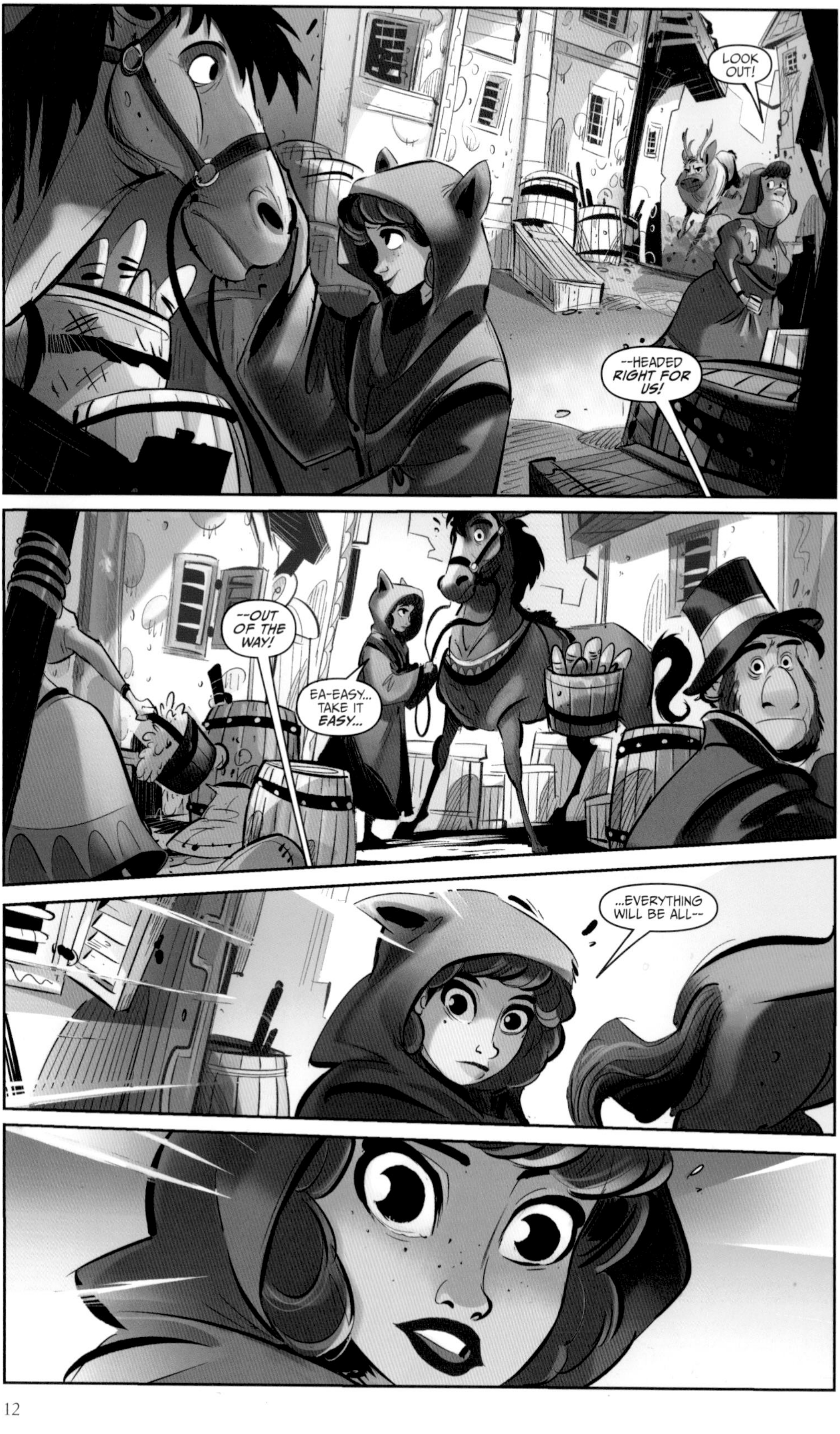
LOOK OUT!
--HEADED RIGHT FOR US!
--OUT OF THE WAY!
EA-EASY... TAKE IT EASY...
...EVERYTHING WILL BE ALL--

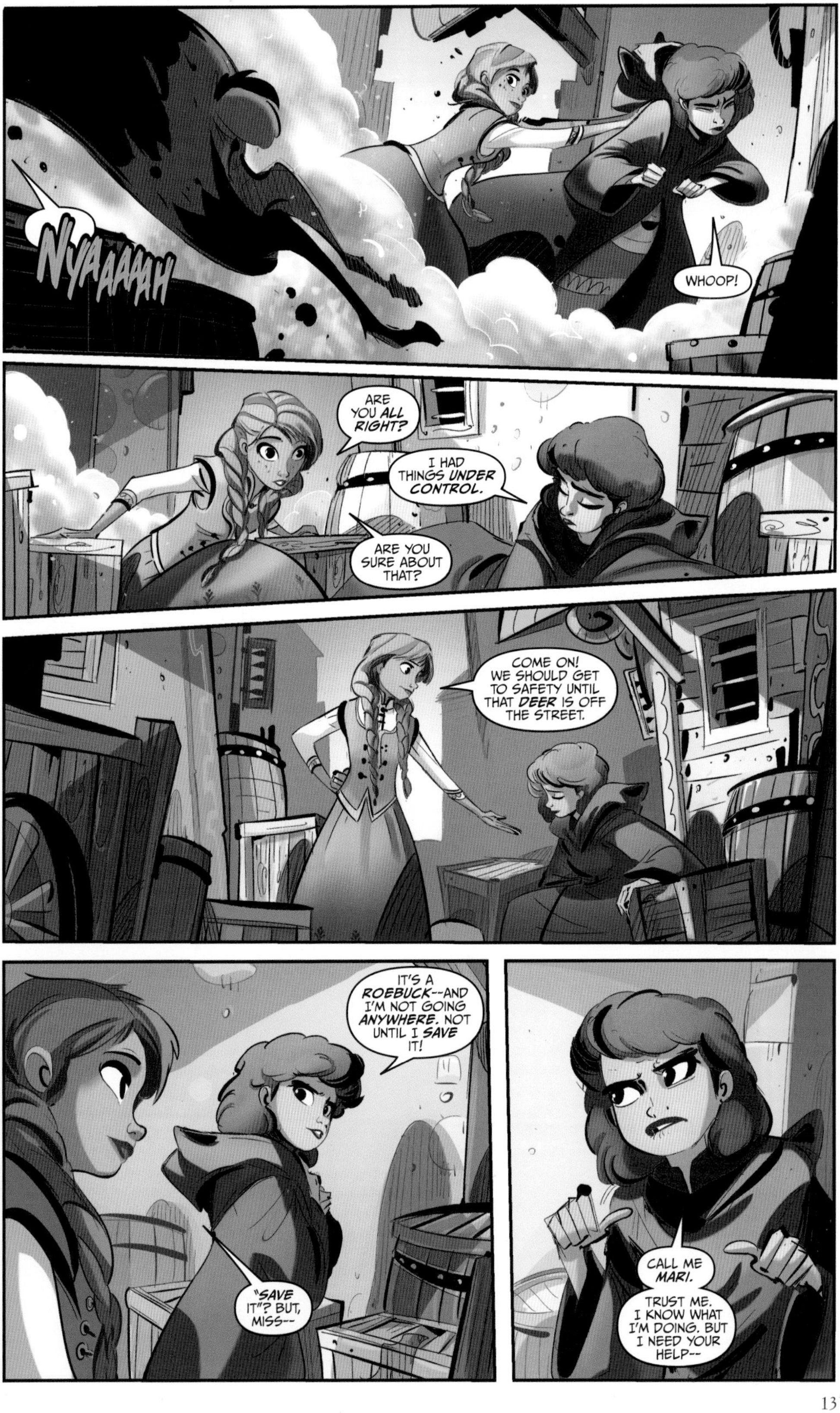
NYAAAAAH
WHOOP!
ARE YOU ALL RIGHT?
I HAD THINGS UNDER CONTROL.
ARE YOU SURE ABOUT THAT?
COME ON! WE SHOULD GET TO SAFETY UNTIL THAT DEER IS OFF THE STREET.
IT'S A ROEBUCK--AND I'M NOT GOING ANYWHERE. NOT UNTIL I SAVE IT!
"SAVE IT"? BUT, MISS--
CALL ME MARI.
TRUST ME. I KNOW WHAT I'M DOING. BUT I NEED YOUR HELP--

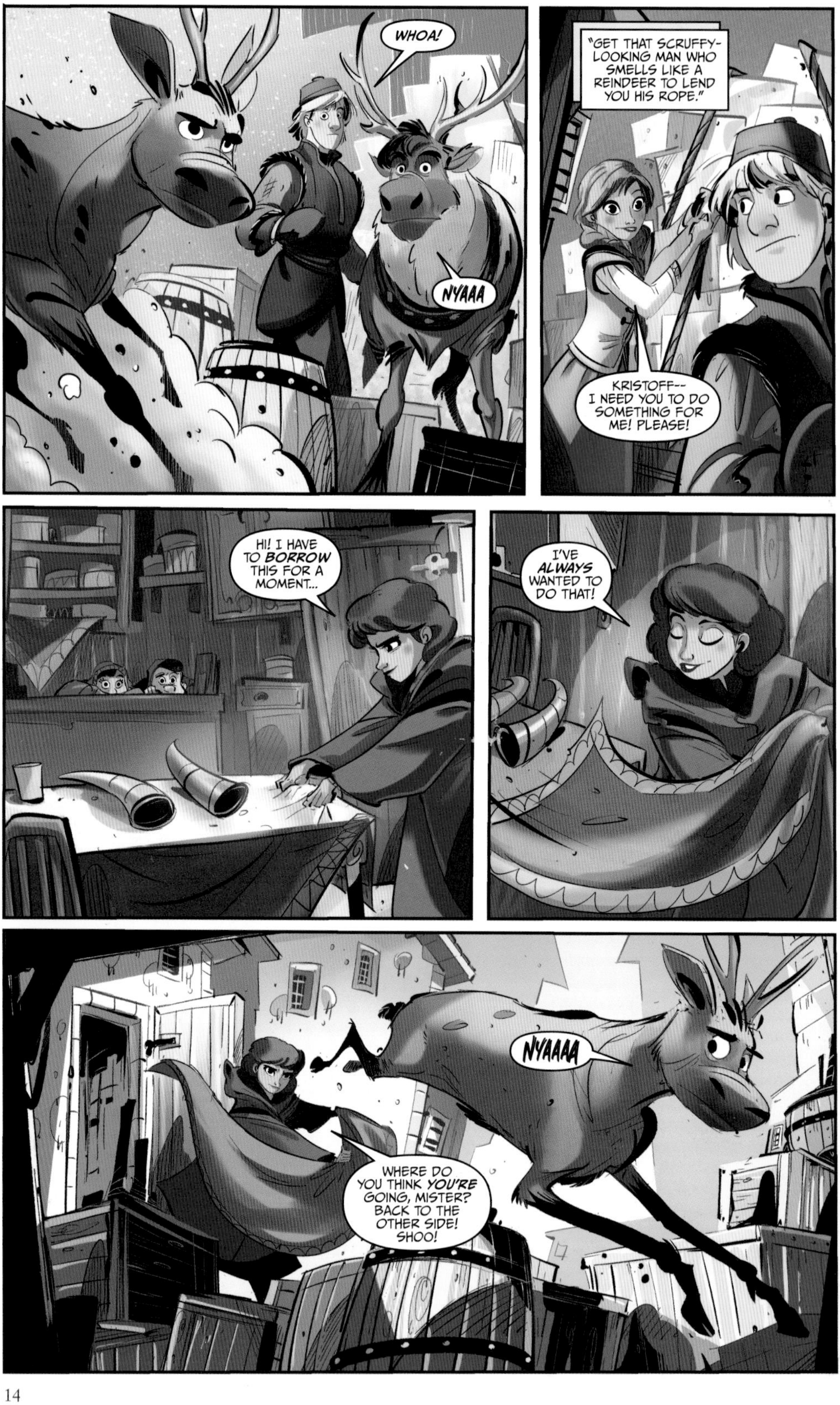
WHOA!
NYAAA
"GET THAT SCRUFFY-LOOKING MAN WHO SMELLS LIKE A REINDEER TO LEND YOU HIS ROPE."
KRISTOFF-- I NEED YOU TO DO SOMETHING FOR ME! PLEASE!
HI! I HAVE TO BORROW THIS FOR A MOMENT...
I'VE ALWAYS WANTED TO DO THAT!
NYAAAA
WHERE DO YOU THINK YOU'RE GOING, MISTER? BACK TO THE OTHER SIDE! SHOO!

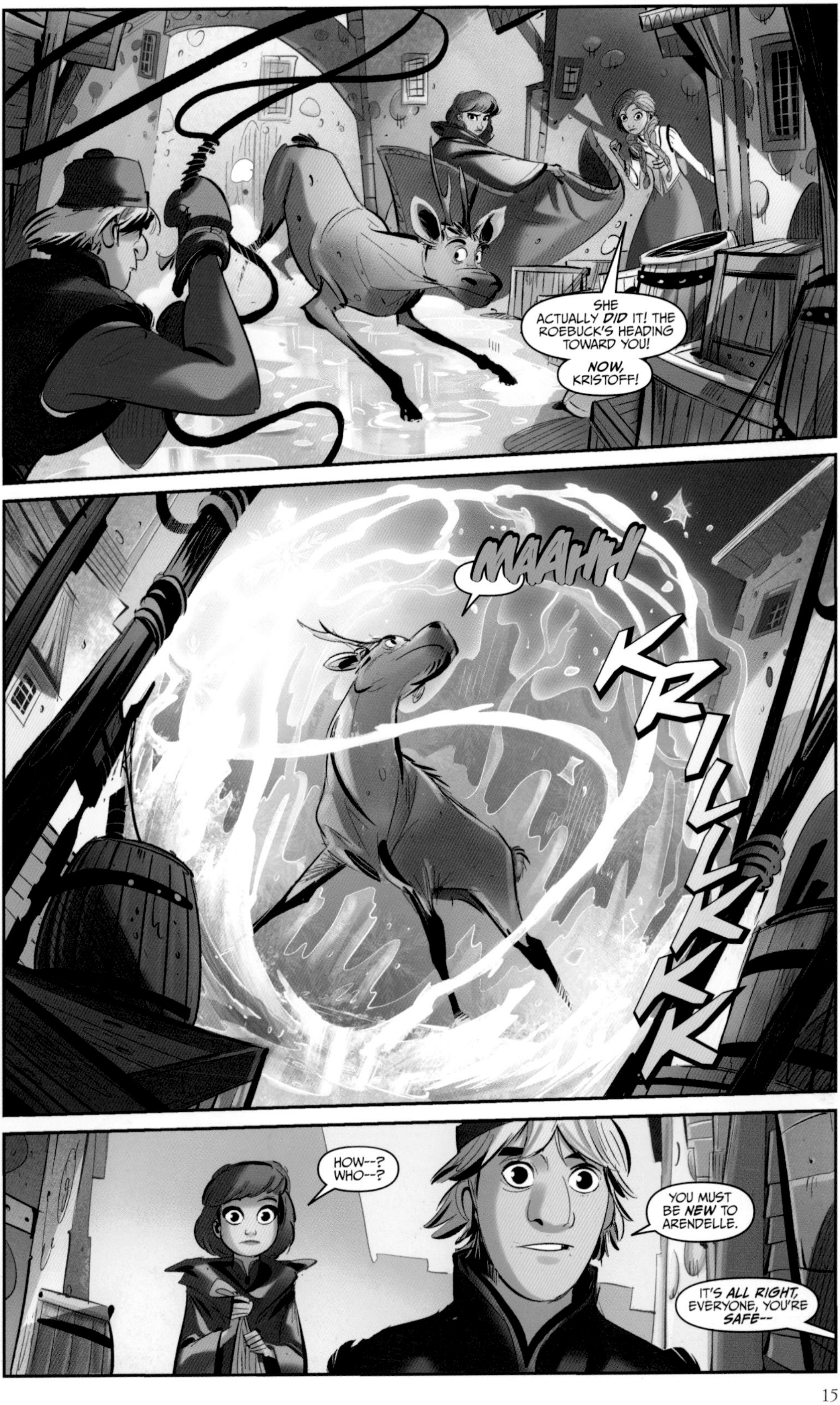
SHE ACTUALLY DID IT! THE ROEBUCK'S HEADING TOWARD YOU!
NOW, KRISTOFF!
MAAHH
KRILLKKK
HOW--? WHO--?
YOU MUST BE NEW TO ARENDELLE.
IT'S ALL RIGHT, EVERYONE, YOU'RE SAFE--

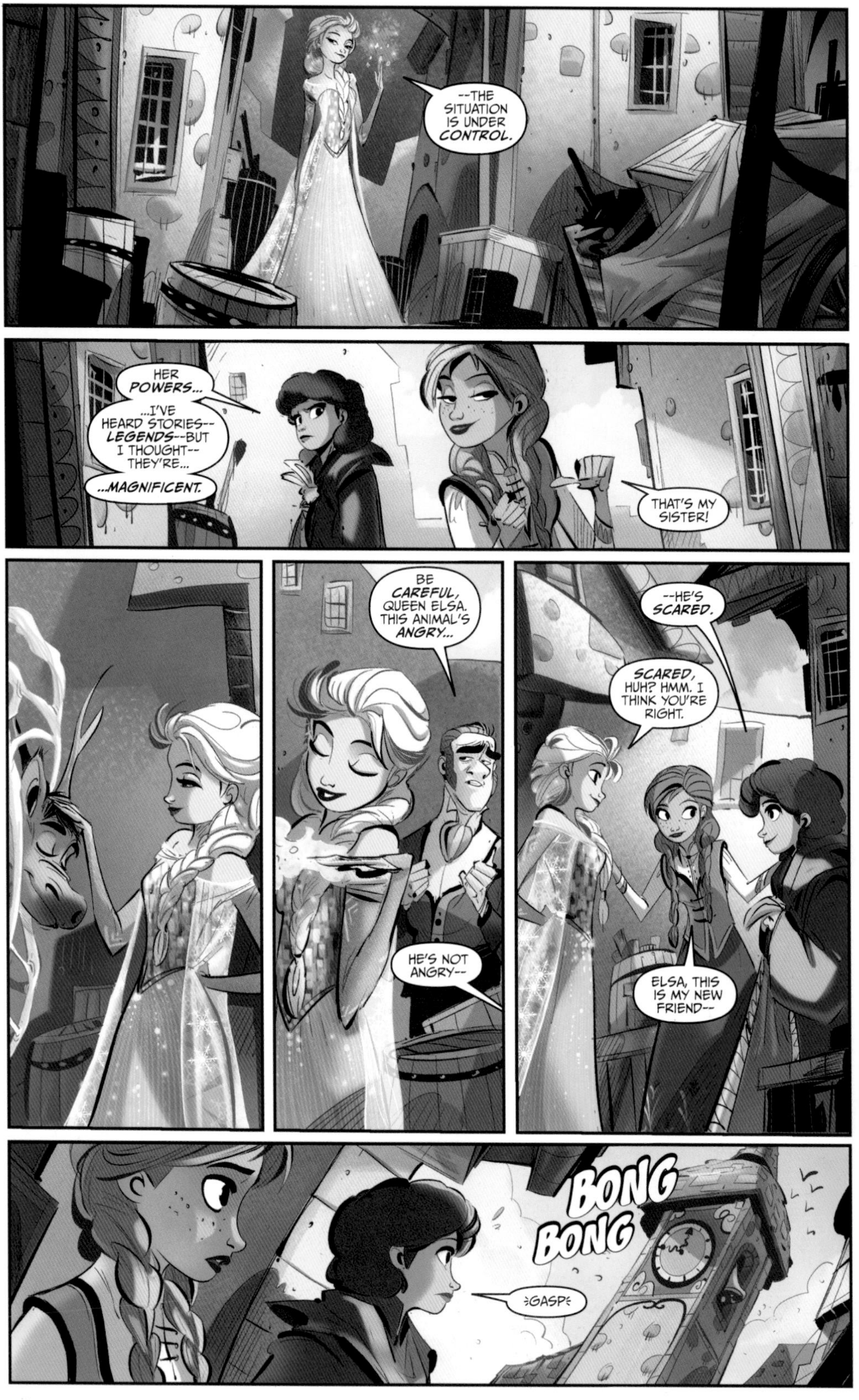
--THE SITUATION IS UNDER CONTROL.
HER POWERS...
...I'VE HEARD STORIES--LEGENDS--BUT I THOUGHT--THEY'RE...
...MAGNIFICENT.
THAT'S MY SISTER!
BE CAREFUL, QUEEN ELSA. THIS ANIMAL'S ANGRY...
HE'S NOT ANGRY--
--HE'S SCARED.
SCARED, HUH? HMM. I THINK YOU'RE RIGHT.
ELSA, THIS IS MY NEW FRIEND--
BONG
BONG
GASP

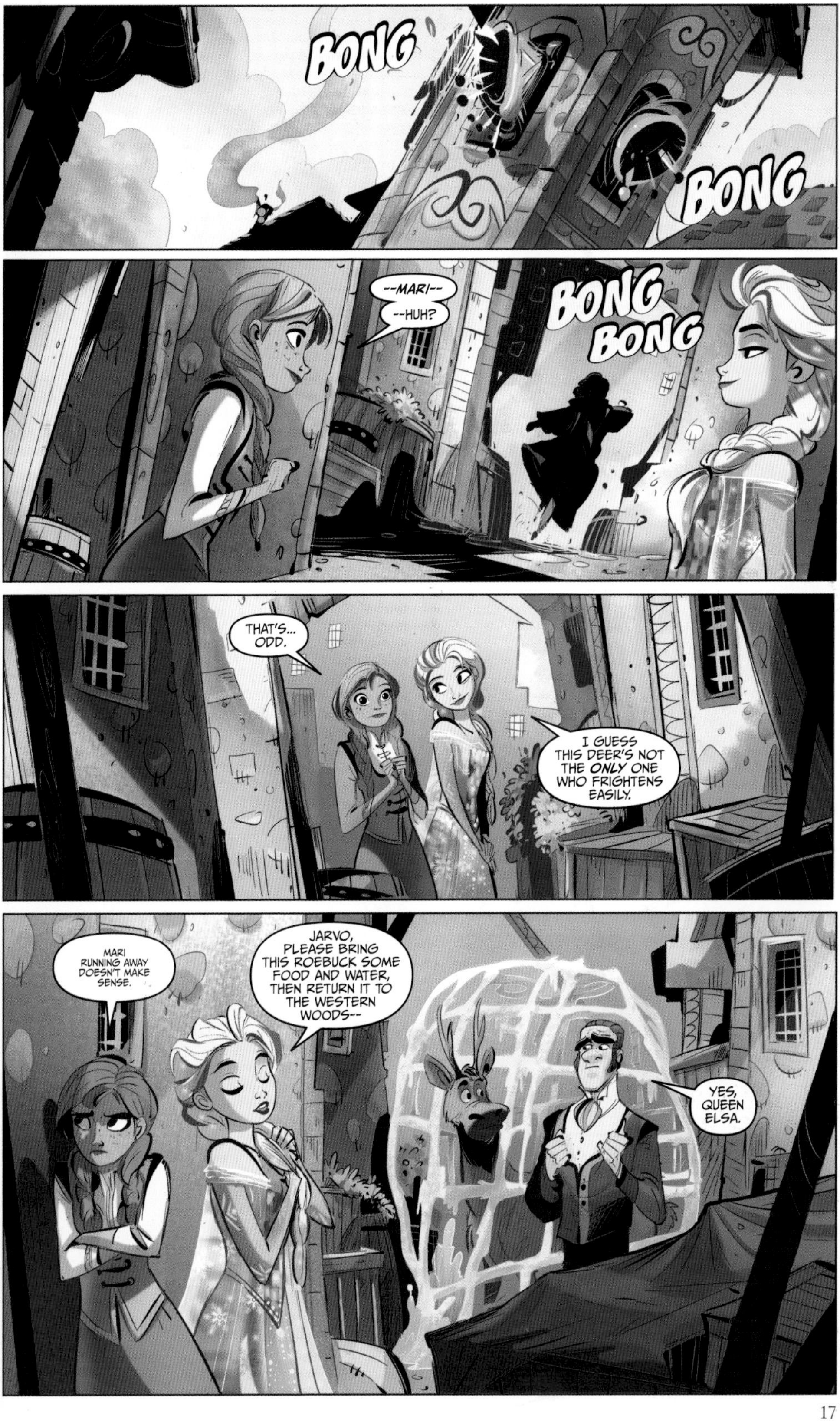
BONG
BONG
--MARI--
--HUH?
BONG
BONG
THAT'S... ODD.
I GUESS THIS DEER'S NOT THE *ONLY* ONE WHO FRIGHTENS EASILY.
MARI RUNNING AWAY DOESN'T MAKE SENSE.
JARVO, PLEASE BRING THIS ROEBUCK SOME FOOD AND WATER, THEN RETURN IT TO THE WESTERN WOODS--
YES, QUEEN ELSA.

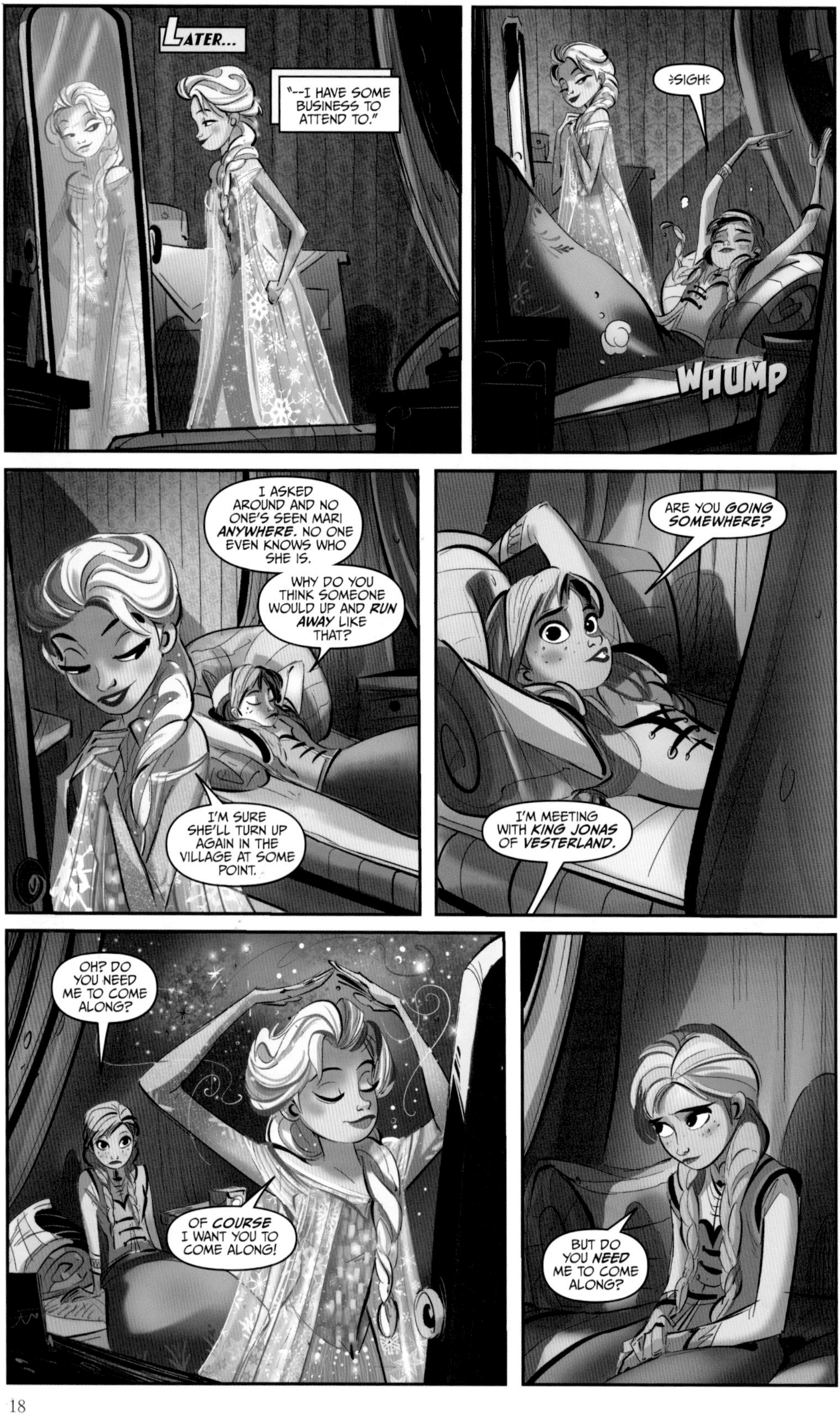
LATER...
"--I HAVE SOME BUSINESS TO ATTEND TO."
SIGH
WHUMP
I ASKED AROUND AND NO ONE'S SEEN MARI ANYWHERE. NO ONE EVEN KNOWS WHO SHE IS.
WHY DO YOU THINK SOMEONE WOULD UP AND RUN AWAY LIKE THAT?
I'M SURE SHE'LL TURN UP AGAIN IN THE VILLAGE AT SOME POINT.
ARE YOU GOING SOMEWHERE?
I'M MEETING WITH KING JONAS OF VESTERLAND.
OH? DO YOU NEED ME TO COME ALONG?
OF COURSE I WANT YOU TO COME ALONG!
BUT DO YOU NEED ME TO COME ALONG?

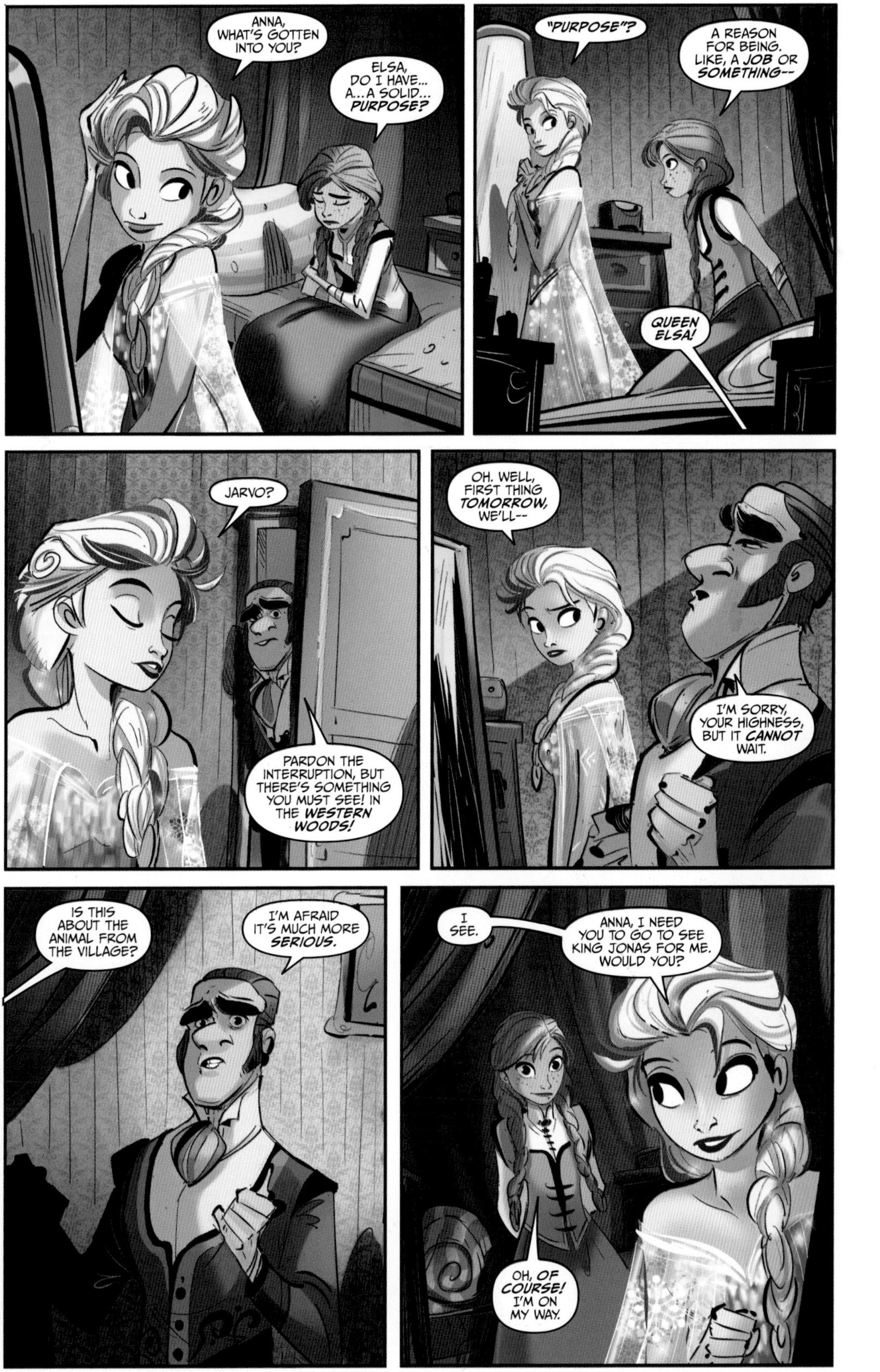
ANNA, WHAT'S GOTTEN INTO YOU?
ELSA, DO I HAVE... A...A SOLID... PURPOSE?
"PURPOSE"?
A REASON FOR BEING. LIKE, A JOB OR SOMETHING--
QUEEN ELSA!
JARVO?
PARDON THE INTERRUPTION, BUT THERE'S SOMETHING YOU MUST SEE! IN THE WESTERN WOODS!
OH. WELL, FIRST THING TOMORROW, WE'LL--
I'M SORRY, YOUR HIGHNESS, BUT IT CANNOT WAIT.
IS THIS ABOUT THE ANIMAL FROM THE VILLAGE?
I'M AFRAID IT'S MUCH MORE SERIOUS.
I SEE.
ANNA, I NEED YOU TO GO TO SEE KING JONAS FOR ME. WOULD YOU?
OH, OF COURSE! I'M ON MY WAY.

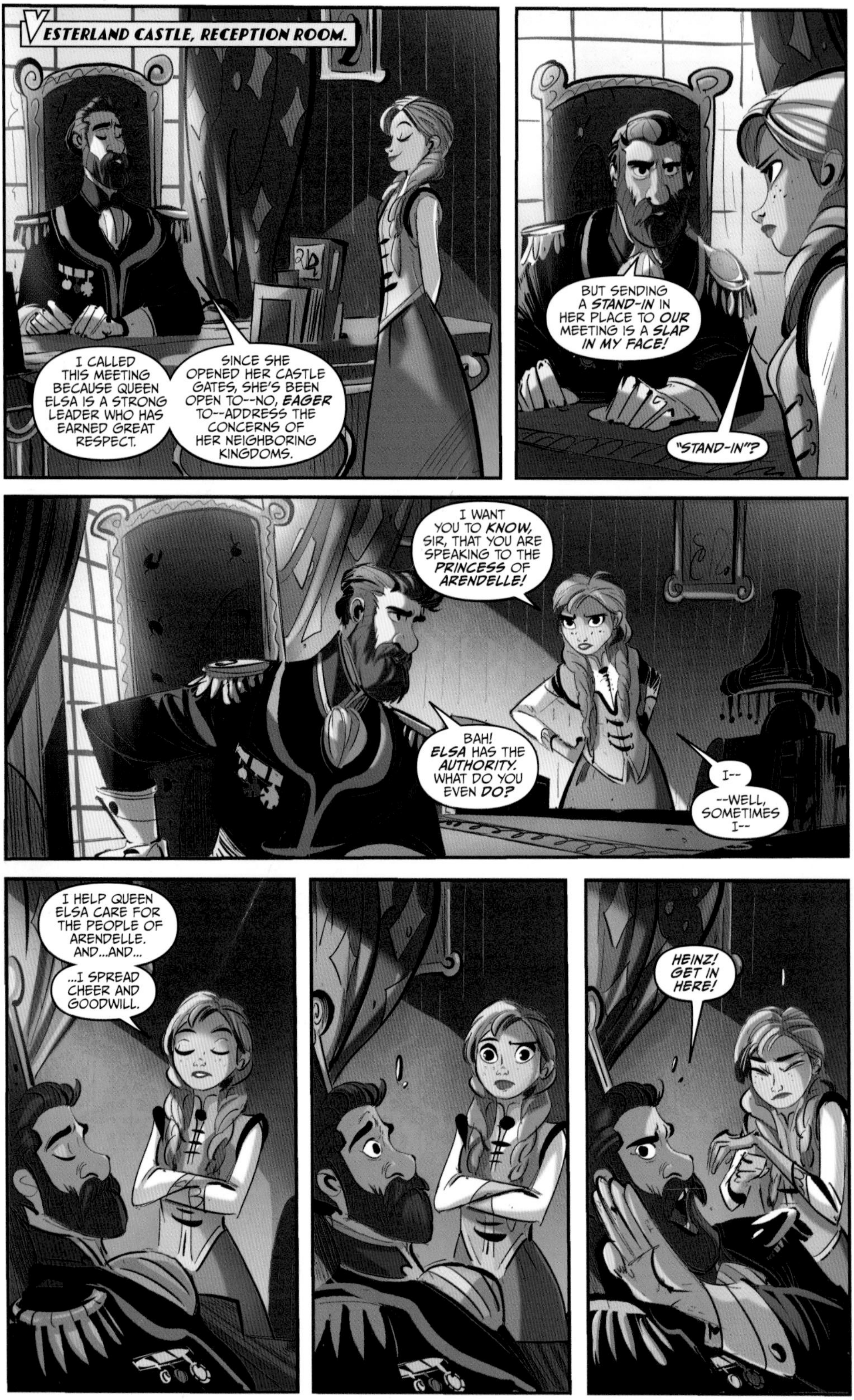
VESTERLAND CASTLE, RECEPTION ROOM.
I CALLED THIS MEETING BECAUSE QUEEN ELSA IS A STRONG LEADER WHO HAS EARNED GREAT RESPECT.
SINCE SHE OPENED HER CASTLE GATES, SHE'S BEEN OPEN TO--NO, EAGER TO--ADDRESS THE CONCERNS OF HER NEIGHBORING KINGDOMS.
BUT SENDING A STAND-IN IN HER PLACE TO OUR MEETING IS A SLAP IN MY FACE!
"STAND-IN"?
I WANT YOU TO KNOW, SIR, THAT YOU ARE SPEAKING TO THE PRINCESS OF ARENDELLE!
BAH! ELSA HAS THE AUTHORITY. WHAT DO YOU EVEN DO?
I--
--WELL, SOMETIMES I--
I HELP QUEEN ELSA CARE FOR THE PEOPLE OF ARENDELLE. AND...AND...
...I SPREAD CHEER AND GOODWILL.
HEINZ! GET IN HERE!

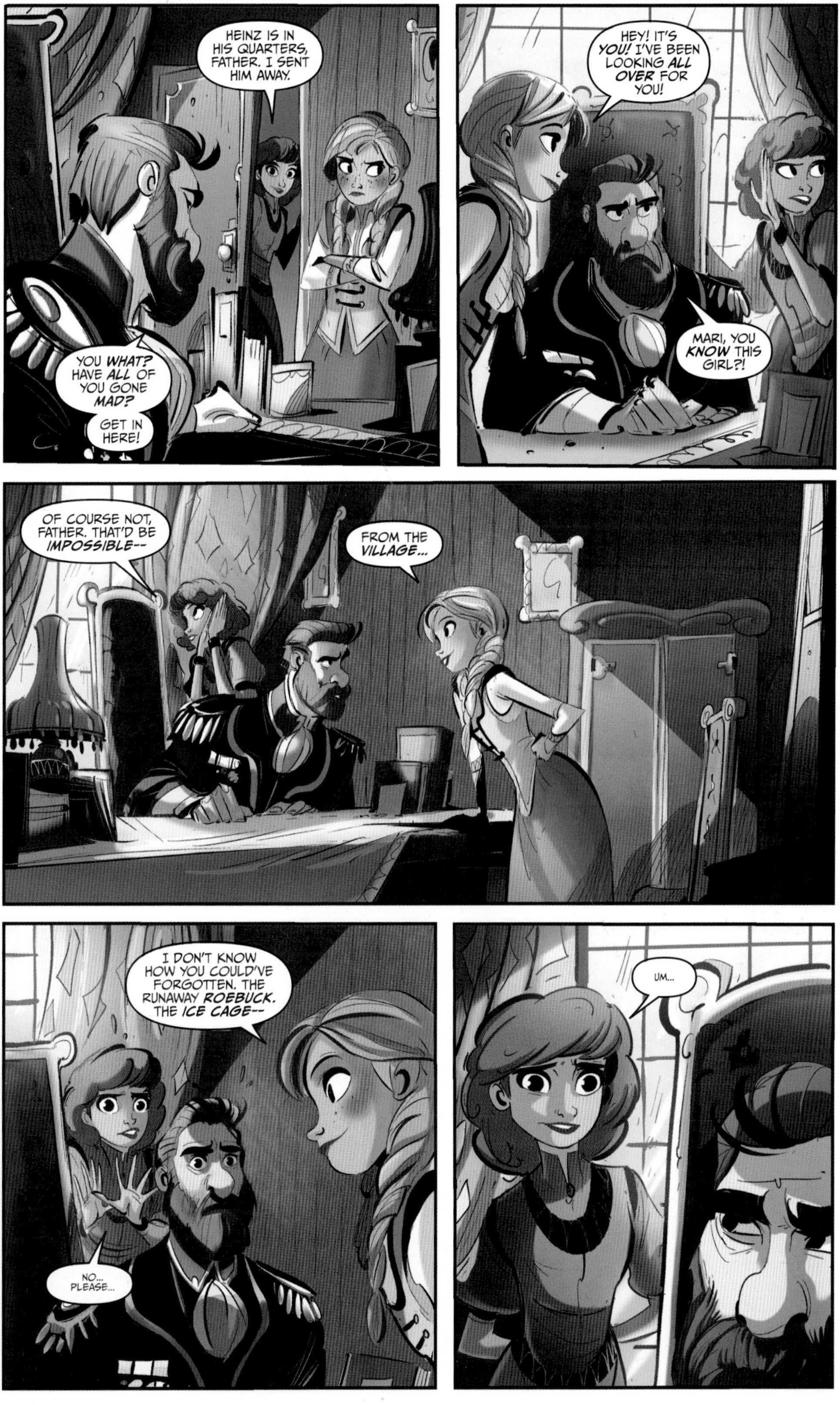

HEINZ IS IN HIS QUARTERS, FATHER. I SENT HIM AWAY.
YOU WHAT? HAVE ALL OF YOU GONE MAD?
GET IN HERE!
HEY! IT'S YOU! I'VE BEEN LOOKING ALL OVER FOR YOU!
MARI, YOU KNOW THIS GIRL?!
OF COURSE NOT, FATHER. THAT'D BE IMPOSSIBLE--
FROM THE VILLAGE...
I DON'T KNOW HOW YOU COULD'VE FORGOTTEN. THE RUNAWAY ROEBUCK. THE ICE CAGE--
NO... PLEASE...
UM...

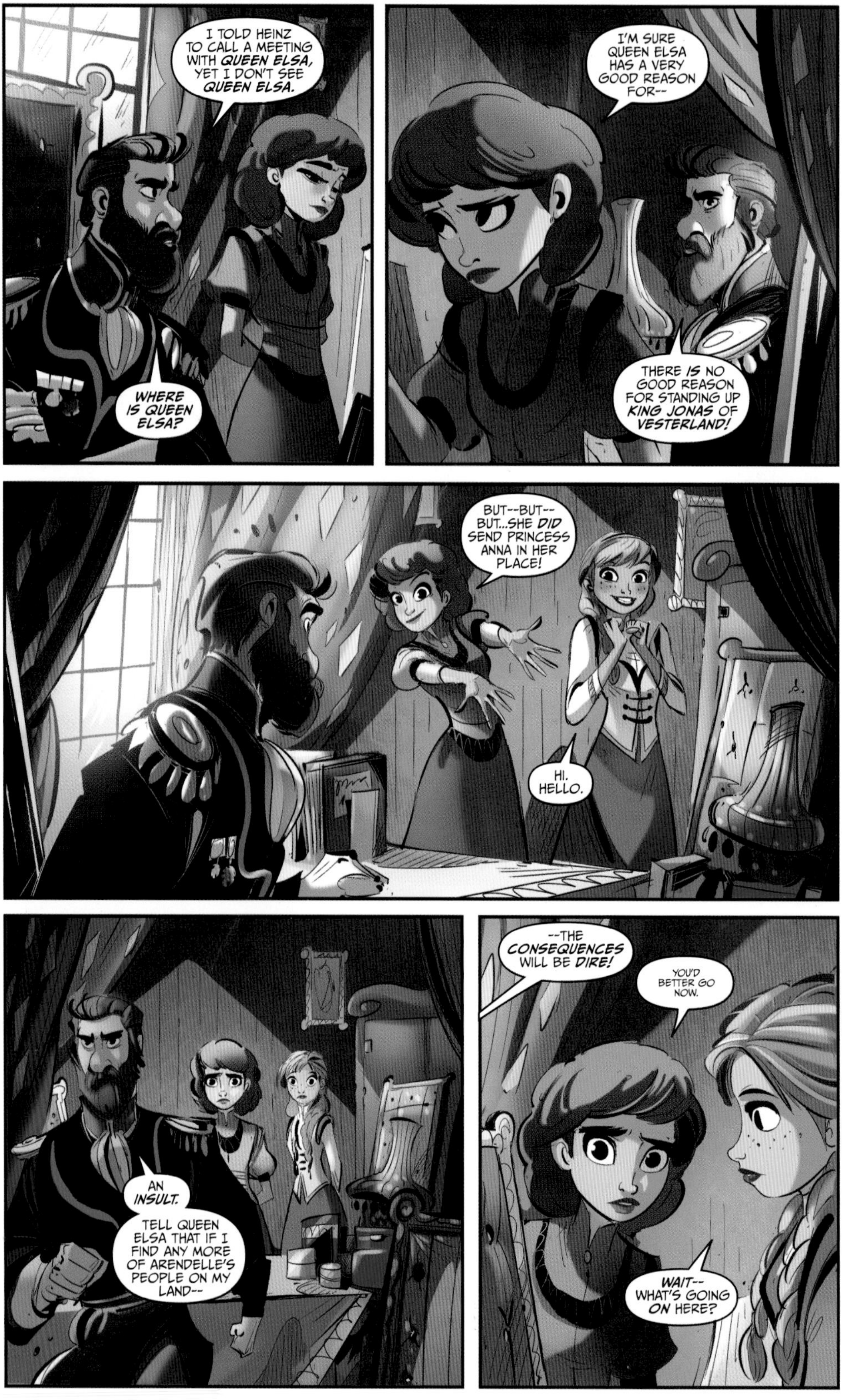
I TOLD HEINZ TO CALL A MEETING WITH *QUEEN ELSA,* YET I DON'T SEE *QUEEN ELSA.*
WHERE IS QUEEN ELSA?
I'M SURE QUEEN ELSA HAS A VERY GOOD REASON FOR--
THERE *IS* NO GOOD REASON FOR STANDING UP *KING JONAS* OF *VESTERLAND!*
BUT--BUT-- BUT...SHE *DID* SEND PRINCESS ANNA IN HER PLACE!
HI. HELLO.
AN *INSULT.*
TELL QUEEN ELSA THAT IF I FIND ANY MORE OF ARENDELLE'S PEOPLE ON MY LAND--
--THE *CONSEQUENCES* WILL BE *DIRE!*
YOU'D BETTER GO NOW.
WAIT-- WHAT'S GOING *ON* HERE?

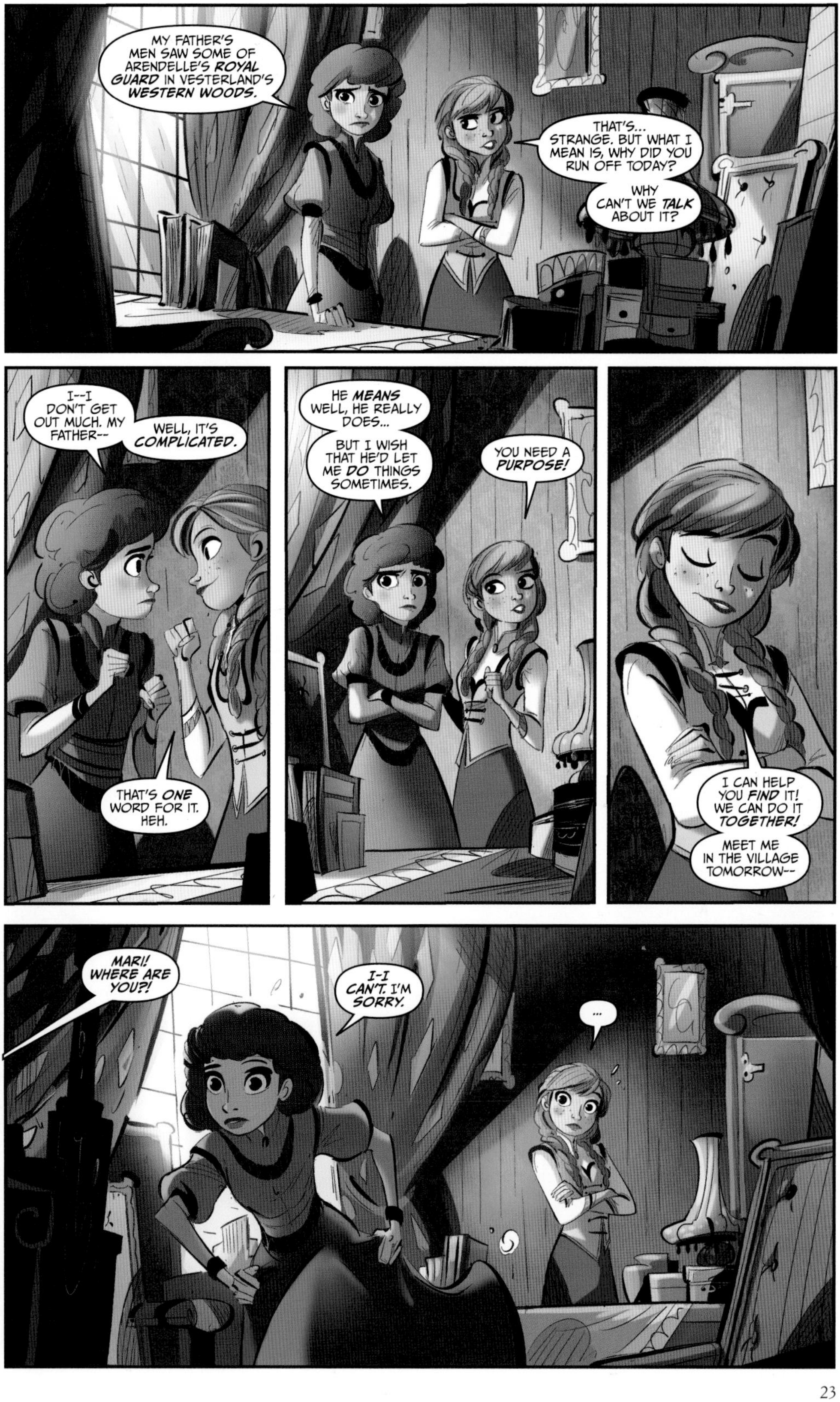
MY FATHER'S MEN SAW SOME OF ARENDELLE'S ROYAL GUARD IN VESTERLAND'S WESTERN WOODS.
THAT'S... STRANGE. BUT WHAT I MEAN IS, WHY DID YOU RUN OFF TODAY?
WHY CAN'T WE TALK ABOUT IT?
I--I DON'T GET OUT MUCH. MY FATHER--
WELL, IT'S COMPLICATED.
THAT'S ONE WORD FOR IT. HEH.
HE MEANS WELL, HE REALLY DOES...
BUT I WISH THAT HE'D LET ME DO THINGS SOMETIMES.
YOU NEED A PURPOSE!
I CAN HELP YOU FIND IT! WE CAN DO IT TOGETHER!
MEET ME IN THE VILLAGE TOMORROW--
MARI! WHERE ARE YOU?!
I-I CAN'T. I'M SORRY.
...

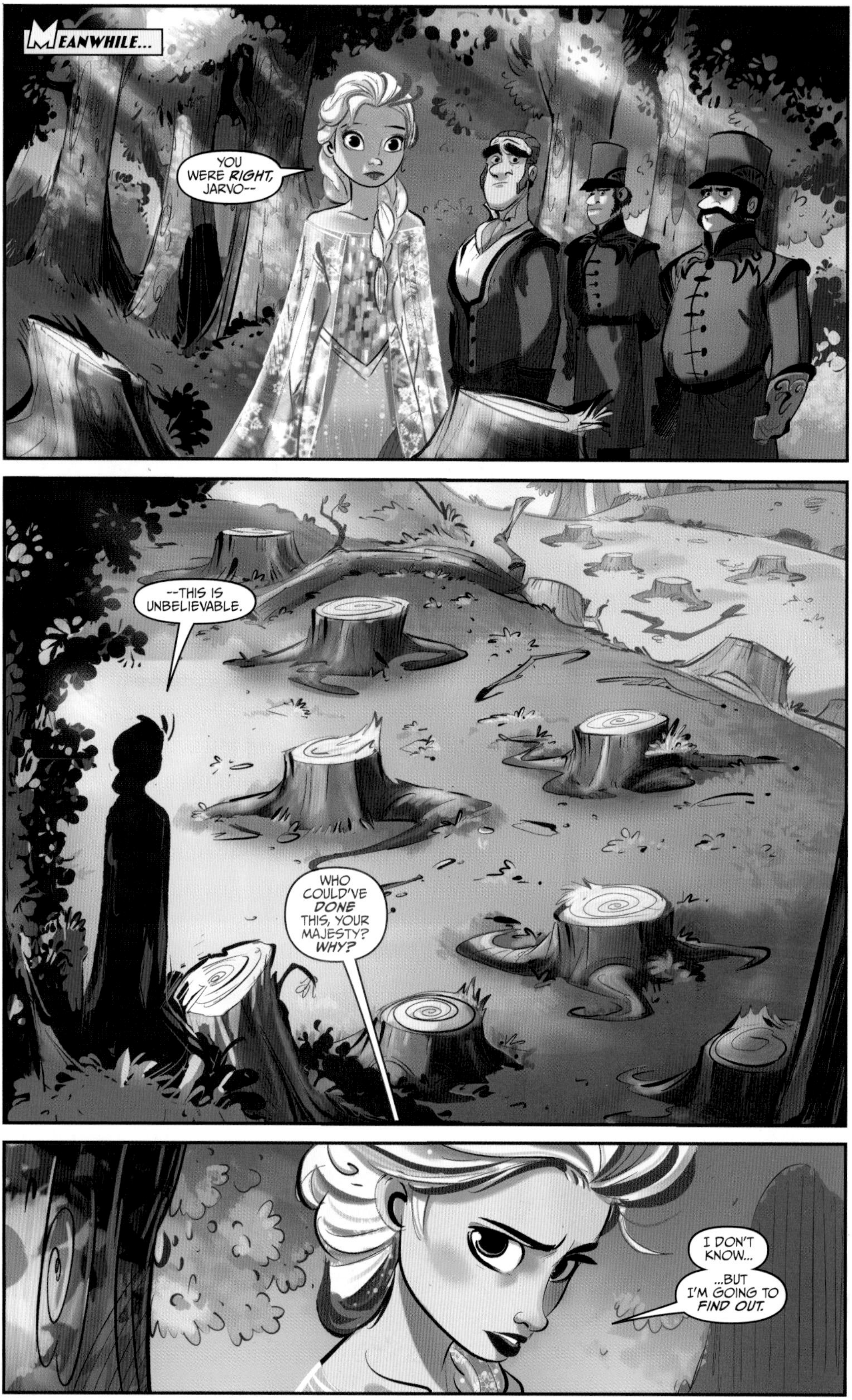
MEANWHILE...
YOU WERE RIGHT, JARVO--
--THIS IS UNBELIEVABLE.
WHO COULD'VE DONE THIS, YOUR MAJESTY? WHY?
I DON'T KNOW...
...BUT I'M GOING TO FIND OUT.

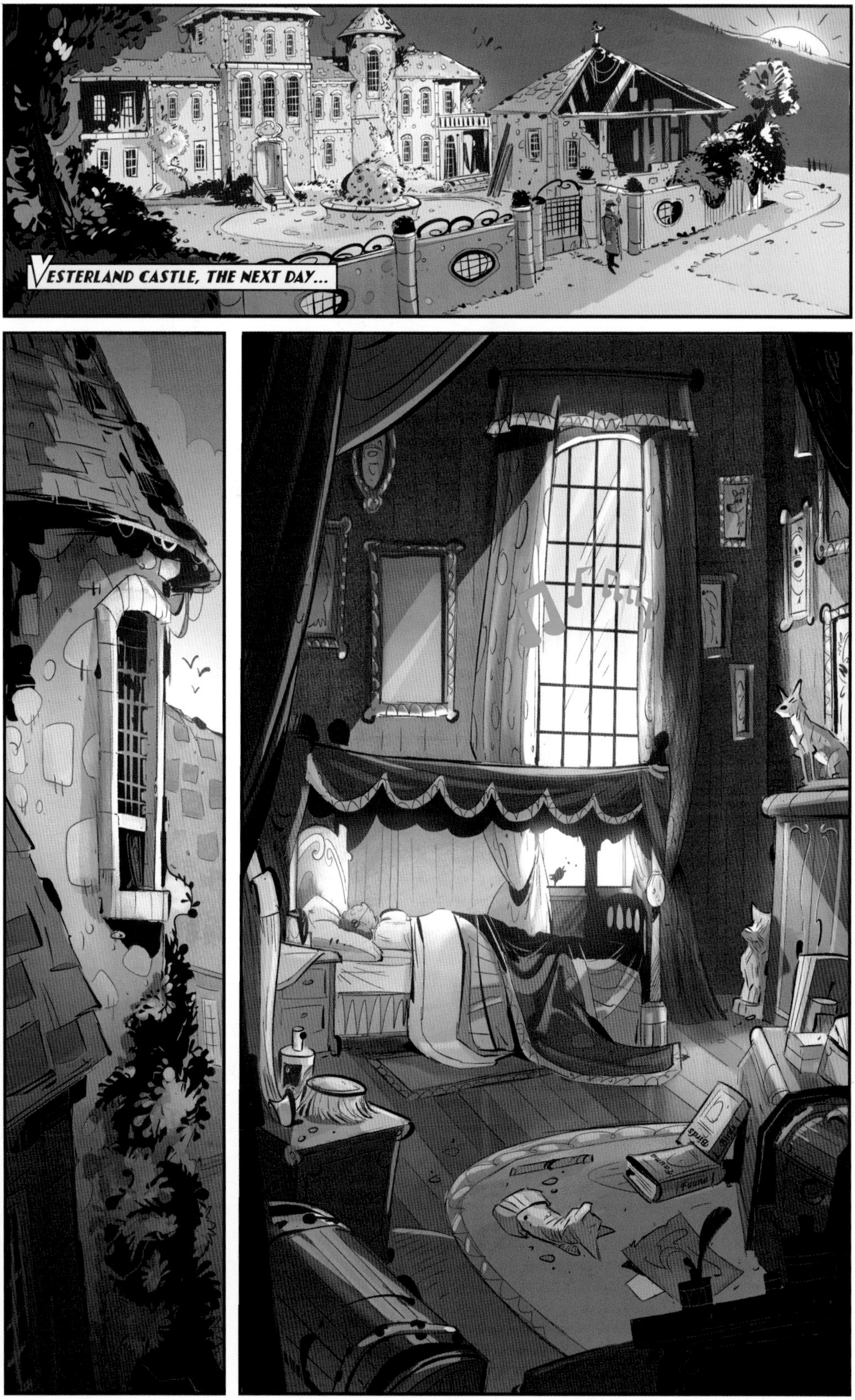
VESTERLAND CASTLE, THE NEXT DAY...
Birds
Fauna

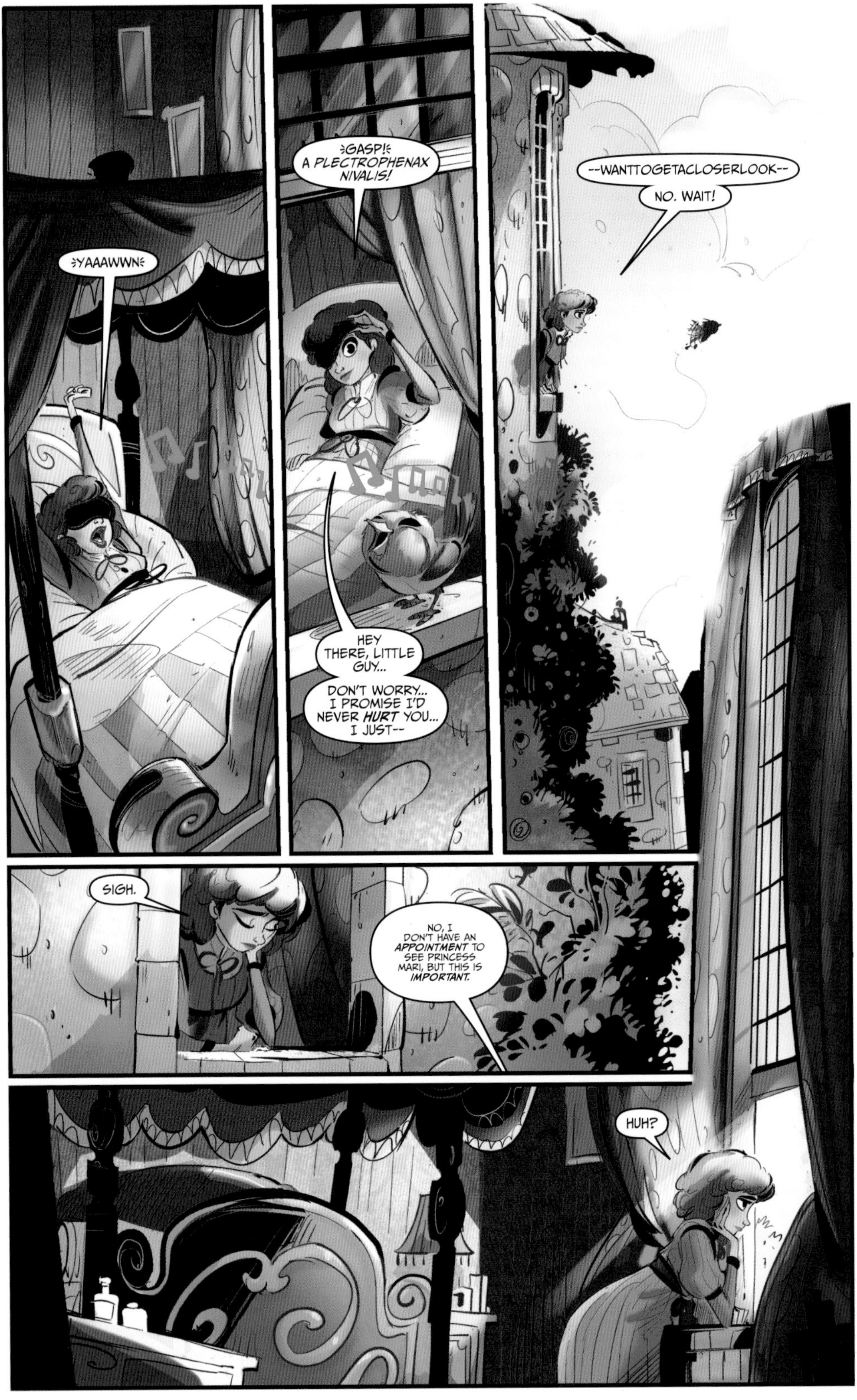

YAAAWWN
GASP! A PLECTROPHENAX NIVALIS!
HEY THERE, LITTLE GUY...
DON'T WORRY... I PROMISE I'D NEVER HURT YOU... I JUST--
--WANTTOGETACLOSERLOOK--
NO. WAIT!
SIGH.
NO, I DON'T HAVE AN APPOINTMENT TO SEE PRINCESS MARI, BUT THIS IS IMPORTANT.
HUH?

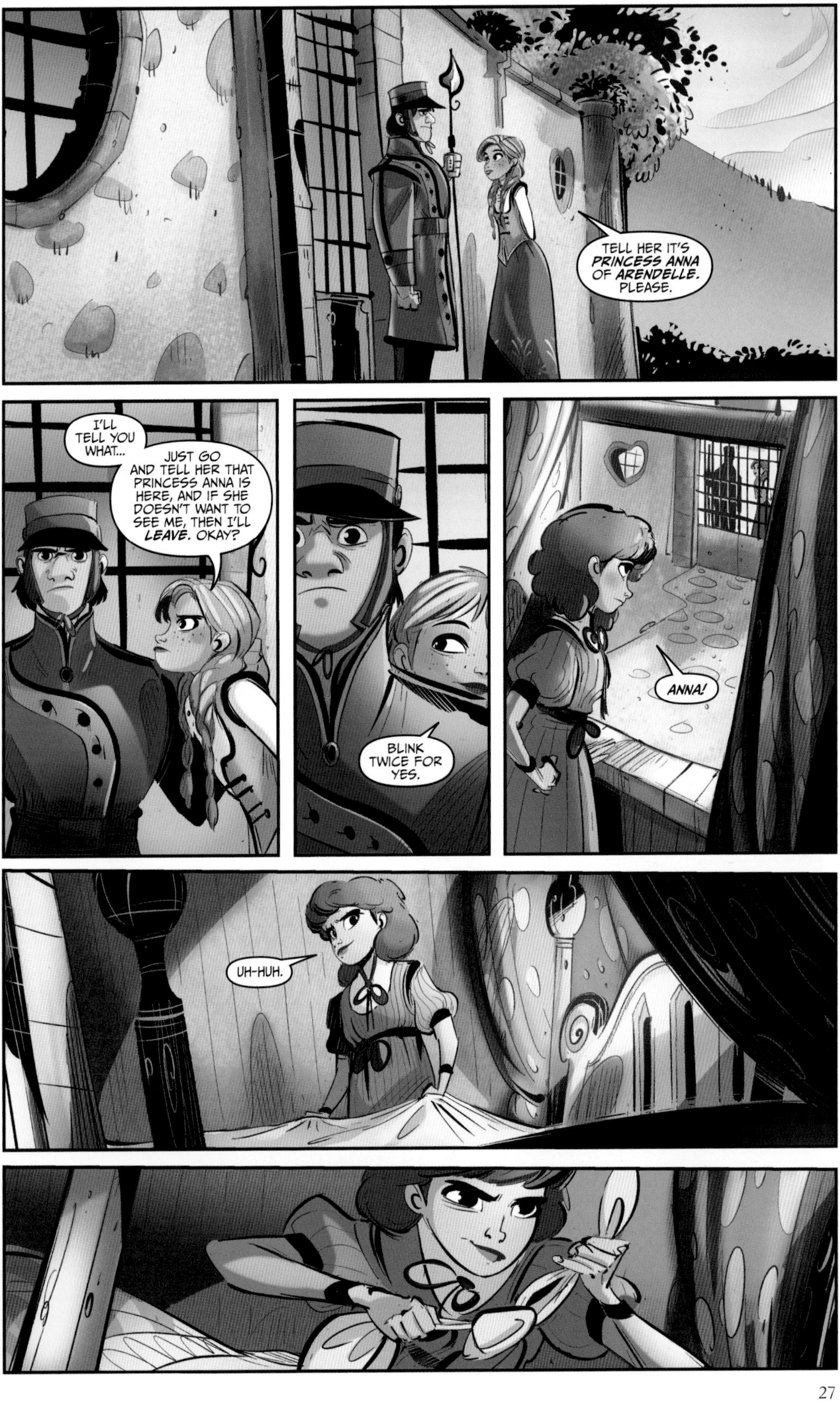
TELL HER IT'S PRINCESS ANNA OF ARENDELLE. PLEASE.
I'LL TELL YOU WHAT...
JUST GO AND TELL HER THAT PRINCESS ANNA IS HERE, AND IF SHE DOESN'T WANT TO SEE ME, THEN I'LL LEAVE. OKAY?
BLINK TWICE FOR YES.
ANNA!
UH-HUH.

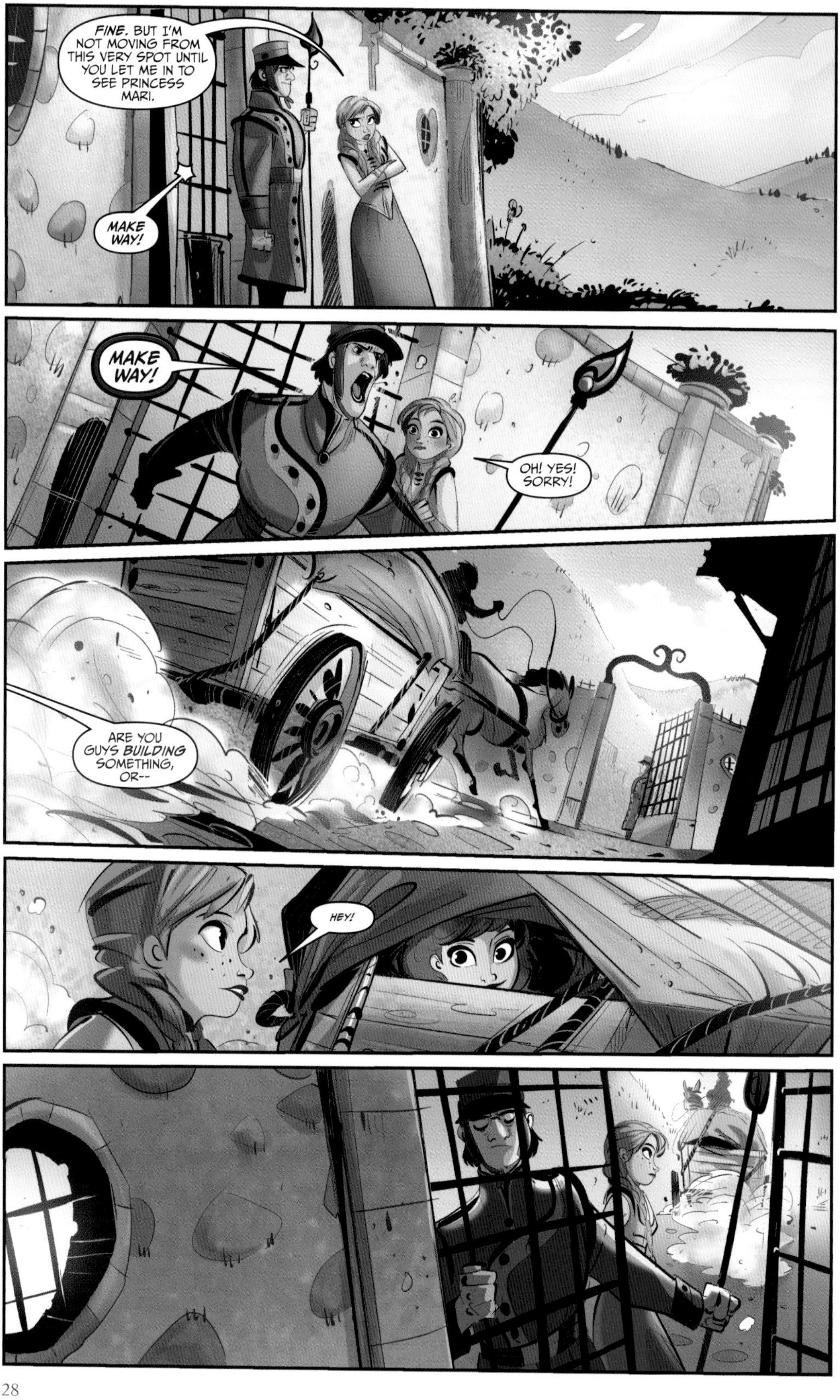
FINE. BUT I'M NOT MOVING FROM THIS VERY SPOT UNTIL YOU LET ME IN TO SEE PRINCESS MARI.
MAKE WAY!
MAKE WAY!
OH! YES! SORRY!
ARE YOU GUYS BUILDING SOMETHING, OR--
HEY!

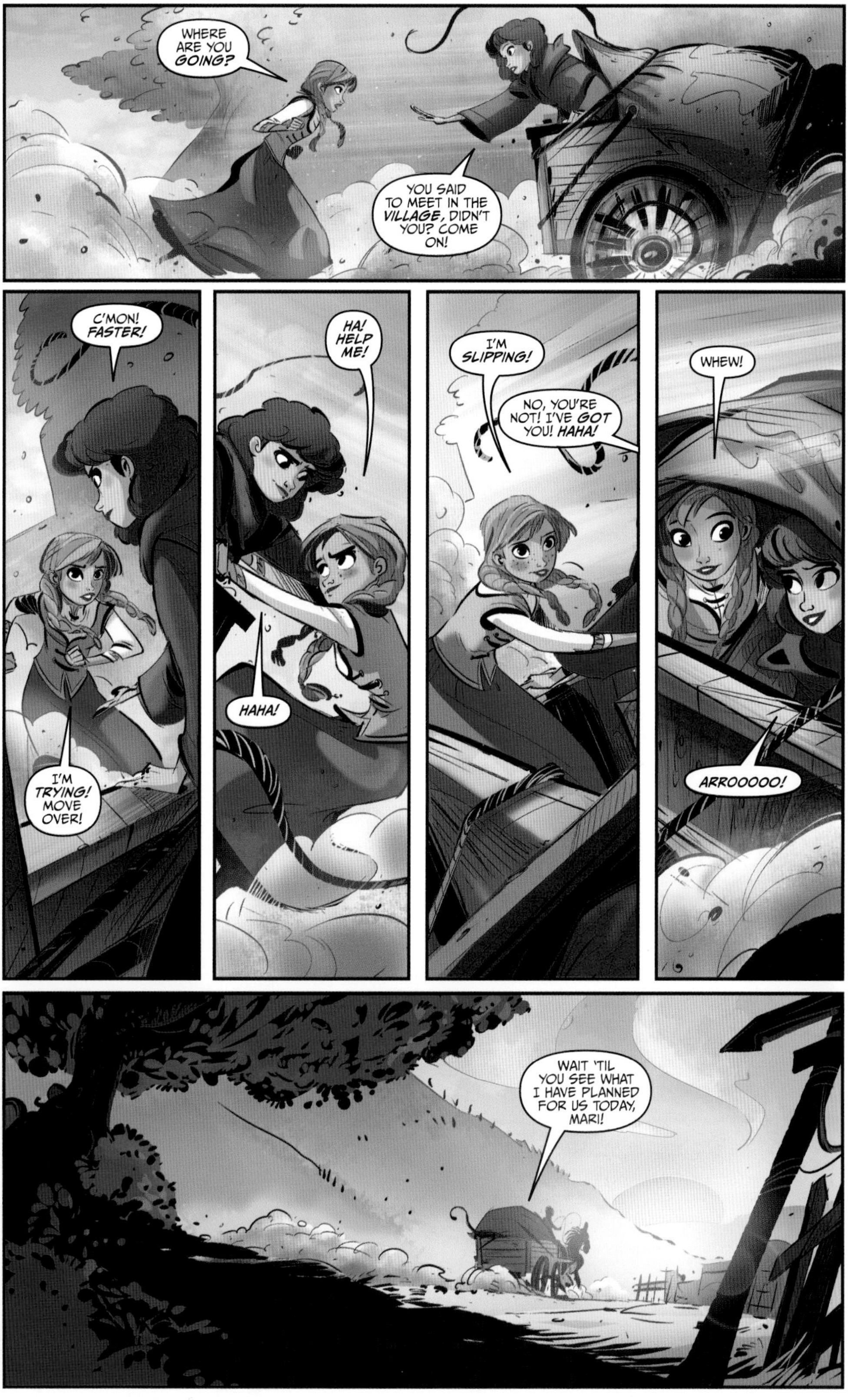
WHERE ARE YOU GOING?
YOU SAID TO MEET IN THE VILLAGE, DIDN'T YOU? COME ON!
C'MON! FASTER!
I'M TRYING! MOVE OVER!
HA! HELP ME!
HAHA!
I'M SLIPPING!
NO, YOU'RE NOT! I'VE GOT YOU! HAHA!
WHEW!
ARROOOOO!
WAIT 'TIL YOU SEE WHAT I HAVE PLANNED FOR US TODAY, MARI!

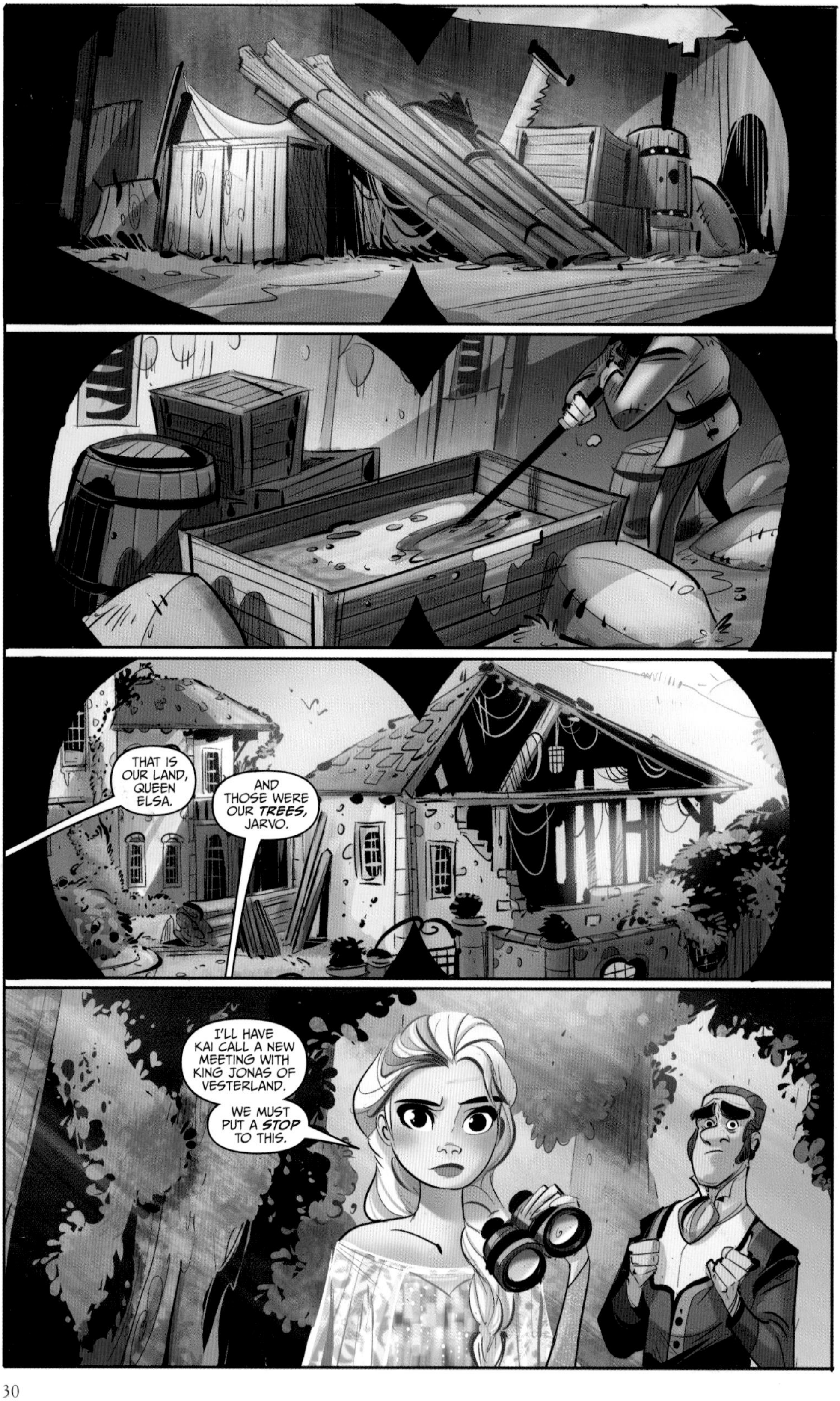
THAT IS OUR LAND, QUEEN ELSA.
AND THOSE WERE OUR TREES, JARVO.
I'LL HAVE KAI CALL A NEW MEETING WITH KING JONAS OF VESTERLAND.
WE MUST PUT A STOP TO THIS.

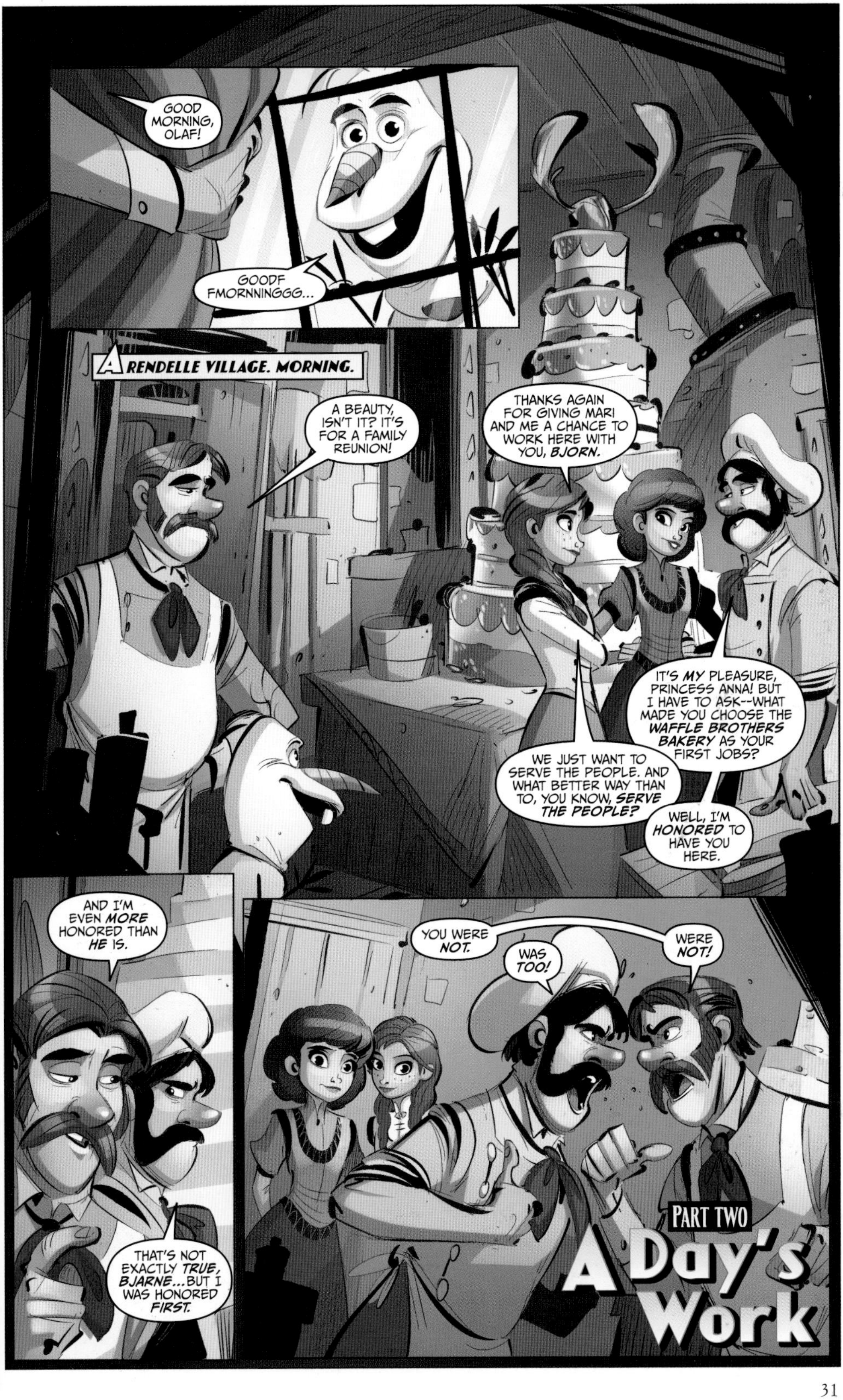
GOOD MORNING, OLAF!
GOODF FMORNNINGGG...
ARENDELLE VILLAGE. MORNING.
A BEAUTY, ISN'T IT? IT'S FOR A FAMILY REUNION!
THANKS AGAIN FOR GIVING MARI AND ME A CHANCE TO WORK HERE WITH YOU, BJORN.
IT'S MY PLEASURE, PRINCESS ANNA! BUT I HAVE TO ASK--WHAT MADE YOU CHOOSE THE WAFFLE BROTHERS BAKERY AS YOUR FIRST JOBS?
WE JUST WANT TO SERVE THE PEOPLE. AND WHAT BETTER WAY THAN TO, YOU KNOW, SERVE THE PEOPLE?
WELL, I'M HONORED TO HAVE YOU HERE.
AND I'M EVEN MORE HONORED THAN HE IS.
THAT'S NOT EXACTLY TRUE, BJARNE...BUT I WAS HONORED FIRST.
YOU WERE NOT.
WAS TOO!
WERE NOT!
PART TWO
A Day's Work

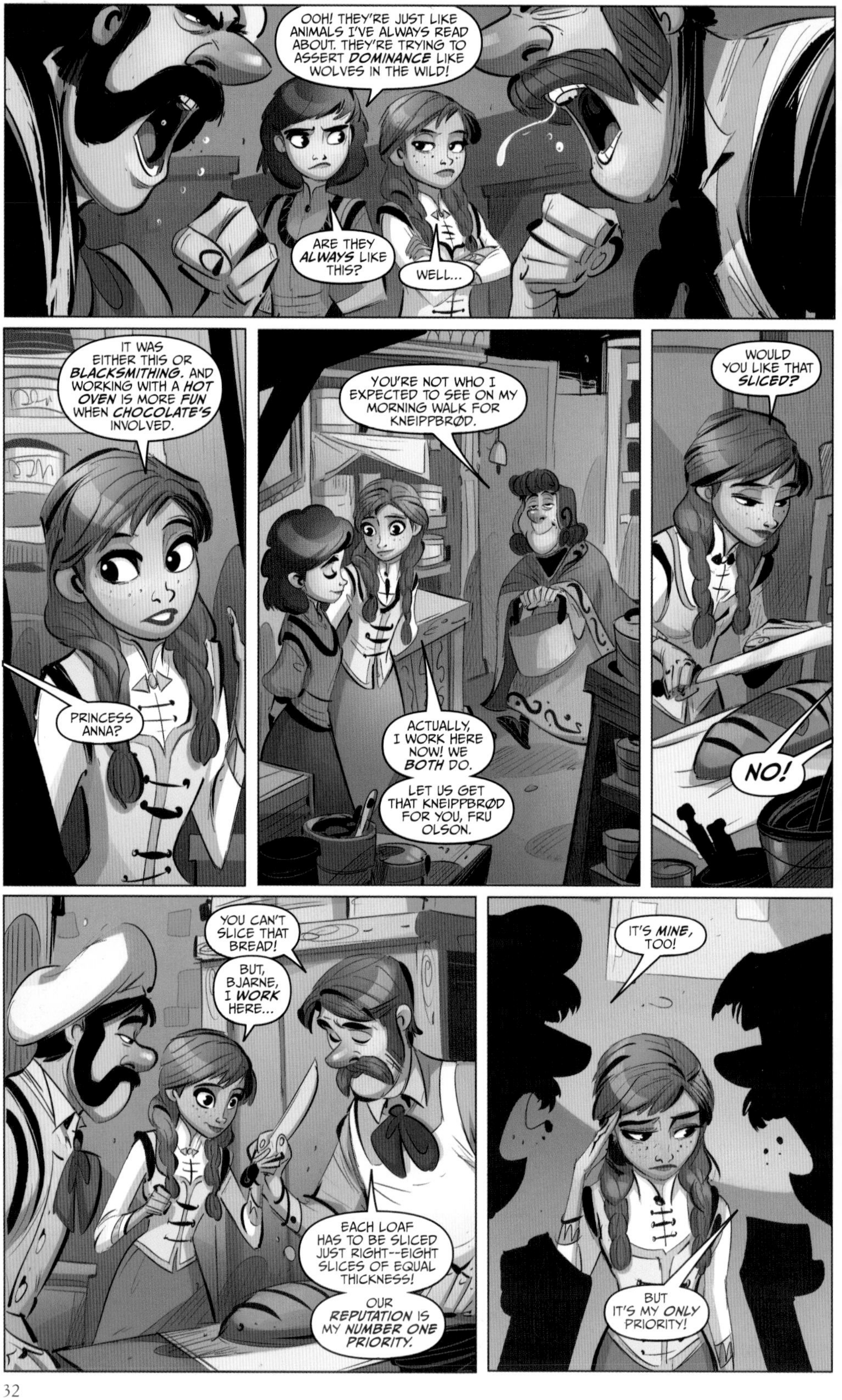

OOH! THEY'RE JUST LIKE ANIMALS I'VE ALWAYS READ ABOUT. THEY'RE TRYING TO ASSERT DOMINANCE LIKE WOLVES IN THE WILD!
ARE THEY ALWAYS LIKE THIS?
WELL...
IT WAS EITHER THIS OR BLACKSMITHING. AND WORKING WITH A HOT OVEN IS MORE FUN WHEN CHOCOLATE'S INVOLVED.
PRINCESS ANNA?
YOU'RE NOT WHO I EXPECTED TO SEE ON MY MORNING WALK FOR KNEIPPBRØD.
ACTUALLY, I WORK HERE NOW! WE BOTH DO.
LET US GET THAT KNEIPPBRØD FOR YOU, FRU OLSON.
WOULD YOU LIKE THAT SLICED?
NO!
YOU CAN'T SLICE THAT BREAD!
BUT, BJARNE, I WORK HERE...
EACH LOAF HAS TO BE SLICED JUST RIGHT--EIGHT SLICES OF EQUAL THICKNESS!
OUR REPUTATION IS MY NUMBER ONE PRIORITY.
IT'S MINE, TOO!
BUT IT'S MY ONLY PRIORITY!

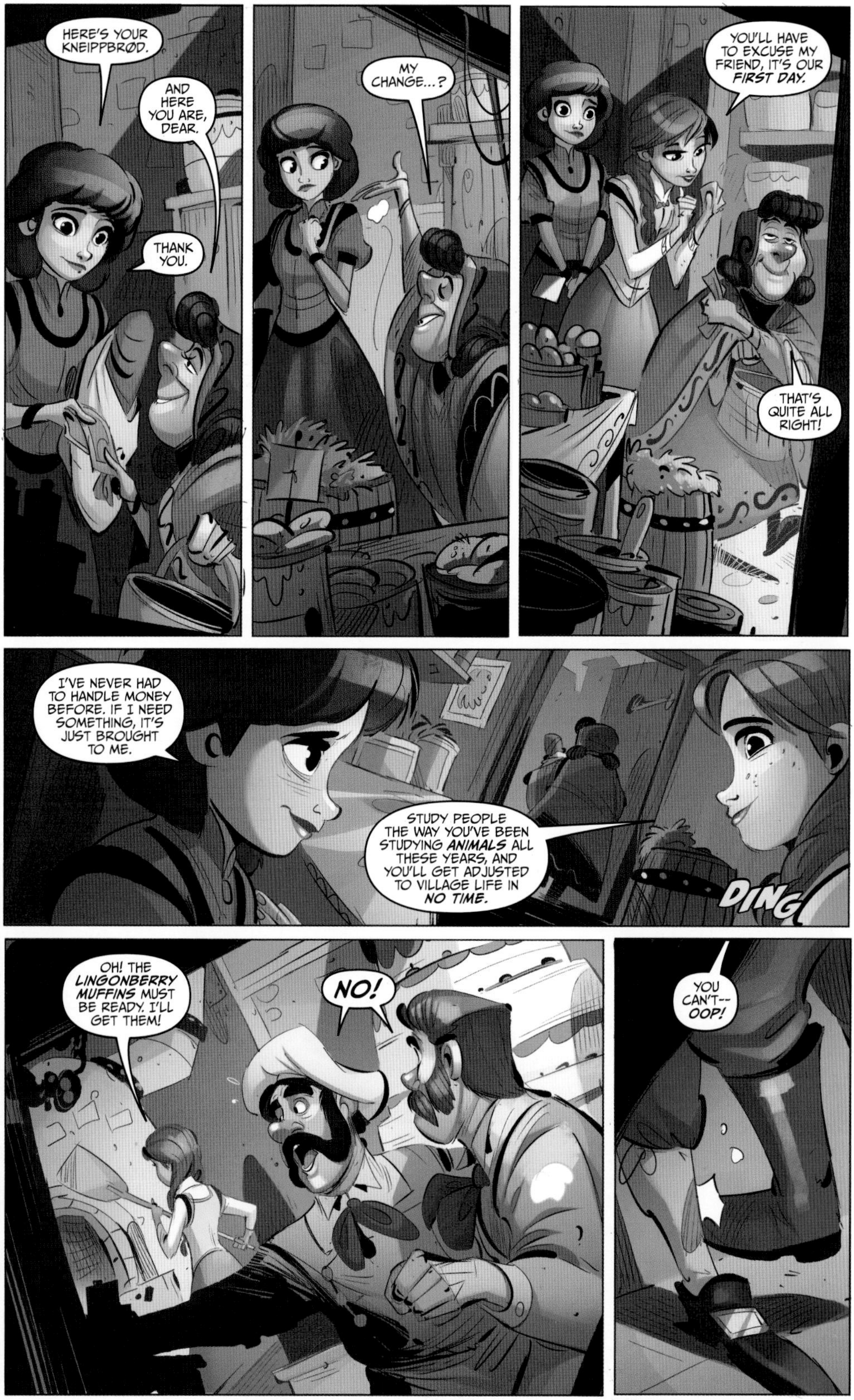
HERE'S YOUR KNEIPPBRØD.
AND HERE YOU ARE, DEAR.
THANK YOU.
MY CHANGE...?
YOU'LL HAVE TO EXCUSE MY FRIEND, IT'S OUR FIRST DAY.
THAT'S QUITE ALL RIGHT!
I'VE NEVER HAD TO HANDLE MONEY BEFORE. IF I NEED SOMETHING, IT'S JUST BROUGHT TO ME.
STUDY PEOPLE THE WAY YOU'VE BEEN STUDYING ANIMALS ALL THESE YEARS, AND YOU'LL GET ADJUSTED TO VILLAGE LIFE IN NO TIME.
DING
OH! THE LINGONBERRY MUFFINS MUST BE READY. I'LL GET THEM!
NO!
YOU CAN'T-- OOP!

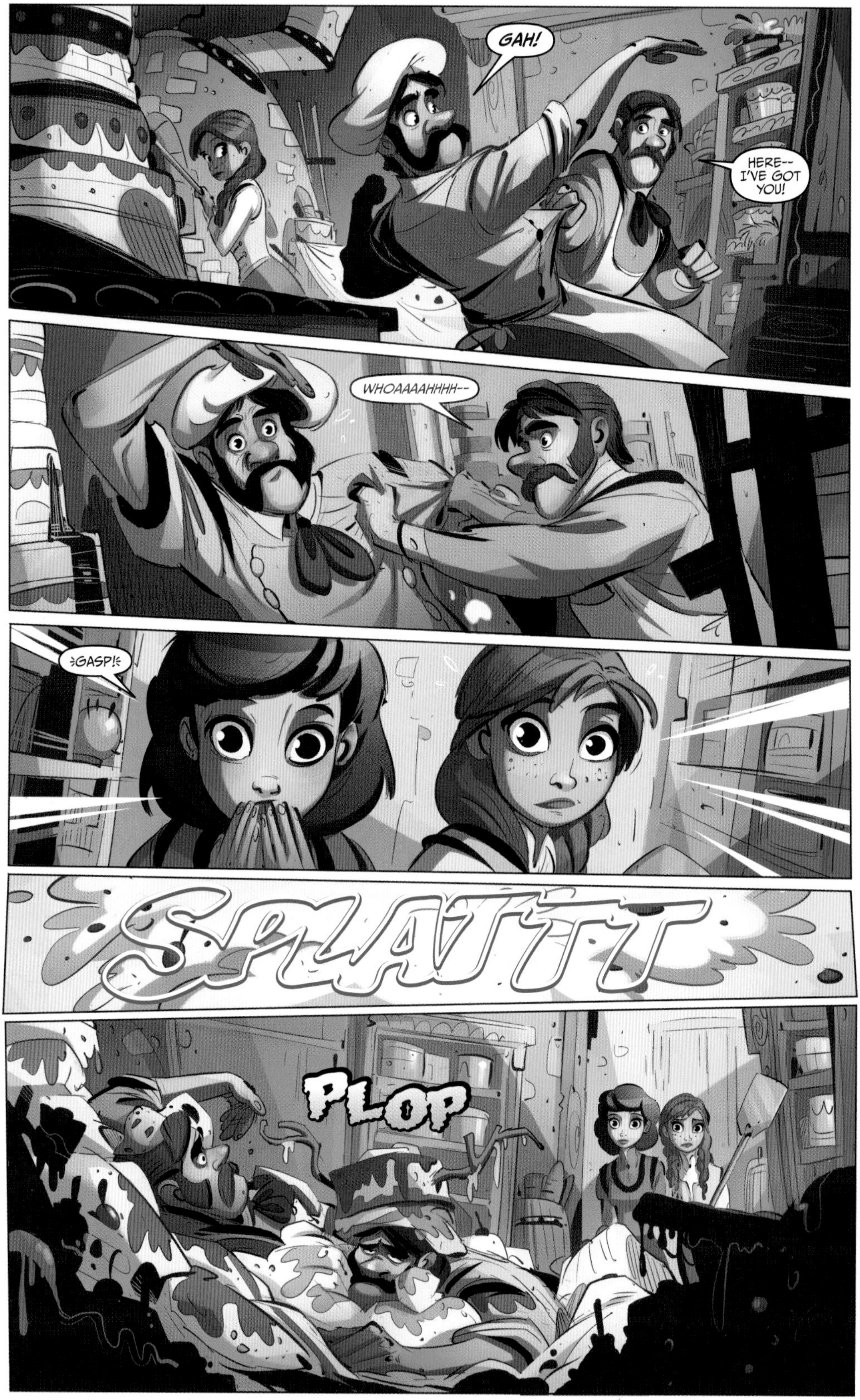

GAH!
HERE-- I'VE GOT YOU!
WHOAAAAHHHH--
GASP!
SPLATTT
PLOP

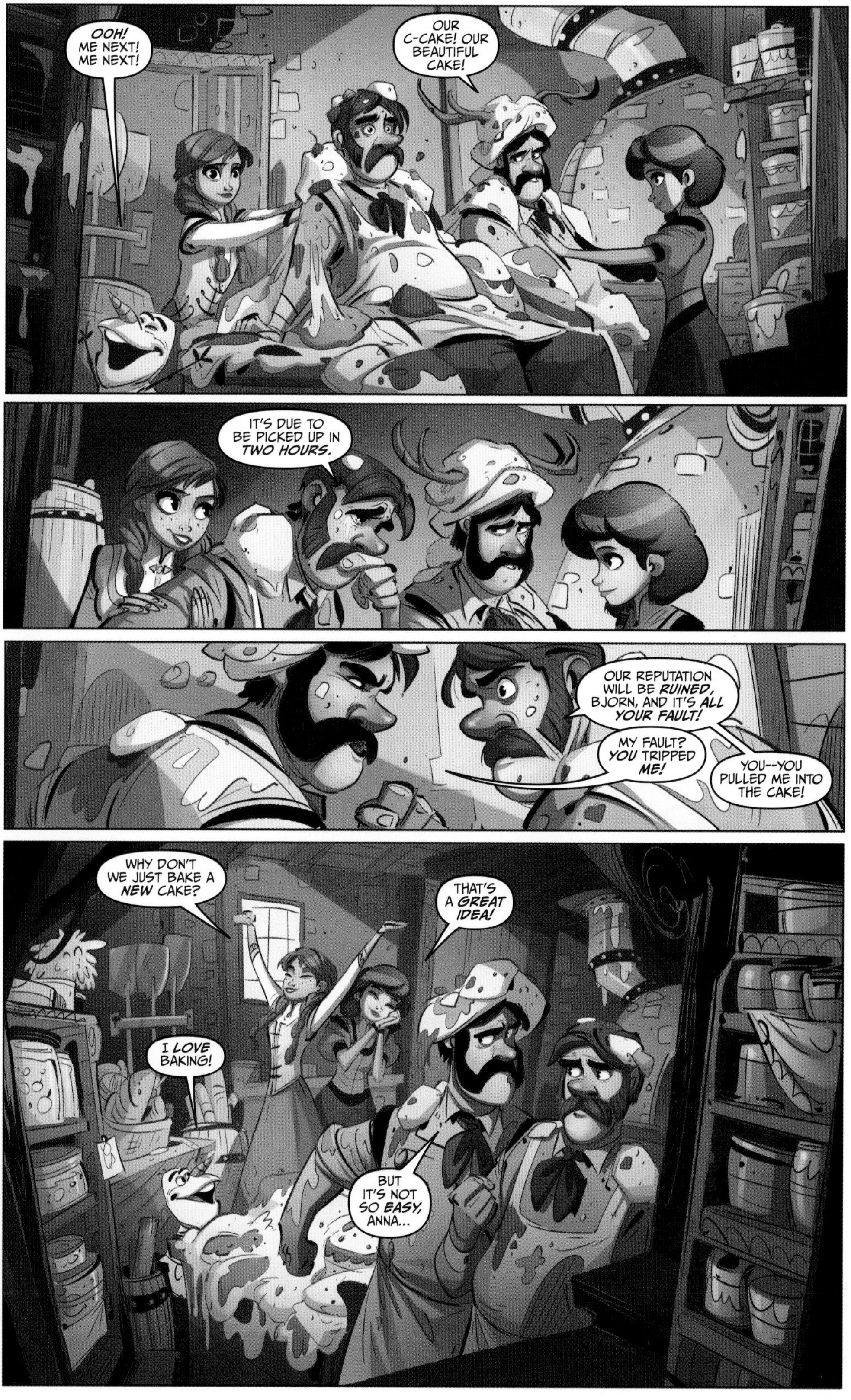
OOH! ME NEXT! ME NEXT!
OUR C-CAKE! OUR BEAUTIFUL CAKE!
IT'S DUE TO BE PICKED UP IN TWO HOURS.
OUR REPUTATION WILL BE RUINED, BJORN, AND IT'S ALL YOUR FAULT!
MY FAULT? YOU TRIPPED ME!
YOU--YOU PULLED ME INTO THE CAKE!
WHY DON'T WE JUST BAKE A NEW CAKE?
THAT'S A GREAT IDEA!
I LOVE BAKING!
BUT IT'S NOT SO EASY, ANNA...

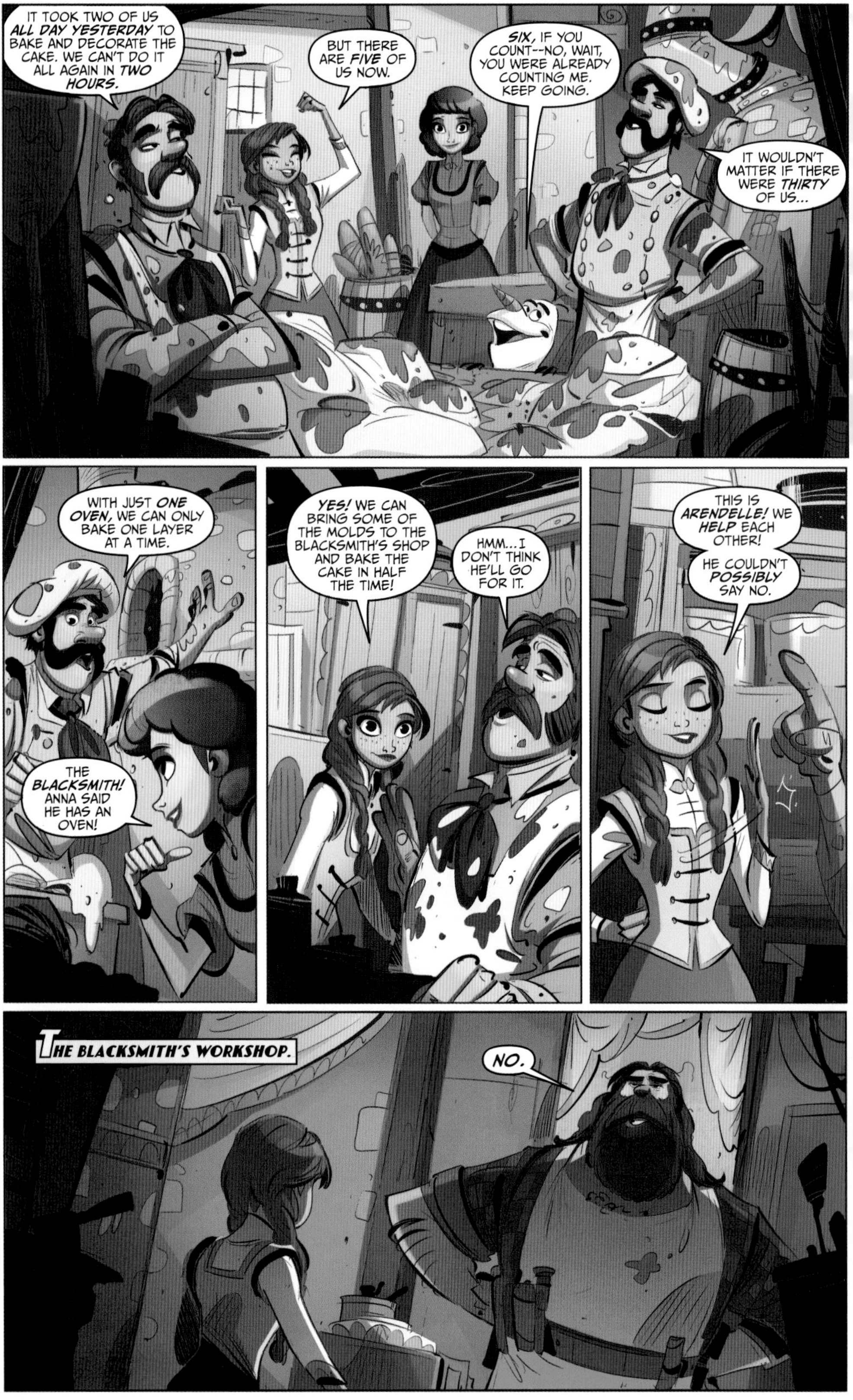
IT TOOK TWO OF US ALL DAY YESTERDAY TO BAKE AND DECORATE THE CAKE. WE CAN'T DO IT ALL AGAIN IN TWO HOURS.
BUT THERE ARE FIVE OF US NOW.
SIX, IF YOU COUNT--NO, WAIT, YOU WERE ALREADY COUNTING ME. KEEP GOING.
IT WOULDN'T MATTER IF THERE WERE THIRTY OF US...
WITH JUST ONE OVEN, WE CAN ONLY BAKE ONE LAYER AT A TIME.
THE BLACKSMITH! ANNA SAID HE HAS AN OVEN!
YES! WE CAN BRING SOME OF THE MOLDS TO THE BLACKSMITH'S SHOP AND BAKE THE CAKE IN HALF THE TIME!
HMM...I DON'T THINK HE'LL GO FOR IT.
THIS IS ARENDELLE! WE HELP EACH OTHER!
HE COULDN'T POSSIBLY SAY NO.
THE BLACKSMITH'S WORKSHOP.
NO.

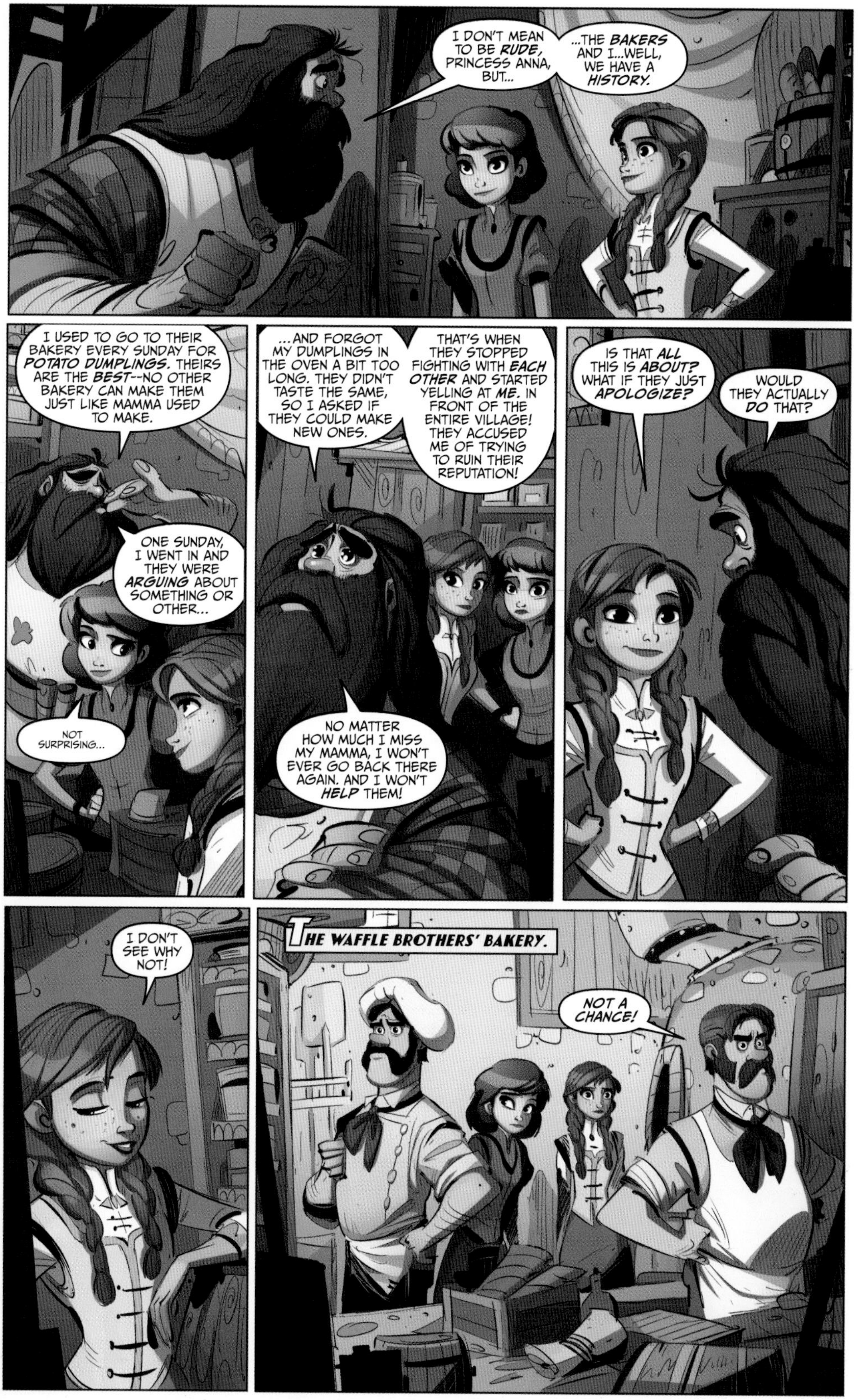
I DON'T MEAN TO BE RUDE, PRINCESS ANNA, BUT...
...THE BAKERS AND I...WELL, WE HAVE A HISTORY.
I USED TO GO TO THEIR BAKERY EVERY SUNDAY FOR POTATO DUMPLINGS. THEIRS ARE THE BEST--NO OTHER BAKERY CAN MAKE THEM JUST LIKE MAMMA USED TO MAKE.
ONE SUNDAY, I WENT IN AND THEY WERE ARGUING ABOUT SOMETHING OR OTHER...
NOT SURPRISING...
...AND FORGOT MY DUMPLINGS IN THE OVEN A BIT TOO LONG. THEY DIDN'T TASTE THE SAME, SO I ASKED IF THEY COULD MAKE NEW ONES.
THAT'S WHEN THEY STOPPED FIGHTING WITH EACH OTHER AND STARTED YELLING AT ME. IN FRONT OF THE ENTIRE VILLAGE! THEY ACCUSED ME OF TRYING TO RUIN THEIR REPUTATION!
NO MATTER HOW MUCH I MISS MY MAMMA, I WON'T EVER GO BACK THERE AGAIN. AND I WON'T HELP THEM!
IS THAT ALL THIS IS ABOUT? WHAT IF THEY JUST APOLOGIZE?
WOULD THEY ACTUALLY DO THAT?
I DON'T SEE WHY NOT!
THE WAFFLE BROTHERS' BAKERY.
NOT A CHANCE!

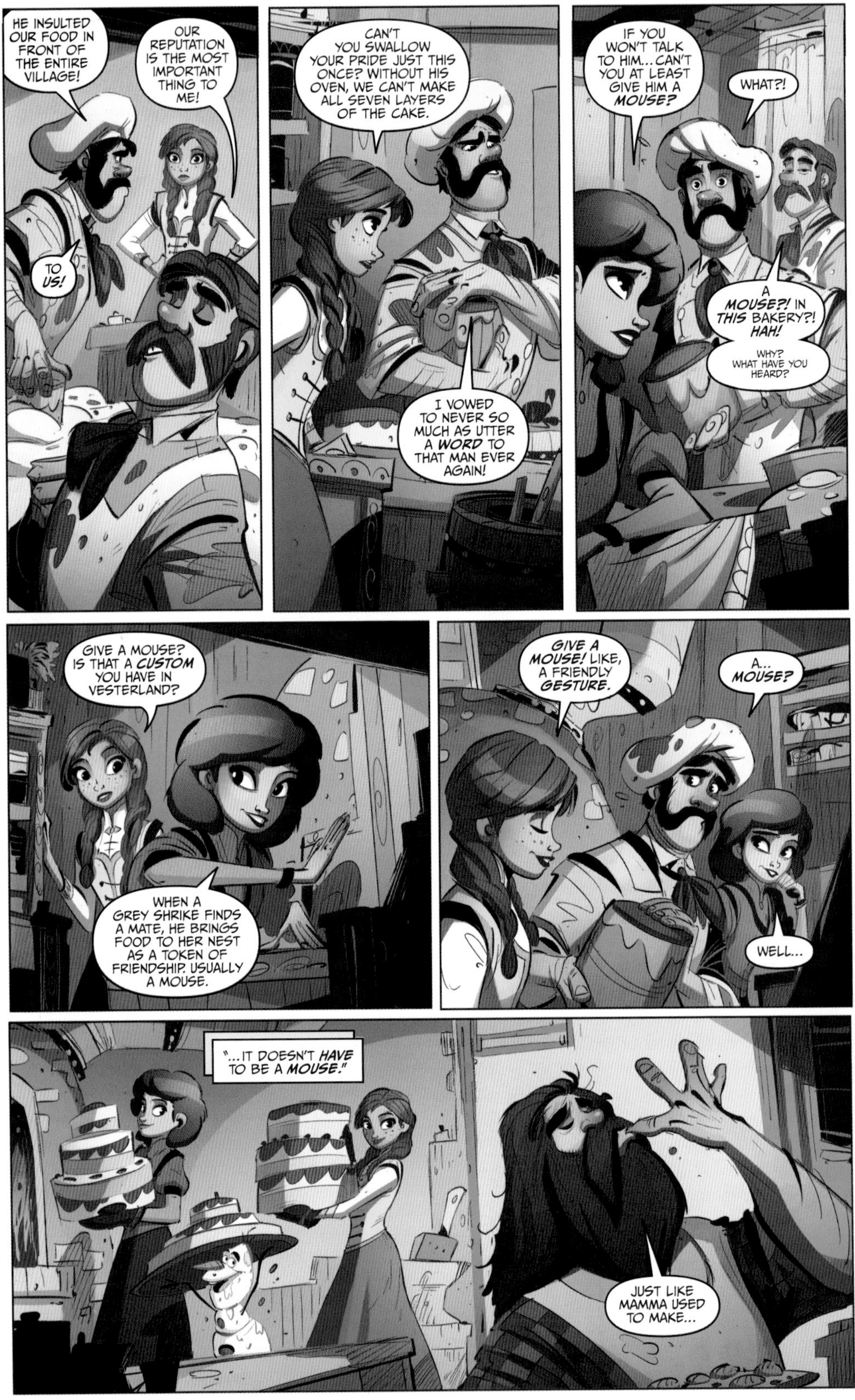
HE INSULTED OUR FOOD IN FRONT OF THE ENTIRE VILLAGE!
OUR REPUTATION IS THE MOST IMPORTANT THING TO ME!
TO US!
CAN'T YOU SWALLOW YOUR PRIDE JUST THIS ONCE? WITHOUT HIS OVEN, WE CAN'T MAKE ALL SEVEN LAYERS OF THE CAKE.
I VOWED TO NEVER SO MUCH AS UTTER A WORD TO THAT MAN EVER AGAIN!
IF YOU WON'T TALK TO HIM... CAN'T YOU AT LEAST GIVE HIM A MOUSE?
WHAT?!
A MOUSE?! IN THIS BAKERY?! HAH!
WHY? WHAT HAVE YOU HEARD?
GIVE A MOUSE? IS THAT A CUSTOM YOU HAVE IN VESTERLAND?
WHEN A GREY SHRIKE FINDS A MATE, HE BRINGS FOOD TO HER NEST AS A TOKEN OF FRIENDSHIP. USUALLY A MOUSE.
GIVE A MOUSE! LIKE, A FRIENDLY GESTURE.
A... MOUSE?
WELL...
"...IT DOESN'T HAVE TO BE A MOUSE."
JUST LIKE MAMMA USED TO MAKE...

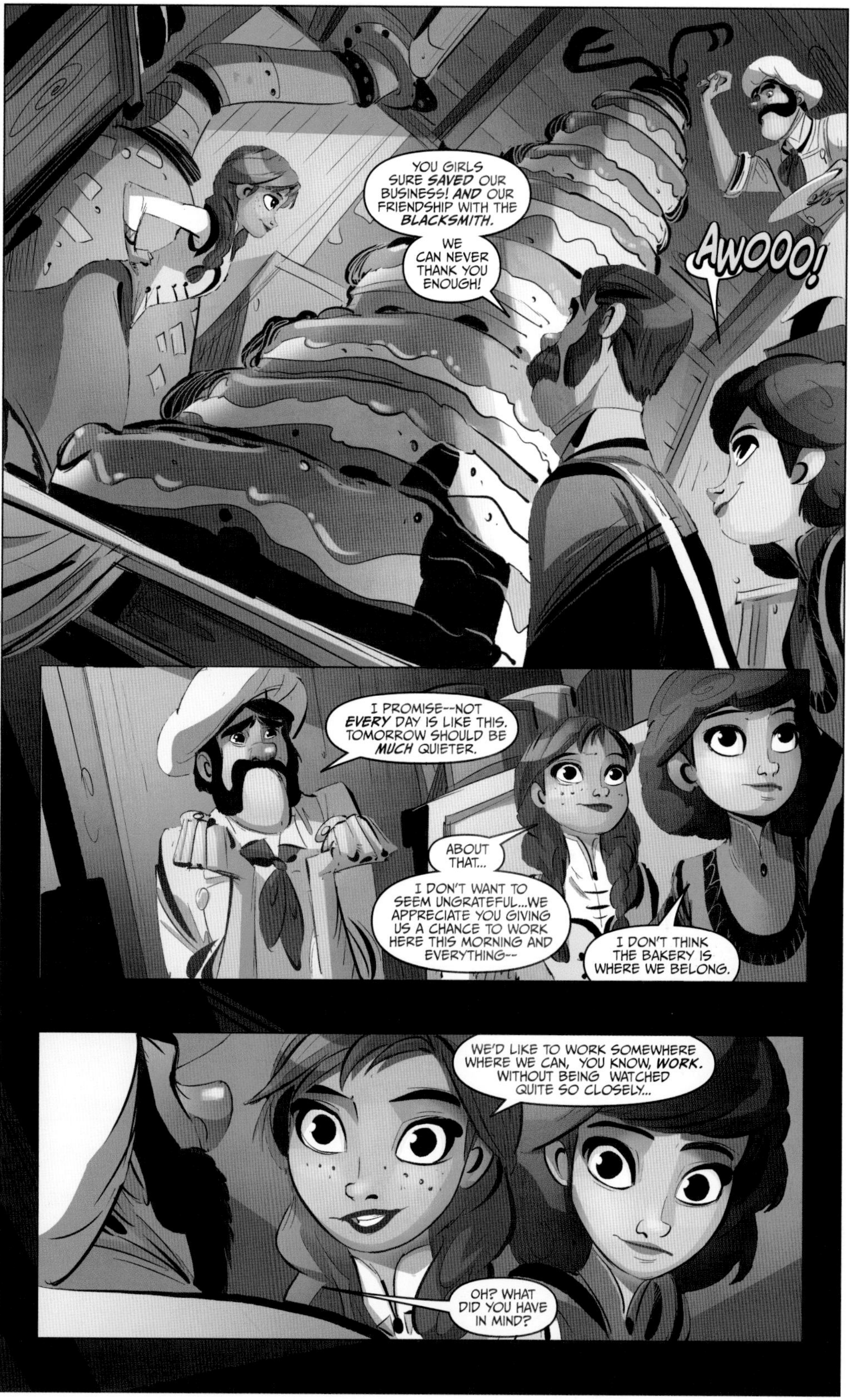

YOU GIRLS SURE SAVED OUR BUSINESS! AND OUR FRIENDSHIP WITH THE BLACKSMITH.
WE CAN NEVER THANK YOU ENOUGH!
AWOOO!
I PROMISE--NOT EVERY DAY IS LIKE THIS. TOMORROW SHOULD BE MUCH QUIETER.
ABOUT THAT...
I DON'T WANT TO SEEM UNGRATEFUL...WE APPRECIATE YOU GIVING US A CHANCE TO WORK HERE THIS MORNING AND EVERYTHING--
I DON'T THINK THE BAKERY IS WHERE WE BELONG.
WE'D LIKE TO WORK SOMEWHERE WHERE WE CAN, YOU KNOW, WORK. WITHOUT BEING WATCHED QUITE SO CLOSELY...
OH? WHAT DID YOU HAVE IN MIND?

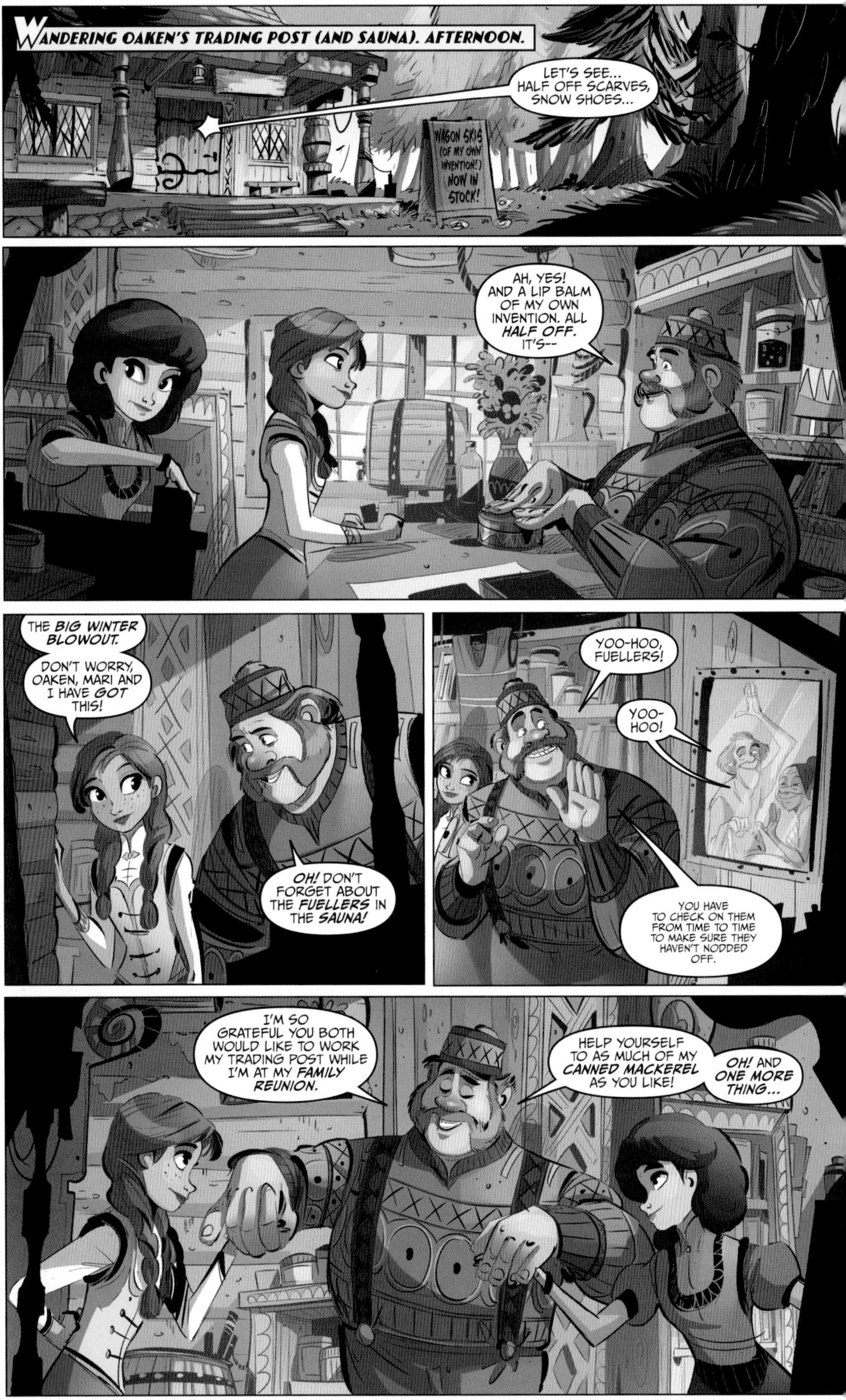
WANDERING OAKEN'S TRADING POST (AND SAUNA). AFTERNOON.
LET'S SEE... HALF OFF SCARVES, SNOW SHOES...
WAGON SKIS (OF MY OWN INVENTION!) NOW IN STOCK!
AH, YES! AND A LIP BALM OF MY OWN INVENTION. ALL HALF OFF. IT'S--
THE BIG WINTER BLOWOUT.
DON'T WORRY, OAKEN, MARI AND I HAVE GOT THIS!
OH! DON'T FORGET ABOUT THE FUELLERS IN THE SAUNA!
YOO-HOO, FUELLERS!
YOO-HOO!
YOU HAVE TO CHECK ON THEM FROM TIME TO TIME TO MAKE SURE THEY HAVEN'T NODDED OFF.
I'M SO GRATEFUL YOU BOTH WOULD LIKE TO WORK MY TRADING POST WHILE I'M AT MY FAMILY REUNION.
HELP YOURSELF TO AS MUCH OF MY CANNED MACKEREL AS YOU LIKE!
OH! AND ONE MORE THING...

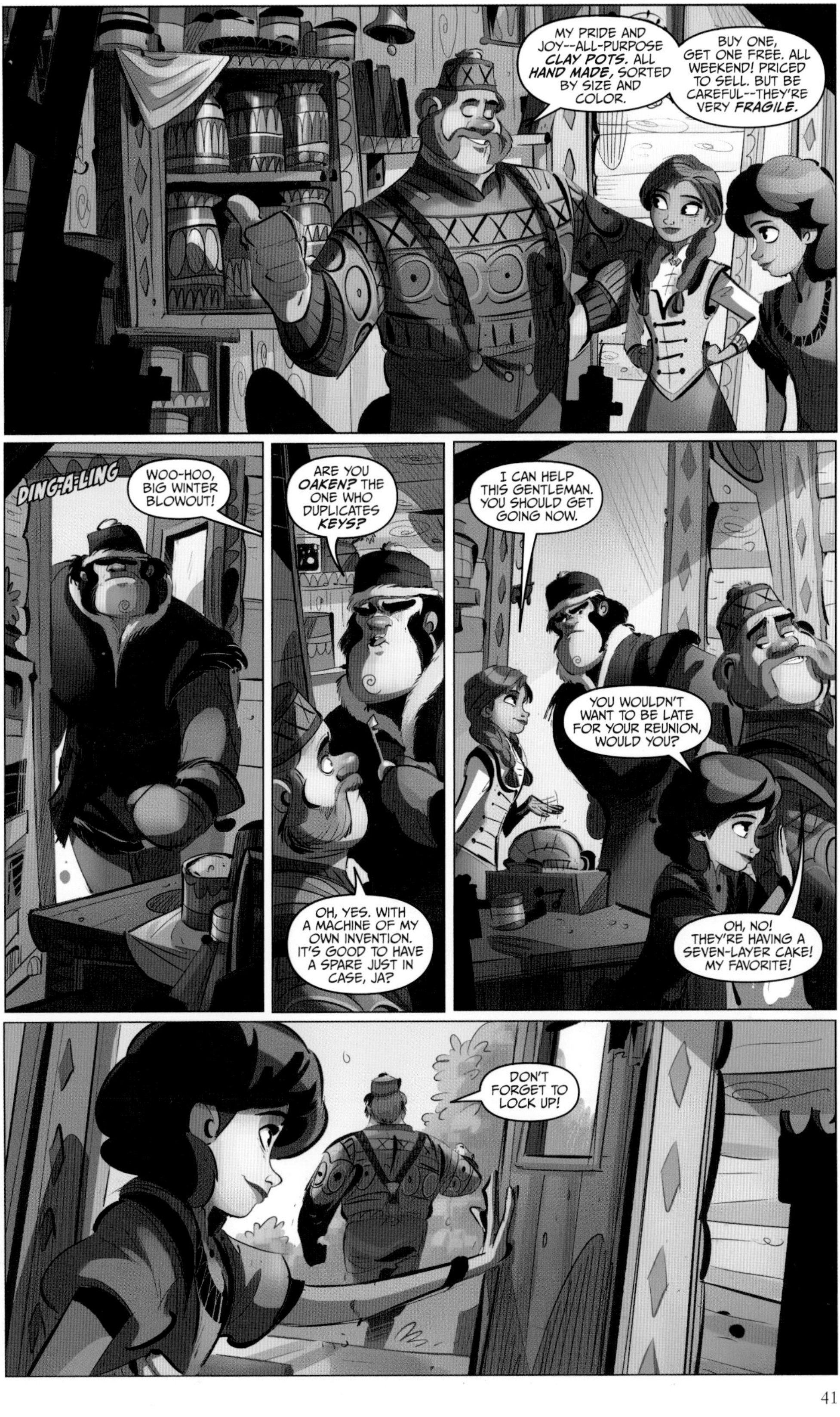

MY PRIDE AND JOY--ALL-PURPOSE CLAY POTS. ALL HAND MADE, SORTED BY SIZE AND COLOR.
BUY ONE, GET ONE FREE. ALL WEEKEND! PRICED TO SELL. BUT BE CAREFUL--THEY'RE VERY FRAGILE.
DING-A-LING
WOO-HOO, BIG WINTER BLOWOUT!
ARE YOU OAKEN? THE ONE WHO DUPLICATES KEYS?
OH, YES. WITH A MACHINE OF MY OWN INVENTION. IT'S GOOD TO HAVE A SPARE JUST IN CASE, JA?
I CAN HELP THIS GENTLEMAN. YOU SHOULD GET GOING NOW.
YOU WOULDN'T WANT TO BE LATE FOR YOUR REUNION, WOULD YOU?
OH, NO! THEY'RE HAVING A SEVEN-LAYER CAKE! MY FAVORITE!
DON'T FORGET TO LOCK UP!

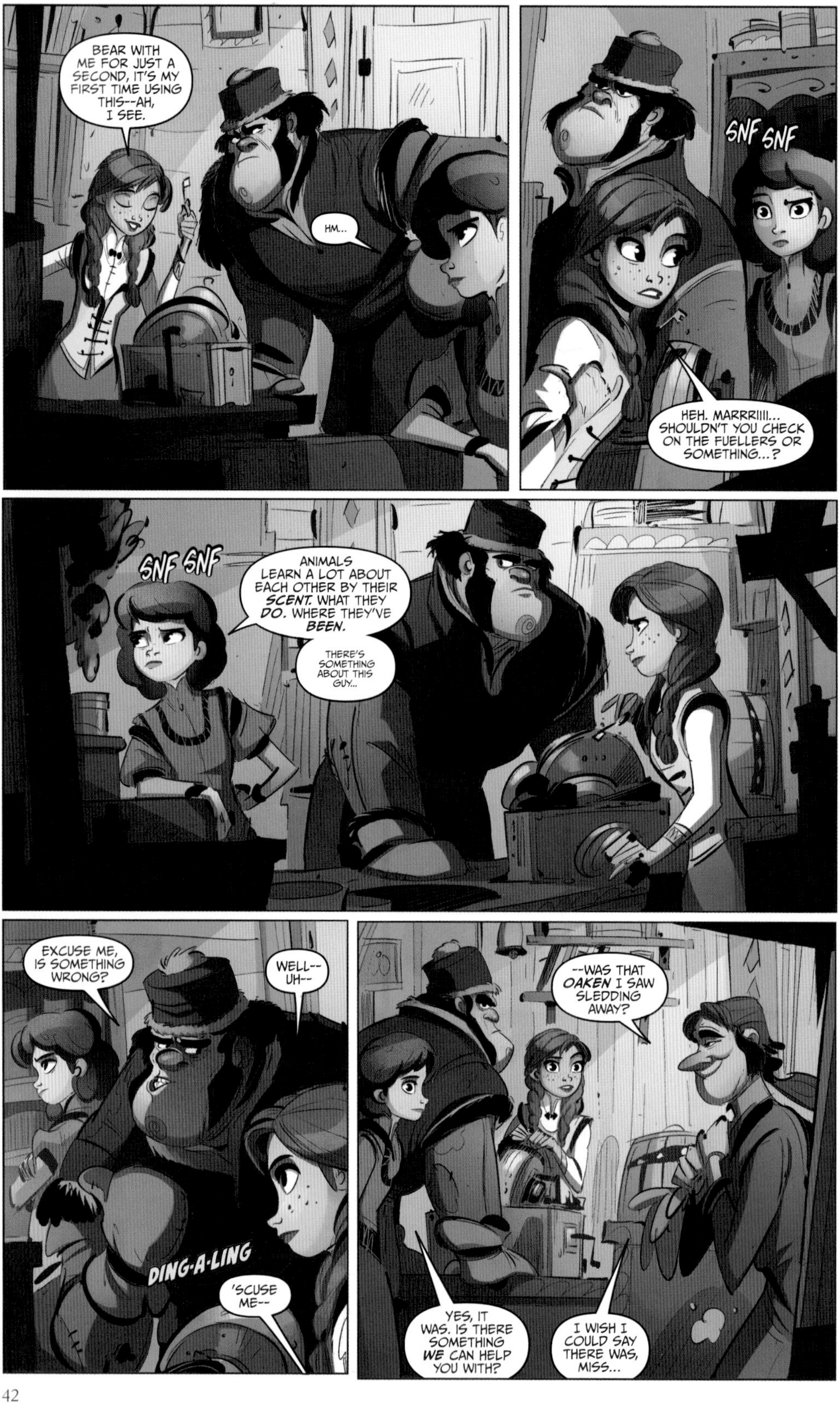
BEAR WITH ME FOR JUST A SECOND, IT'S MY FIRST TIME USING THIS--AH, I SEE.
HM...
SNF SNF
HEH. MARRRIIII... SHOULDN'T YOU CHECK ON THE FUELLERS OR SOMETHING...?
SNF SNF
ANIMALS LEARN A LOT ABOUT EACH OTHER BY THEIR SCENT. WHAT THEY DO. WHERE THEY'VE BEEN.
THERE'S SOMETHING ABOUT THIS GUY...
EXCUSE ME, IS SOMETHING WRONG?
WELL-- UH--
DING-A-LING
'SCUSE ME--
--WAS THAT OAKEN I SAW SLEDDING AWAY?
YES, IT WAS. IS THERE SOMETHING WE CAN HELP YOU WITH?
I WISH I COULD SAY THERE WAS, MISS...

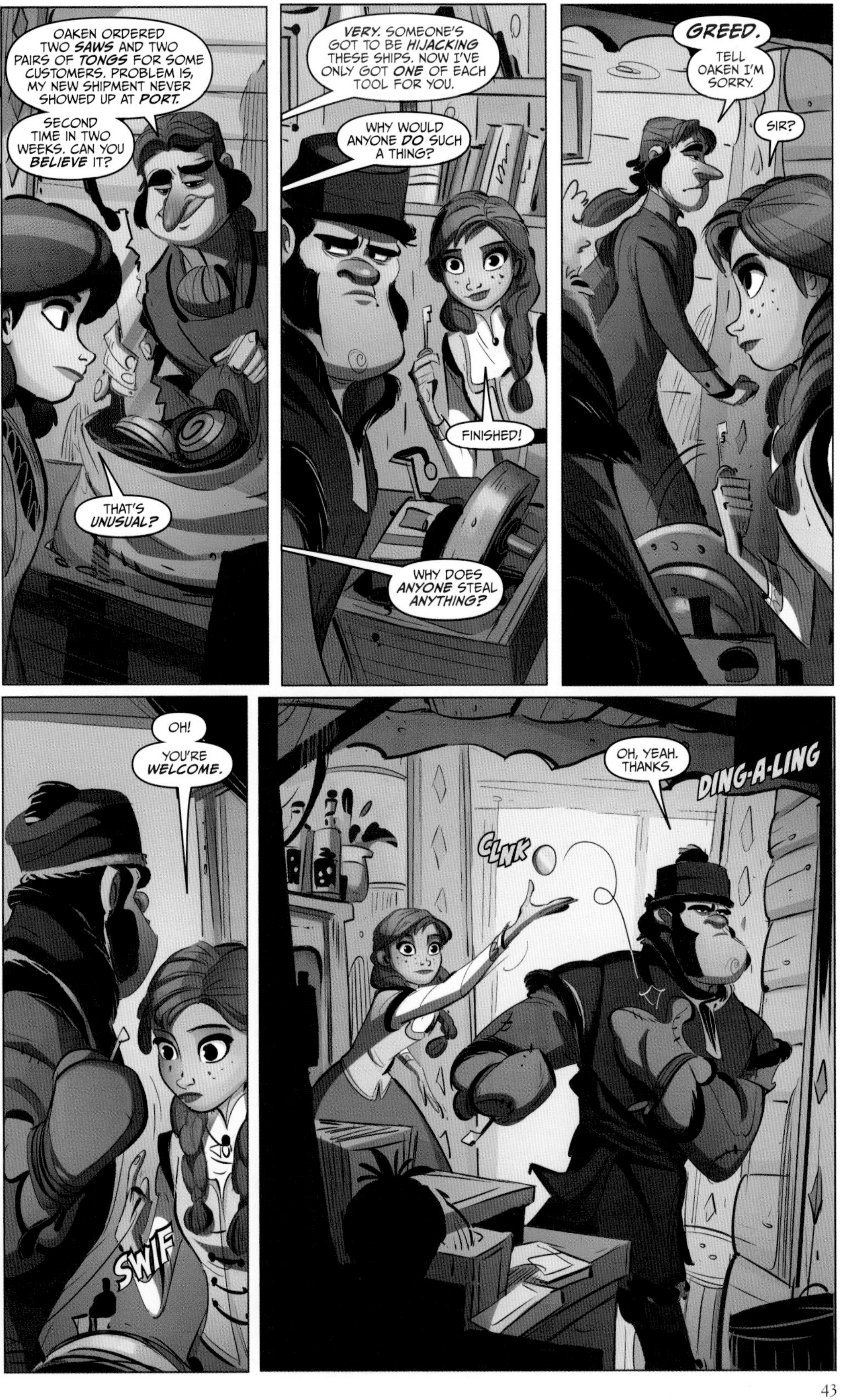
OAKEN ORDERED TWO SAWS AND TWO PAIRS OF TONGS FOR SOME CUSTOMERS. PROBLEM IS, MY NEW SHIPMENT NEVER SHOWED UP AT PORT.
SECOND TIME IN TWO WEEKS. CAN YOU BELIEVE IT?
THAT'S UNUSUAL?
VERY. SOMEONE'S GOT TO BE HIJACKING THESE SHIPS. NOW I'VE ONLY GOT ONE OF EACH TOOL FOR YOU.
WHY WOULD ANYONE DO SUCH A THING?
FINISHED!
WHY DOES ANYONE STEAL ANYTHING?
GREED.
TELL OAKEN I'M SORRY.
SIR?
OH!
YOU'RE WELCOME.
SWIF
OH, YEAH. THANKS.
DING-A-LING
CLNK

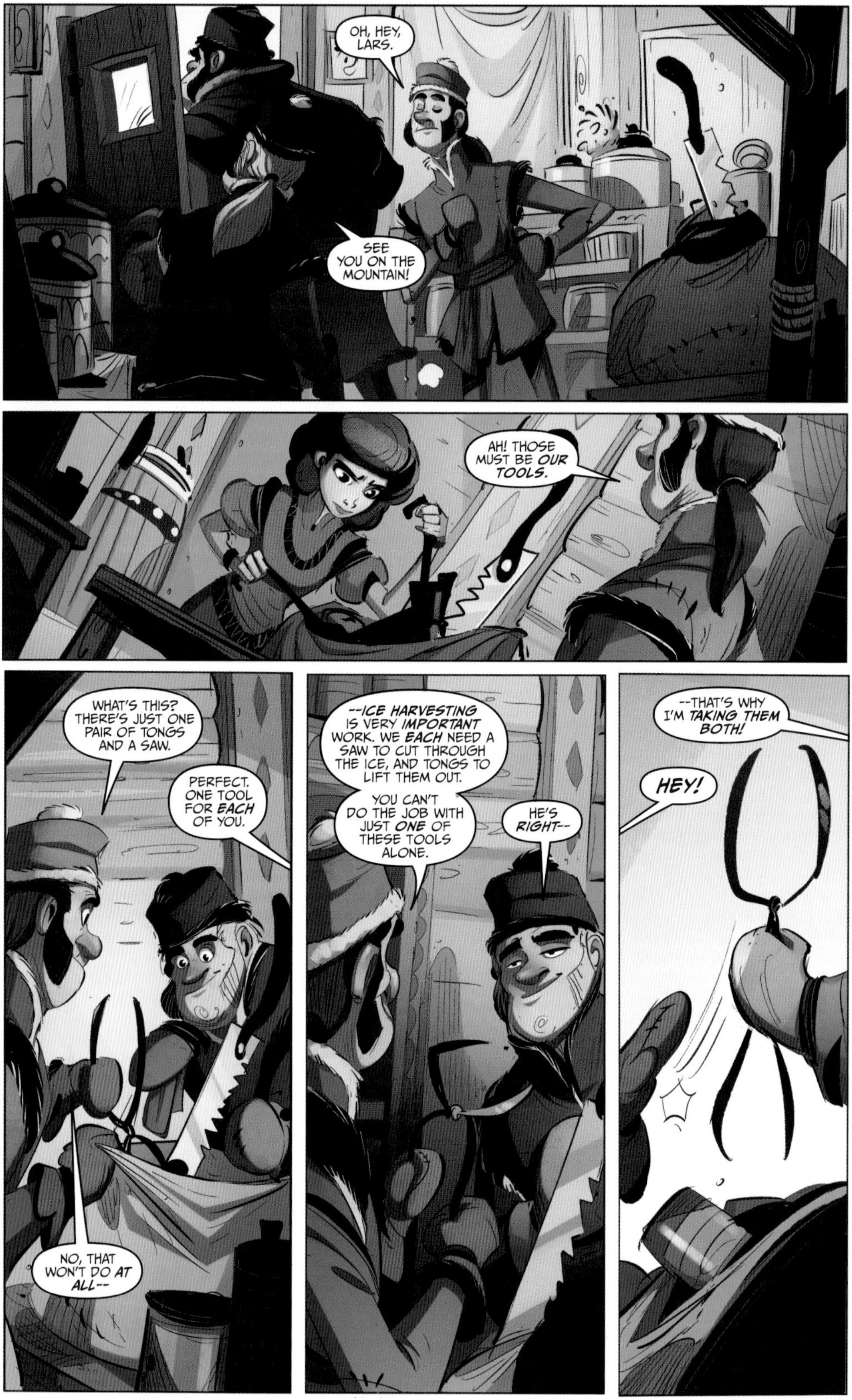
OH, HEY, LARS.
SEE YOU ON THE MOUNTAIN!
AH! THOSE MUST BE *OUR TOOLS.*
WHAT'S THIS? THERE'S JUST ONE PAIR OF TONGS AND A SAW.
PERFECT. ONE TOOL FOR *EACH* OF YOU.
NO, THAT WON'T DO *AT ALL*--
--*ICE HARVESTING* IS VERY *IMPORTANT* WORK. WE *EACH* NEED A SAW TO CUT THROUGH THE ICE, AND TONGS TO LIFT THEM OUT.
YOU CAN'T DO THE JOB WITH JUST *ONE* OF THESE TOOLS ALONE.
HE'S *RIGHT*--
--THAT'S WHY I'M *TAKING THEM BOTH!*
HEY!

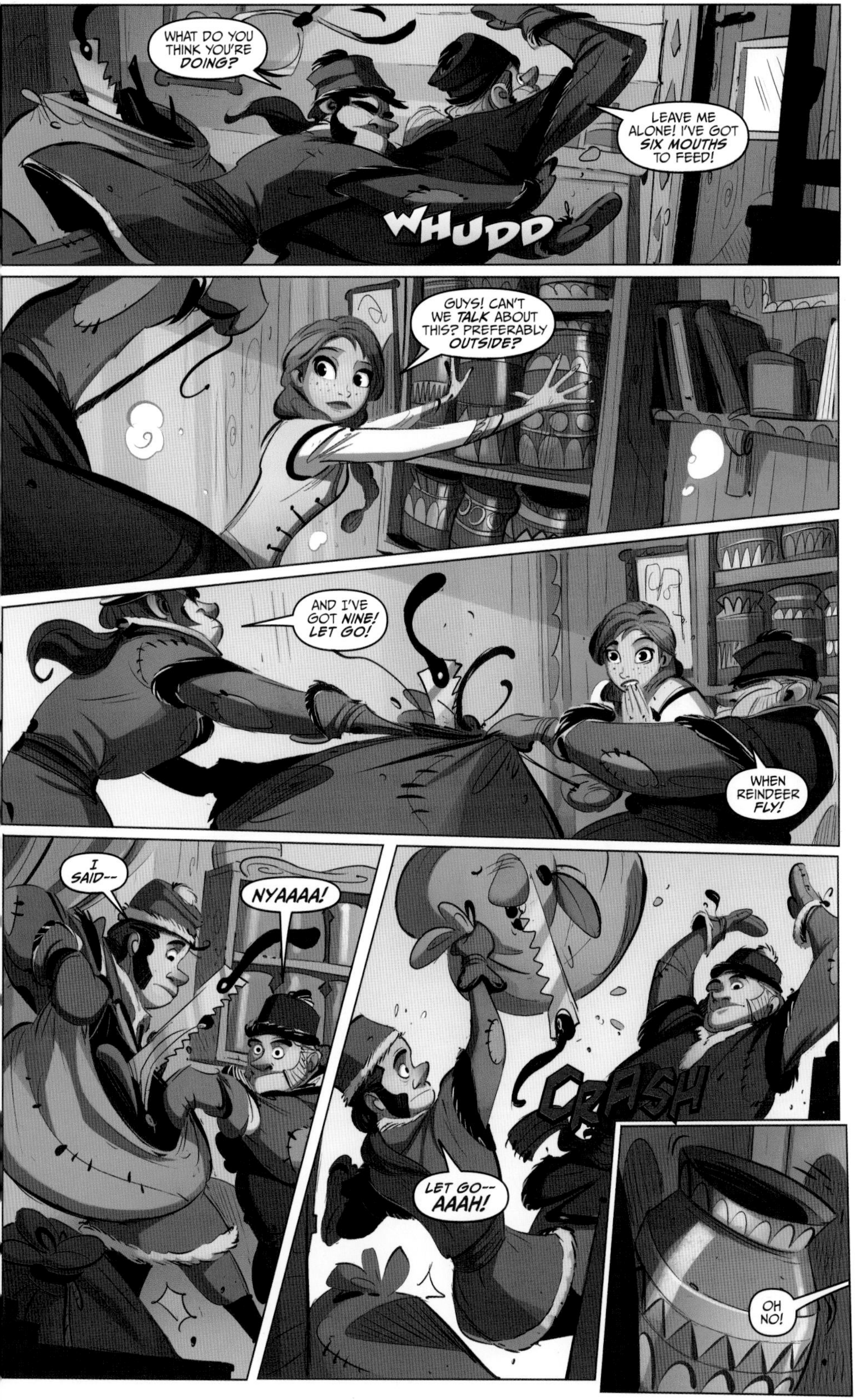
WHAT DO YOU THINK YOU'RE DOING?
LEAVE ME ALONE! I'VE GOT SIX MOUTHS TO FEED!
WHUDD
GUYS! CAN'T WE TALK ABOUT THIS? PREFERABLY OUTSIDE?
AND I'VE GOT NINE! LET GO!
WHEN REINDEER FLY!
I SAID--
NYAAAA!
CRASH
LET GO-- AAAH!
OH NO!

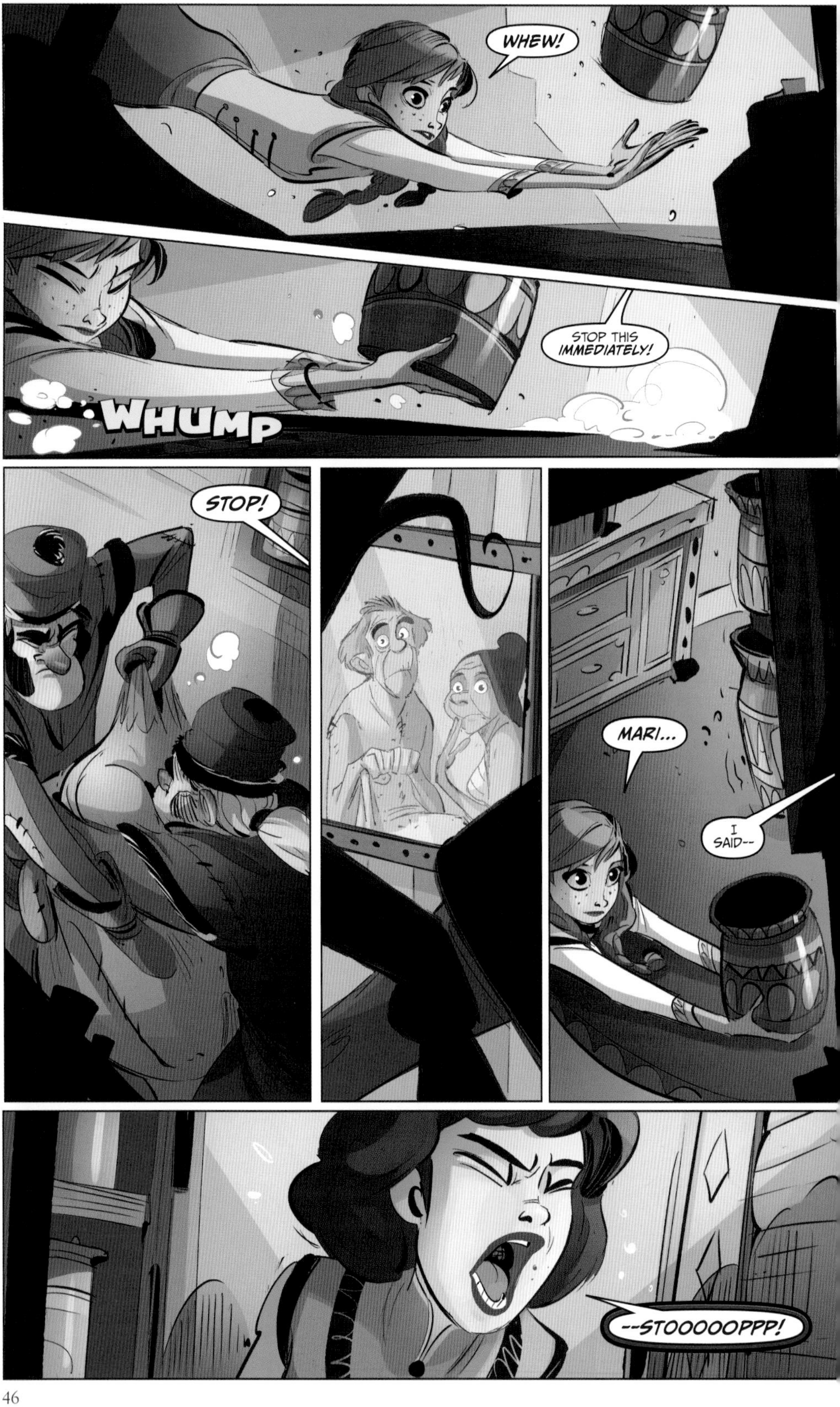
WHEW!
STOP THIS IMMEDIATELY!
WHUMP
STOP!
MARI...
I SAID--
--STOOOOOPPP!

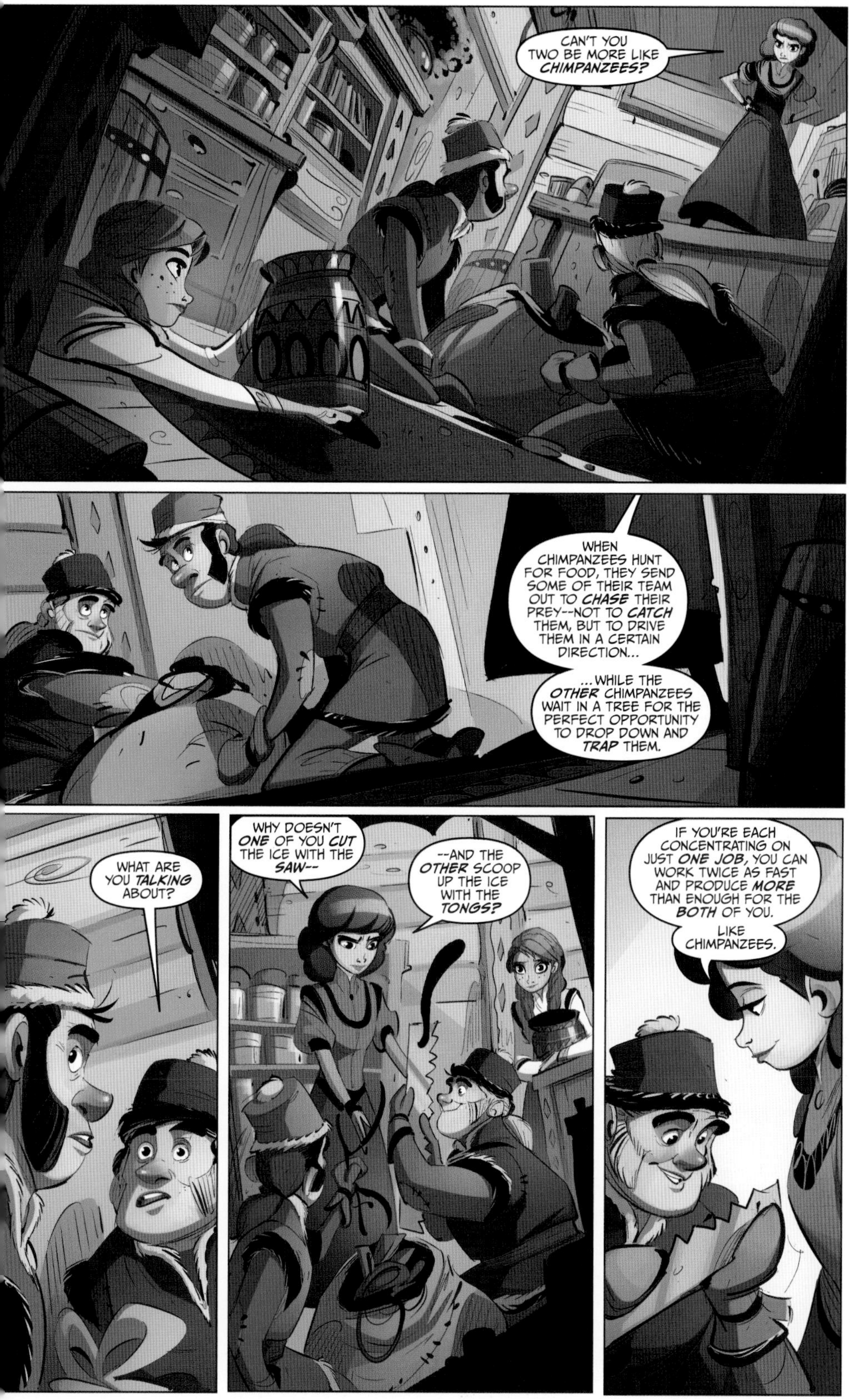

CAN'T YOU TWO BE MORE LIKE CHIMPANZEES?
WHEN CHIMPANZEES HUNT FOR FOOD, THEY SEND SOME OF THEIR TEAM OUT TO CHASE THEIR PREY--NOT TO CATCH THEM, BUT TO DRIVE THEM IN A CERTAIN DIRECTION...
...WHILE THE OTHER CHIMPANZEES WAIT IN A TREE FOR THE PERFECT OPPORTUNITY TO DROP DOWN AND TRAP THEM.
WHAT ARE YOU TALKING ABOUT?
WHY DOESN'T ONE OF YOU CUT THE ICE WITH THE SAW--
--AND THE OTHER SCOOP UP THE ICE WITH THE TONGS?
IF YOU'RE EACH CONCENTRATING ON JUST ONE JOB, YOU CAN WORK TWICE AS FAST AND PRODUCE MORE THAN ENOUGH FOR THE BOTH OF YOU.
LIKE CHIMPANZEES.

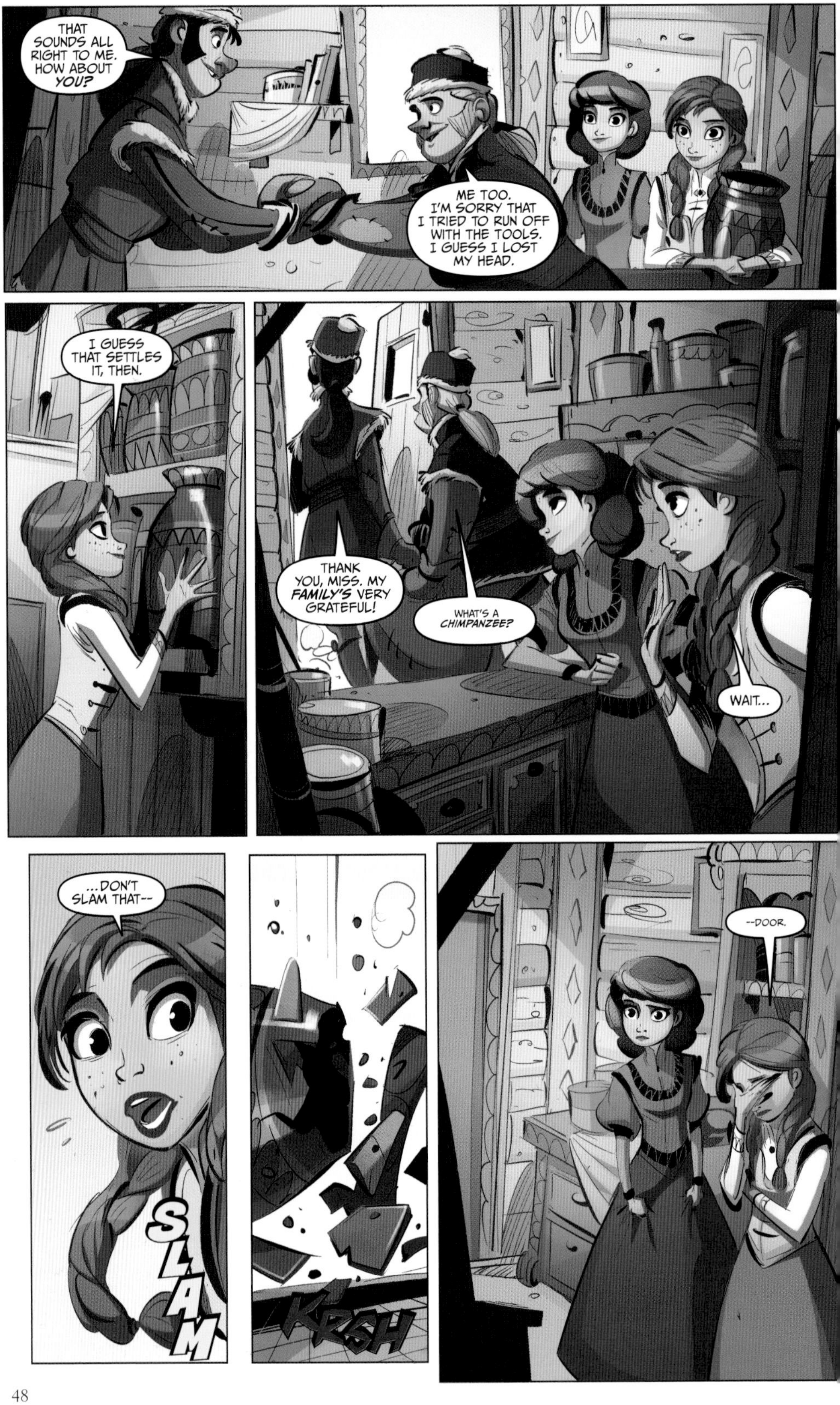
THAT SOUNDS ALL RIGHT TO ME. HOW ABOUT YOU?
ME TOO. I'M SORRY THAT I TRIED TO RUN OFF WITH THE TOOLS. I GUESS I LOST MY HEAD.
I GUESS THAT SETTLES IT, THEN.
THANK YOU, MISS. MY FAMILY'S VERY GRATEFUL!
WHAT'S A CHIMPANZEE?
WAIT...
...DON'T SLAM THAT--
SLAM
KRSH
--DOOR.

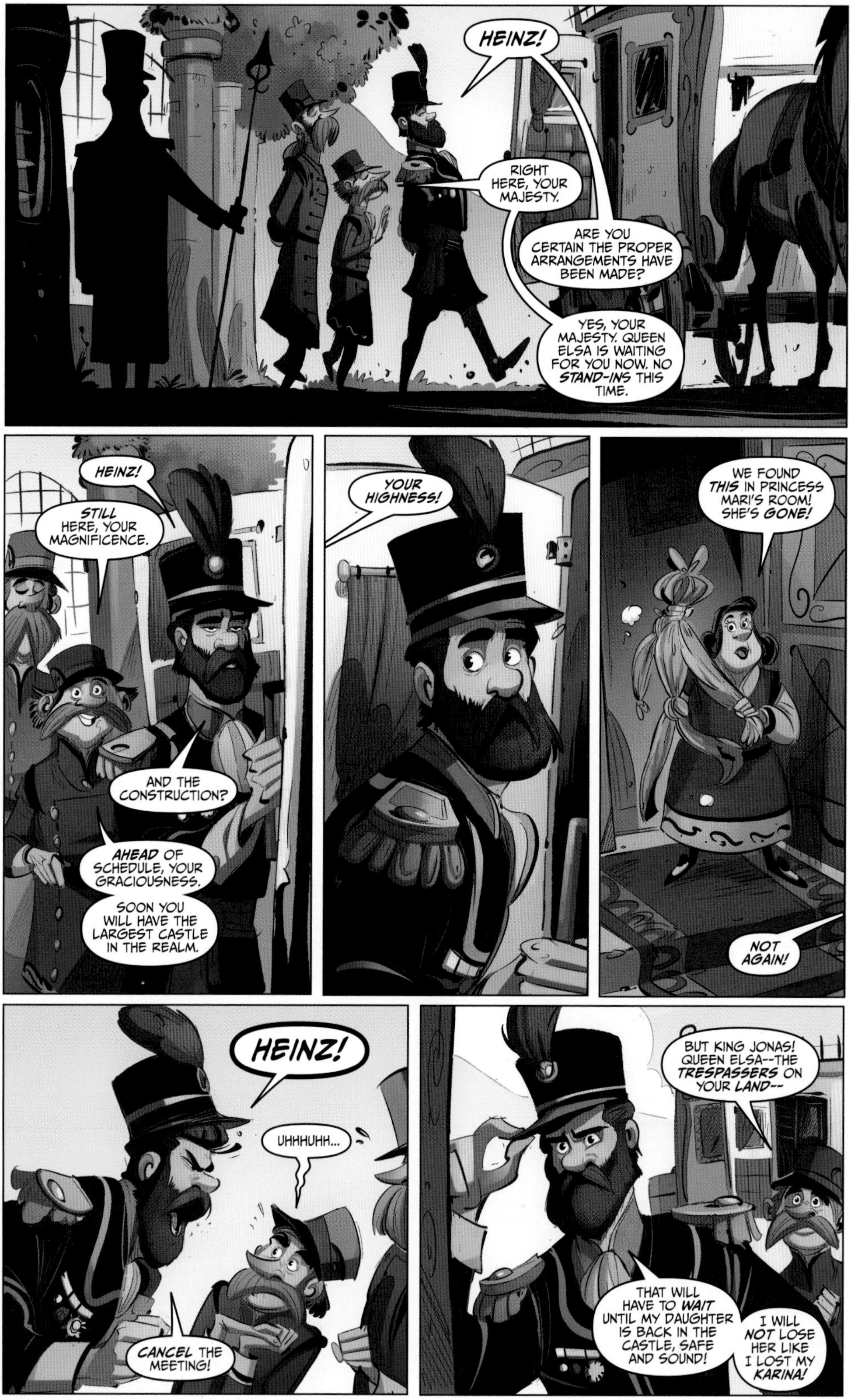
HEINZ!
RIGHT HERE, YOUR MAJESTY.
ARE YOU CERTAIN THE PROPER ARRANGEMENTS HAVE BEEN MADE?
YES, YOUR MAJESTY. QUEEN ELSA IS WAITING FOR YOU NOW. NO STAND-INS THIS TIME.
HEINZ!
STILL HERE, YOUR MAGNIFICENCE.
AND THE CONSTRUCTION?
AHEAD OF SCHEDULE, YOUR GRACIOUSNESS.
SOON YOU WILL HAVE THE LARGEST CASTLE IN THE REALM.
YOUR HIGHNESS!
WE FOUND THIS IN PRINCESS MARI'S ROOM! SHE'S GONE!
NOT AGAIN!
HEINZ!
UHHHUHH...
CANCEL THE MEETING!
BUT KING JONAS! QUEEN ELSA--THE TRESPASSERS ON YOUR LAND--
THAT WILL HAVE TO WAIT UNTIL MY DAUGHTER IS BACK IN THE CASTLE, SAFE AND SOUND!
I WILL NOT LOSE HER LIKE I LOST MY KARINA!

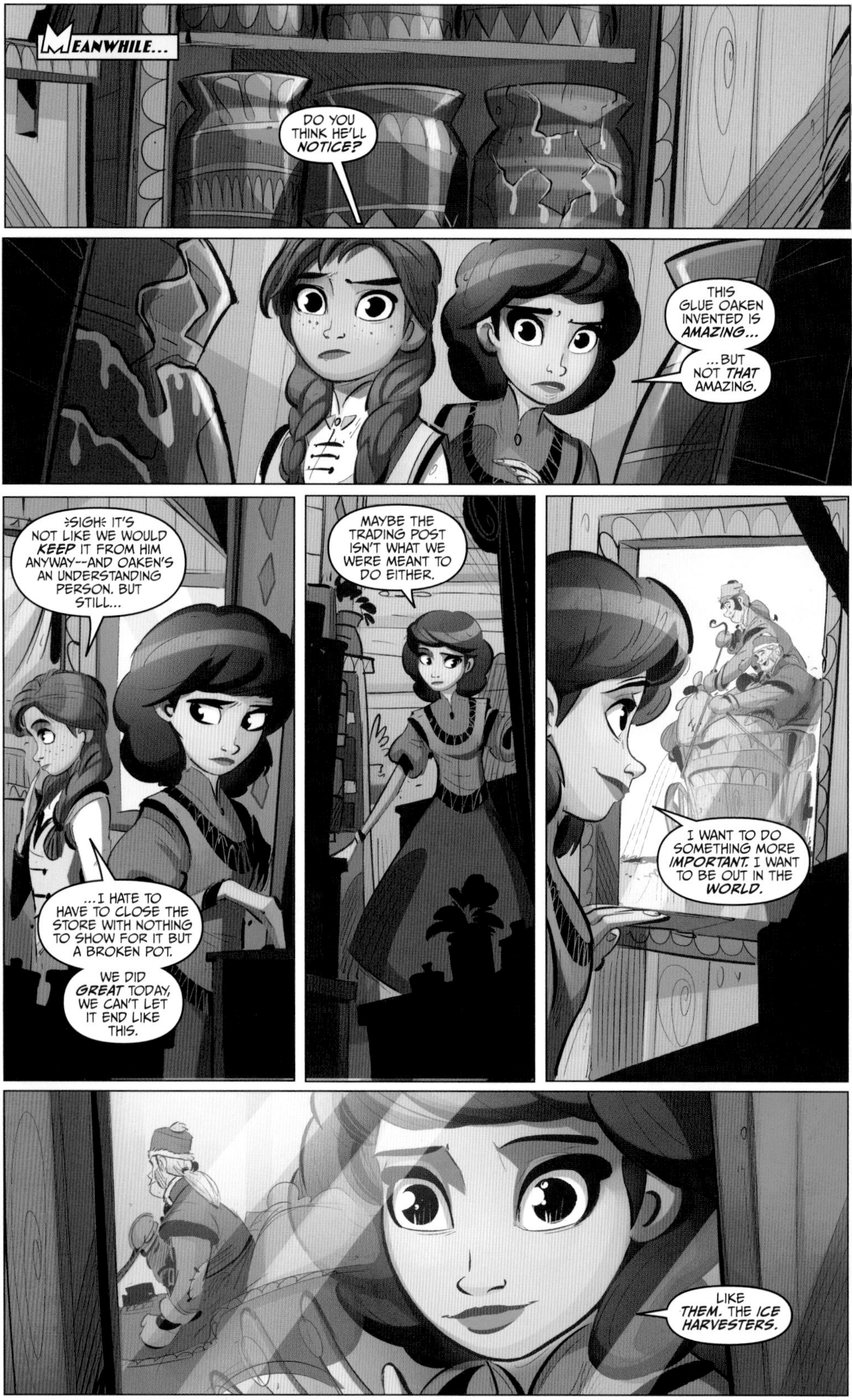
MEANWHILE...
DO YOU THINK HE'LL NOTICE?
THIS GLUE OAKEN INVENTED IS AMAZING...
...BUT NOT THAT AMAZING.
SIGH IT'S NOT LIKE WE WOULD KEEP IT FROM HIM ANYWAY--AND OAKEN'S AN UNDERSTANDING PERSON. BUT STILL...
...I HATE TO HAVE TO CLOSE THE STORE WITH NOTHING TO SHOW FOR IT BUT A BROKEN POT.
WE DID GREAT TODAY, WE CAN'T LET IT END LIKE THIS.
MAYBE THE TRADING POST ISN'T WHAT WE WERE MEANT TO DO EITHER.
I WANT TO DO SOMETHING MORE IMPORTANT. I WANT TO BE OUT IN THE WORLD.
LIKE THEM. THE ICE HARVESTERS.

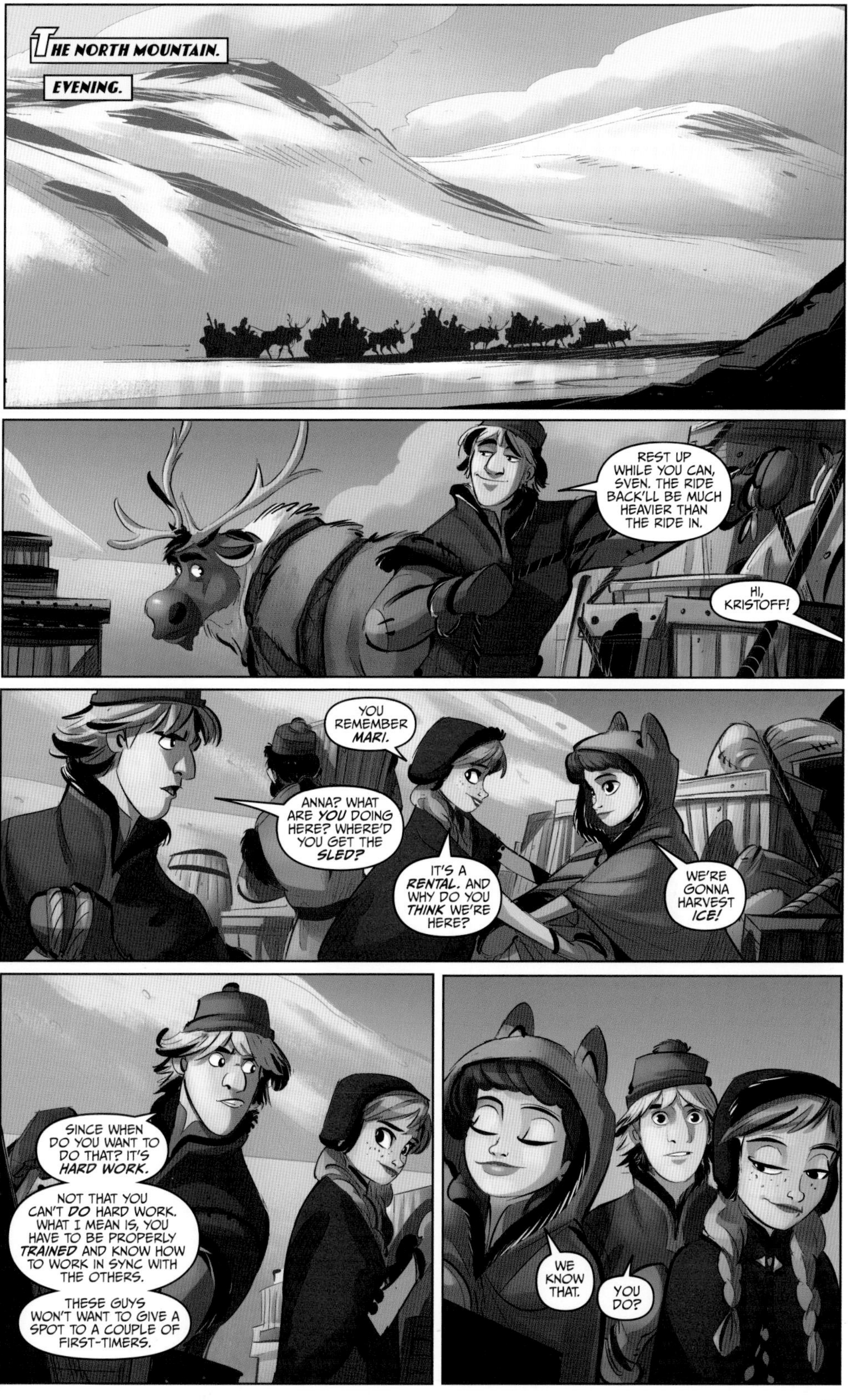
THE NORTH MOUNTAIN.
EVENING.
REST UP WHILE YOU CAN, SVEN. THE RIDE BACK'LL BE MUCH HEAVIER THAN THE RIDE IN.
HI, KRISTOFF!
YOU REMEMBER MARI.
ANNA? WHAT ARE YOU DOING HERE? WHERE'D YOU GET THE SLED?
IT'S A RENTAL. AND WHY DO YOU THINK WE'RE HERE?
WE'RE GONNA HARVEST ICE!
SINCE WHEN DO YOU WANT TO DO THAT? IT'S HARD WORK.
NOT THAT YOU CAN'T DO HARD WORK. WHAT I MEAN IS, YOU HAVE TO BE PROPERLY TRAINED AND KNOW HOW TO WORK IN SYNC WITH THE OTHERS.
THESE GUYS WON'T WANT TO GIVE A SPOT TO A COUPLE OF FIRST-TIMERS.
WE KNOW THAT.
YOU DO?

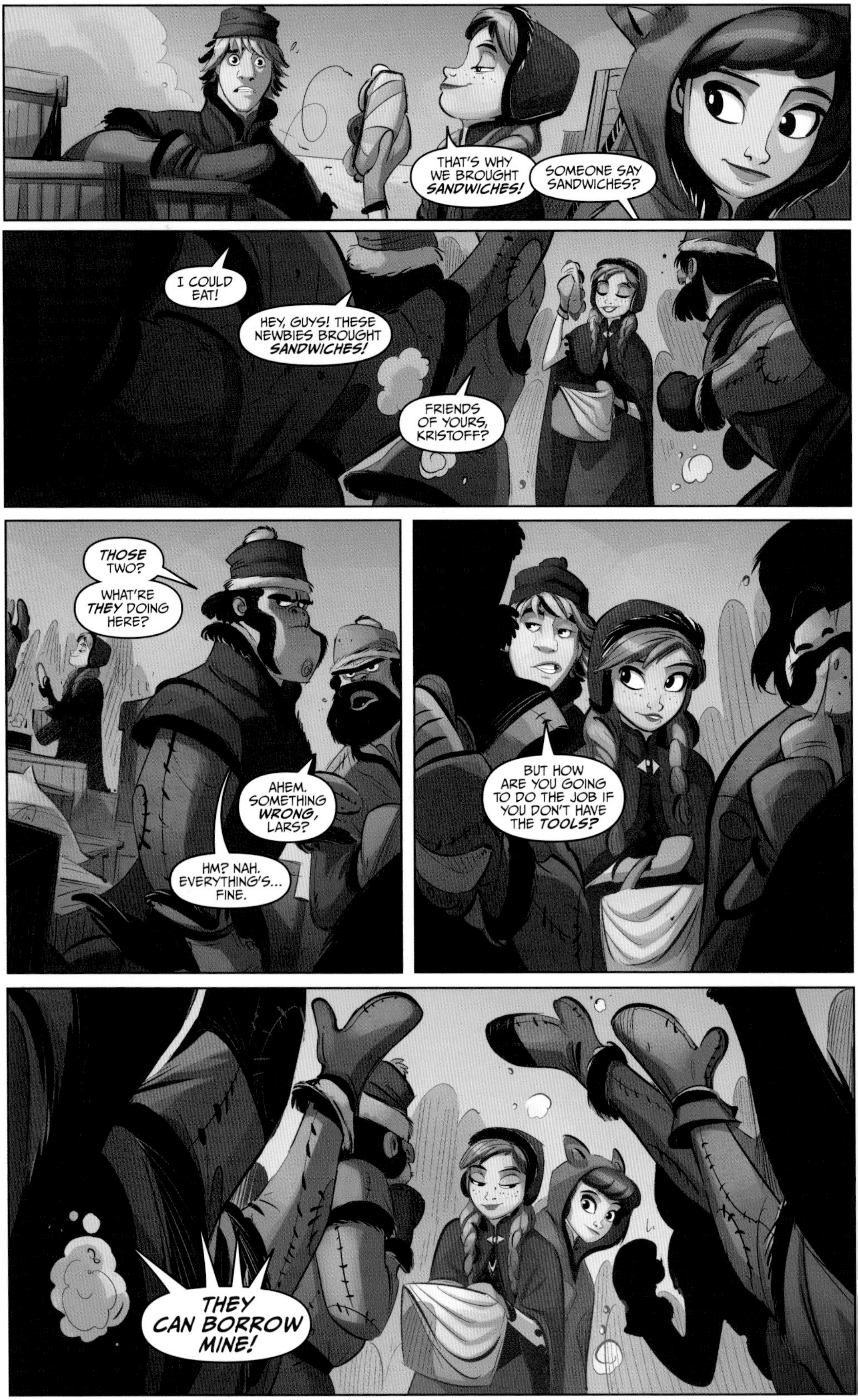
THAT'S WHY WE BROUGHT *SANDWICHES!*
SOMEONE SAY SANDWICHES?
I COULD EAT!
HEY, GUYS! THESE NEWBIES BROUGHT *SANDWICHES!*
FRIENDS OF YOURS, KRISTOFF?
THOSE TWO?
WHAT'RE *THEY* DOING HERE?
AHEM. SOMETHING *WRONG,* LARS?
HM? NAH. EVERYTHING'S... FINE.
BUT HOW ARE YOU GOING TO DO THE JOB IF YOU DON'T HAVE THE *TOOLS?*
THEY CAN BORROW MINE!

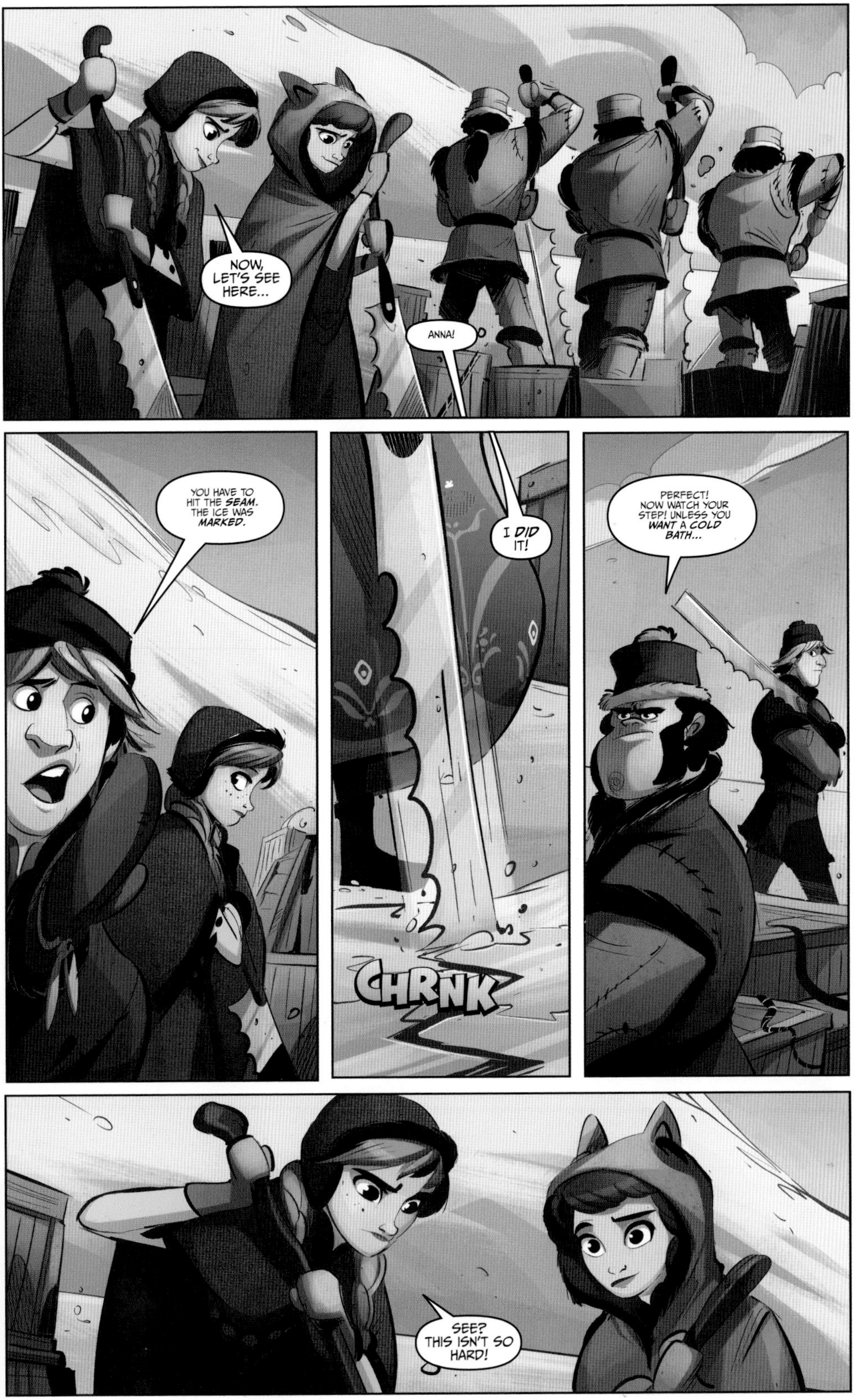
NOW, LET'S SEE HERE...
ANNA!
YOU HAVE TO HIT THE SEAM. THE ICE WAS MARKED.
I DID IT!
CHRNK
PERFECT! NOW WATCH YOUR STEP! UNLESS YOU WANT A COLD BATH...
SEE? THIS ISN'T SO HARD!

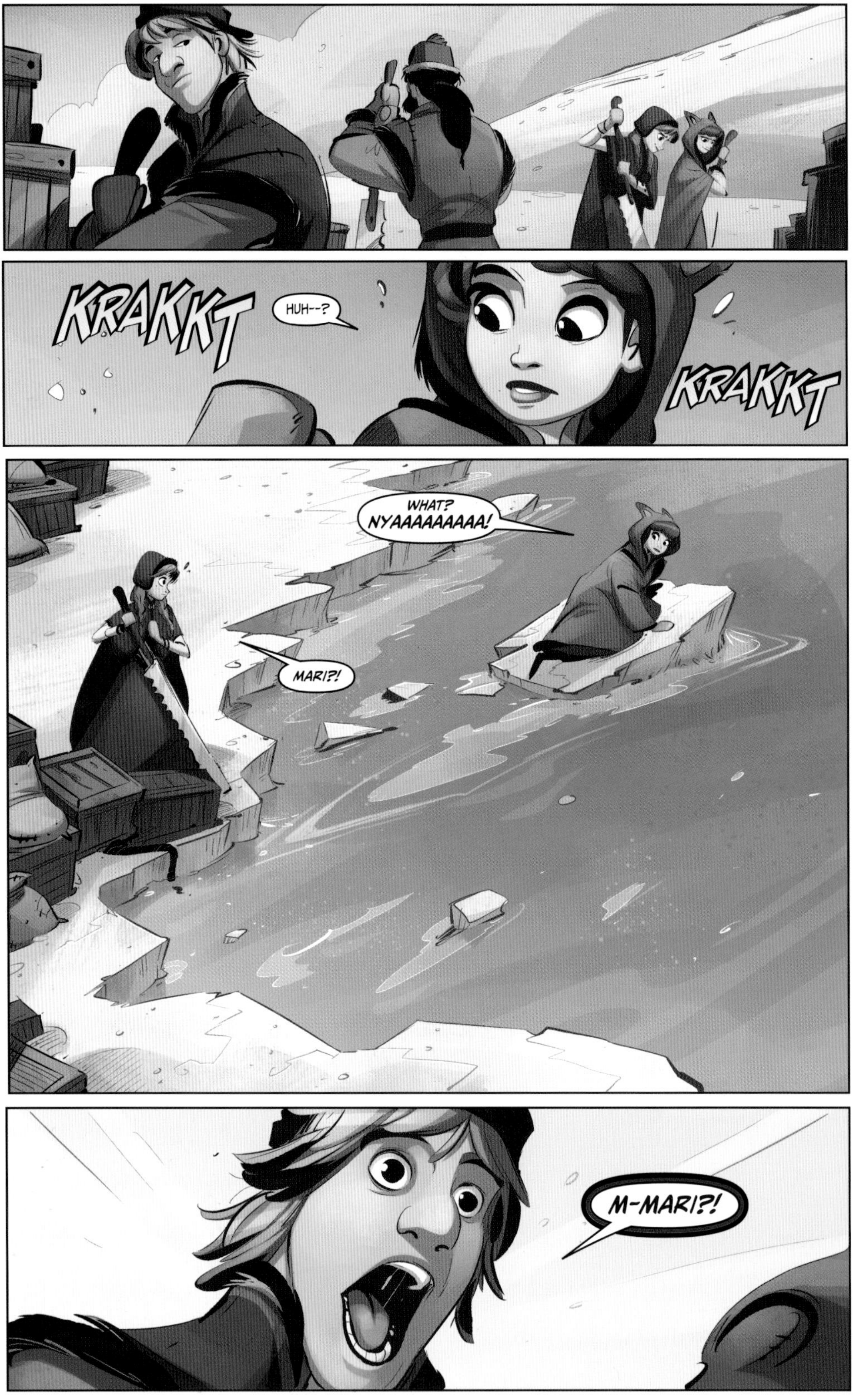
KRAKKT
HUH--?
KRAKKT
WHAT? NYAAAAAAAAA!
MARI?!
M-MARI?!

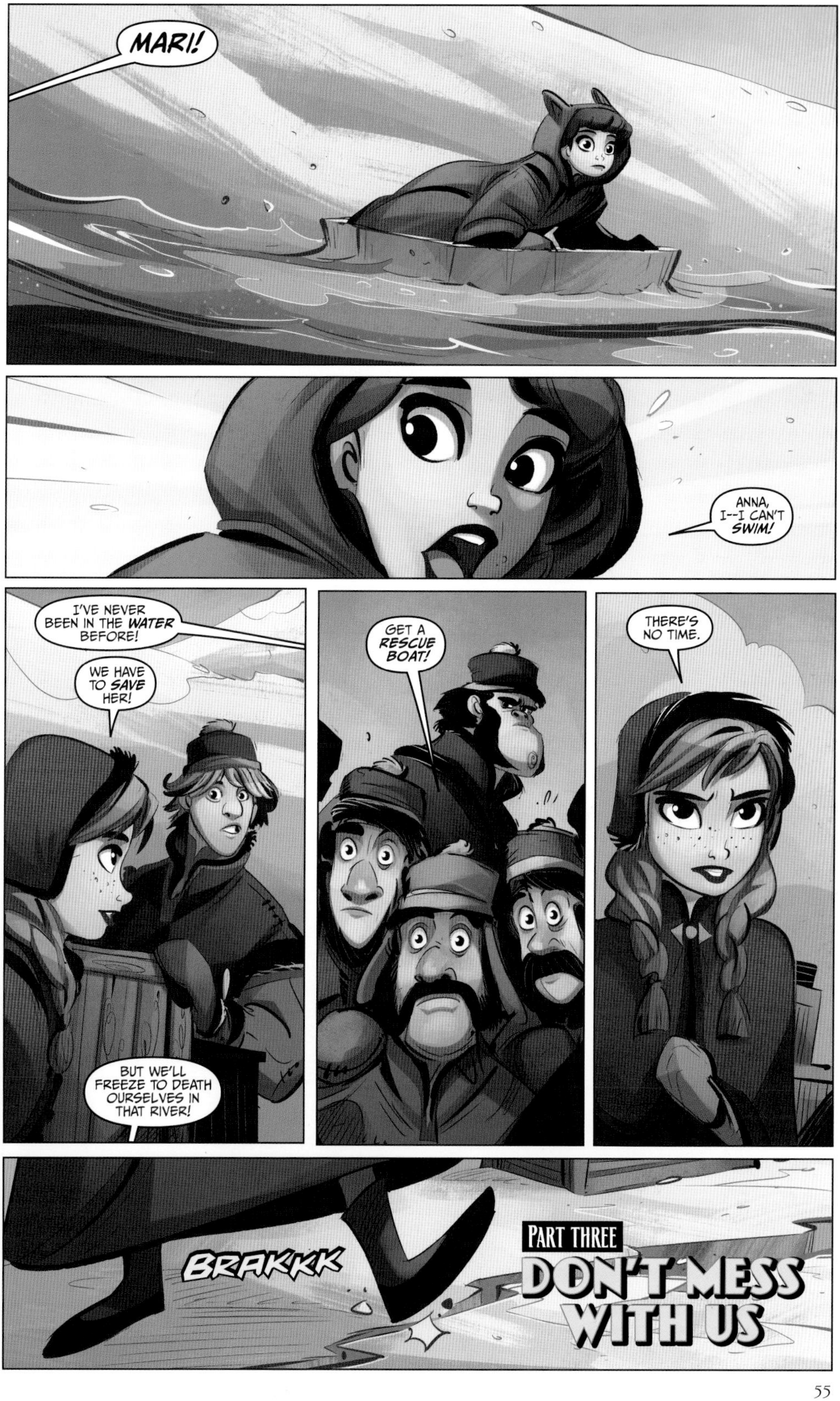
MARI!
ANNA, I--I CAN'T SWIM!
I'VE NEVER BEEN IN THE WATER BEFORE!
WE HAVE TO SAVE HER!
BUT WE'LL FREEZE TO DEATH OURSELVES IN THAT RIVER!
GET A RESCUE BOAT!
THERE'S NO TIME.
BRAKKK
PART THREE
DON'T MESS WITH US

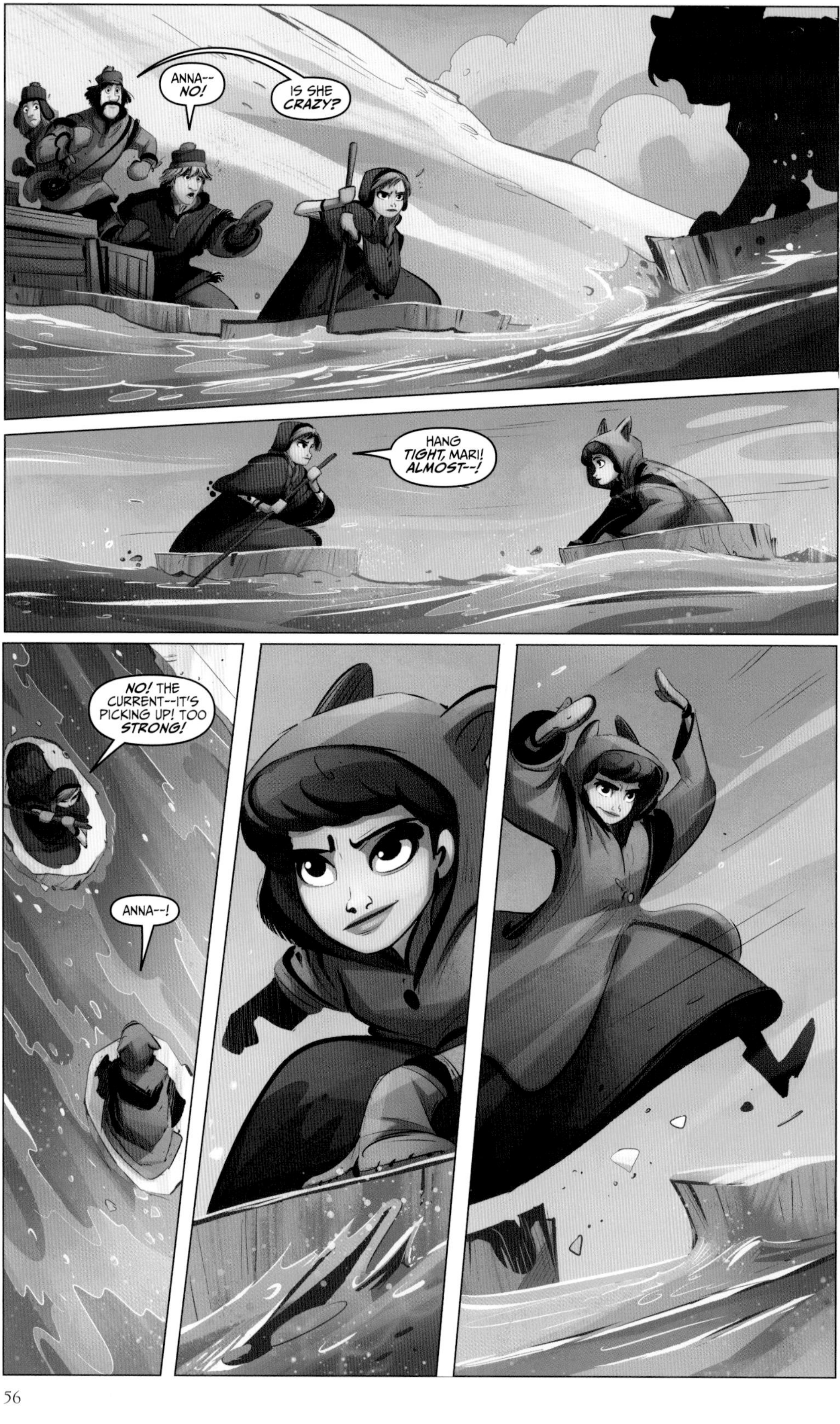
ANNA--
NO!
IS SHE
CRAZY?
HANG
TIGHT, MARI!
ALMOST--!
NO! THE
CURRENT--IT'S
PICKING UP! TOO
STRONG!
ANNA--!

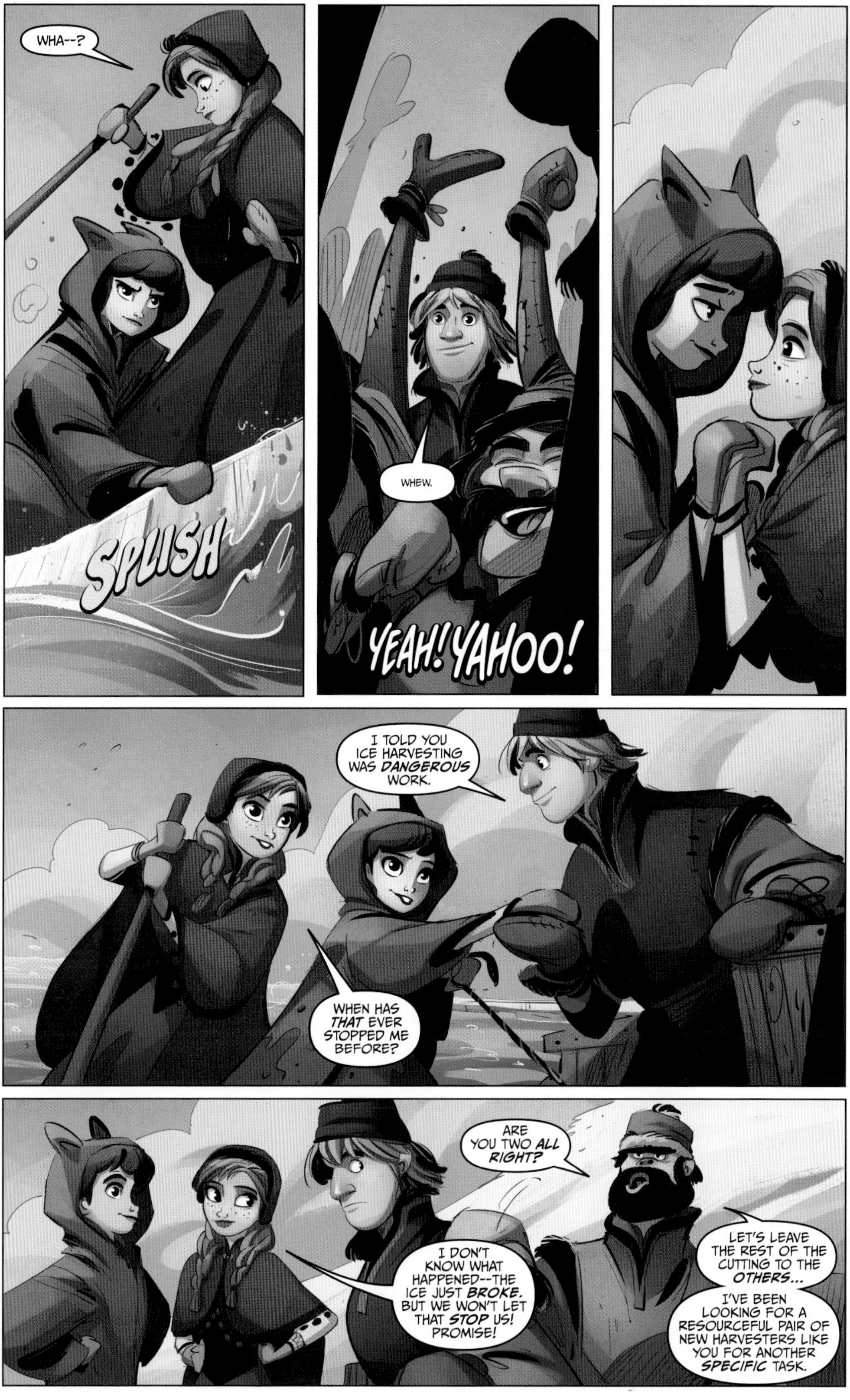

WHA--?
SPLISH
WHEW.
YEAH! YAHOO!
I TOLD YOU ICE HARVESTING WAS DANGEROUS WORK.
WHEN HAS THAT EVER STOPPED ME BEFORE?
ARE YOU TWO ALL RIGHT?
I DON'T KNOW WHAT HAPPENED--THE ICE JUST BROKE. BUT WE WON'T LET THAT STOP US! PROMISE!
LET'S LEAVE THE REST OF THE CUTTING TO THE OTHERS...
I'VE BEEN LOOKING FOR A RESOURCEFUL PAIR OF NEW HARVESTERS LIKE YOU FOR ANOTHER SPECIFIC TASK.

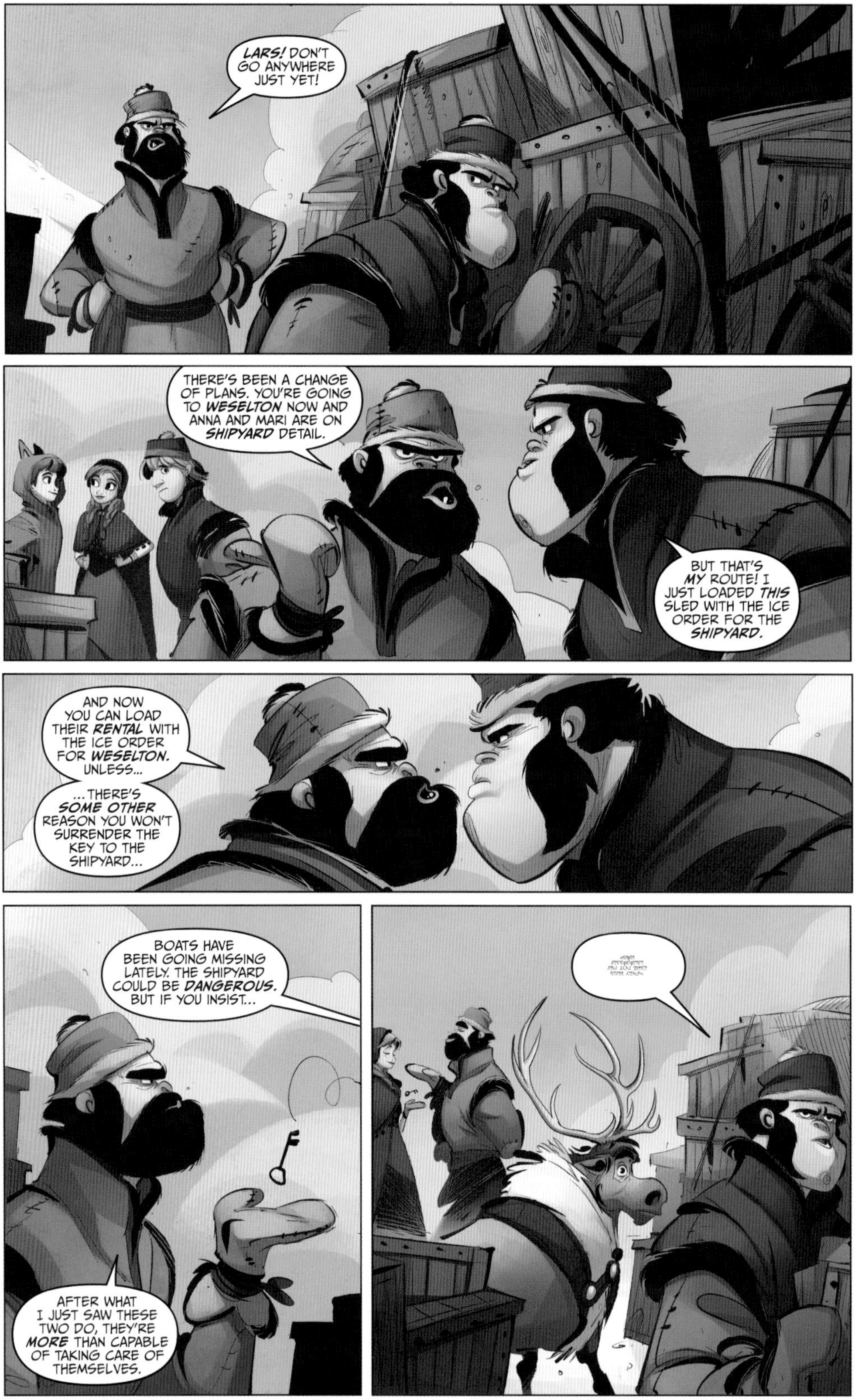
LARS! DON'T GO ANYWHERE JUST YET!
THERE'S BEEN A CHANGE OF PLANS. YOU'RE GOING TO WESELTON NOW AND ANNA AND MARI ARE ON SHIPYARD DETAIL.
BUT THAT'S MY ROUTE! I JUST LOADED THIS SLED WITH THE ICE ORDER FOR THE SHIPYARD.
AND NOW YOU CAN LOAD THEIR RENTAL WITH THE ICE ORDER FOR WESELTON. UNLESS...
...THERE'S SOME OTHER REASON YOU WON'T SURRENDER THE KEY TO THE SHIPYARD...
BOATS HAVE BEEN GOING MISSING LATELY. THE SHIPYARD COULD BE DANGEROUS. BUT IF YOU INSIST...
AFTER WHAT I JUST SAW THESE TWO DO, THEY'RE MORE THAN CAPABLE OF TAKING CARE OF THEMSELVES.

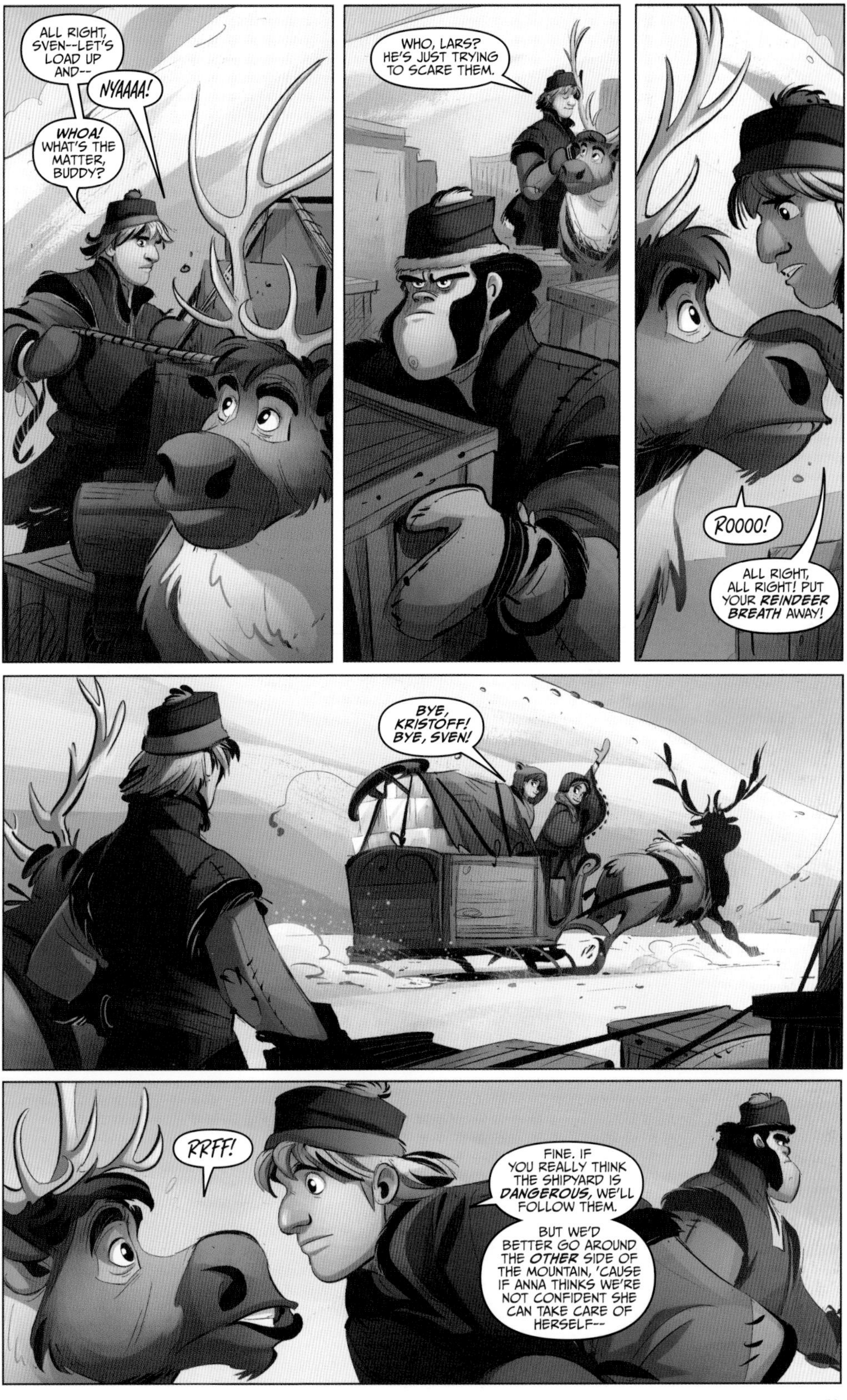
ALL RIGHT, SVEN--LET'S LOAD UP AND--
NYAAAA!
WHOA! WHAT'S THE MATTER, BUDDY?
WHO, LARS? HE'S JUST TRYING TO SCARE THEM.
ROOOO!
ALL RIGHT, ALL RIGHT! PUT YOUR REINDEER BREATH AWAY!
BYE, KRISTOFF! BYE, SVEN!
RRFF!
FINE. IF YOU REALLY THINK THE SHIPYARD IS DANGEROUS, WE'LL FOLLOW THEM.
BUT WE'D BETTER GO AROUND THE OTHER SIDE OF THE MOUNTAIN, 'CAUSE IF ANNA THINKS WE'RE NOT CONFIDENT SHE CAN TAKE CARE OF HERSELF--

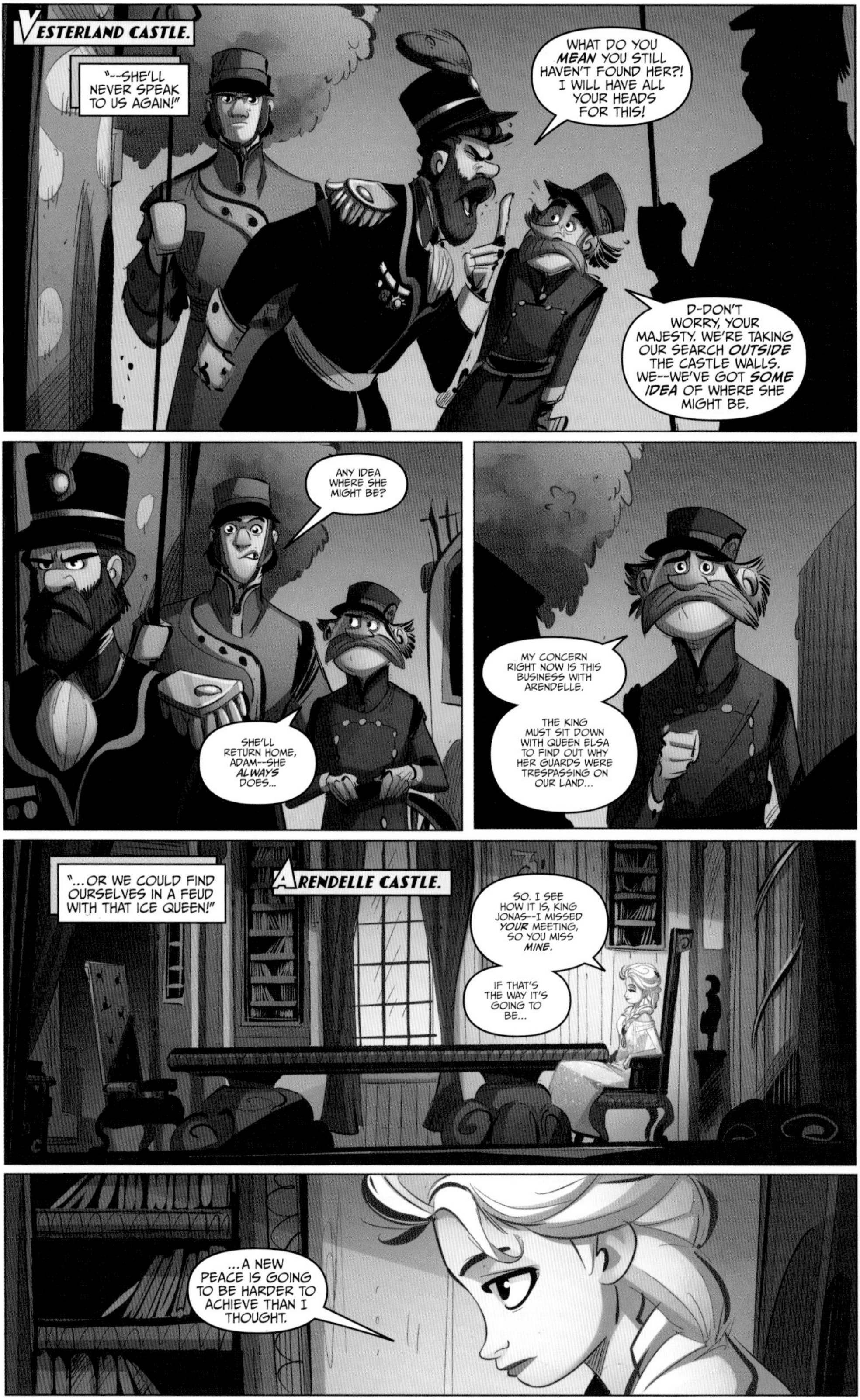
VESTERLAND CASTLE.
"--SHE'LL NEVER SPEAK TO US AGAIN!"
WHAT DO YOU MEAN YOU STILL HAVEN'T FOUND HER?! I WILL HAVE ALL YOUR HEADS FOR THIS!
D-DON'T WORRY, YOUR MAJESTY. WE'RE TAKING OUR SEARCH OUTSIDE THE CASTLE WALLS. WE--WE'VE GOT SOME IDEA OF WHERE SHE MIGHT BE.
ANY IDEA WHERE SHE MIGHT BE?
SHE'LL RETURN HOME, ADAM--SHE ALWAYS DOES...
MY CONCERN RIGHT NOW IS THIS BUSINESS WITH ARENDELLE.
THE KING MUST SIT DOWN WITH QUEEN ELSA TO FIND OUT WHY HER GUARDS WERE TRESPASSING ON OUR LAND...
"...OR WE COULD FIND OURSELVES IN A FEUD WITH THAT ICE QUEEN!"
ARENDELLE CASTLE.
SO. I SEE HOW IT IS, KING JONAS--I MISSED YOUR MEETING, SO YOU MISS MINE.
IF THAT'S THE WAY IT'S GOING TO BE...
...A NEW PEACE IS GOING TO BE HARDER TO ACHIEVE THAN I THOUGHT.

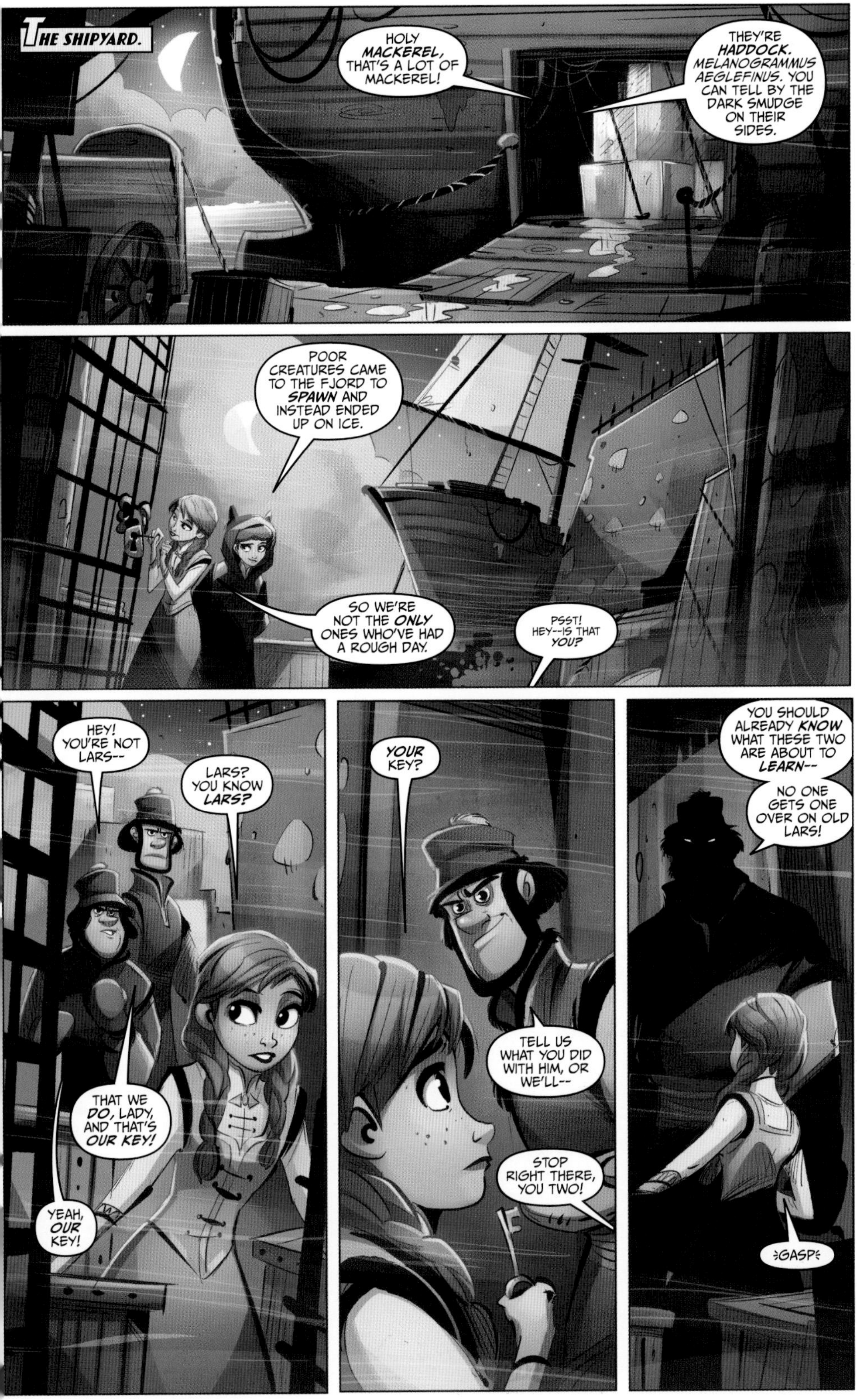
THE SHIPYARD.
HOLY MACKEREL, THAT'S A LOT OF MACKEREL!
THEY'RE HADDOCK. MELANOGRAMMUS AEGLEFINUS. YOU CAN TELL BY THE DARK SMUDGE ON THEIR SIDES.
POOR CREATURES CAME TO THE FJORD TO SPAWN AND INSTEAD ENDED UP ON ICE.
SO WE'RE NOT THE ONLY ONES WHO'VE HAD A ROUGH DAY.
PSST! HEY--IS THAT YOU?
HEY! YOU'RE NOT LARS--
LARS? YOU KNOW LARS?
THAT WE DO, LADY, AND THAT'S OUR KEY!
YEAH, OUR KEY!
YOUR KEY?
TELL US WHAT YOU DID WITH HIM, OR WE'LL--
STOP RIGHT THERE, YOU TWO!
YOU SHOULD ALREADY KNOW WHAT THESE TWO ARE ABOUT TO LEARN--
NO ONE GETS ONE OVER ON OLD LARS!
GASP

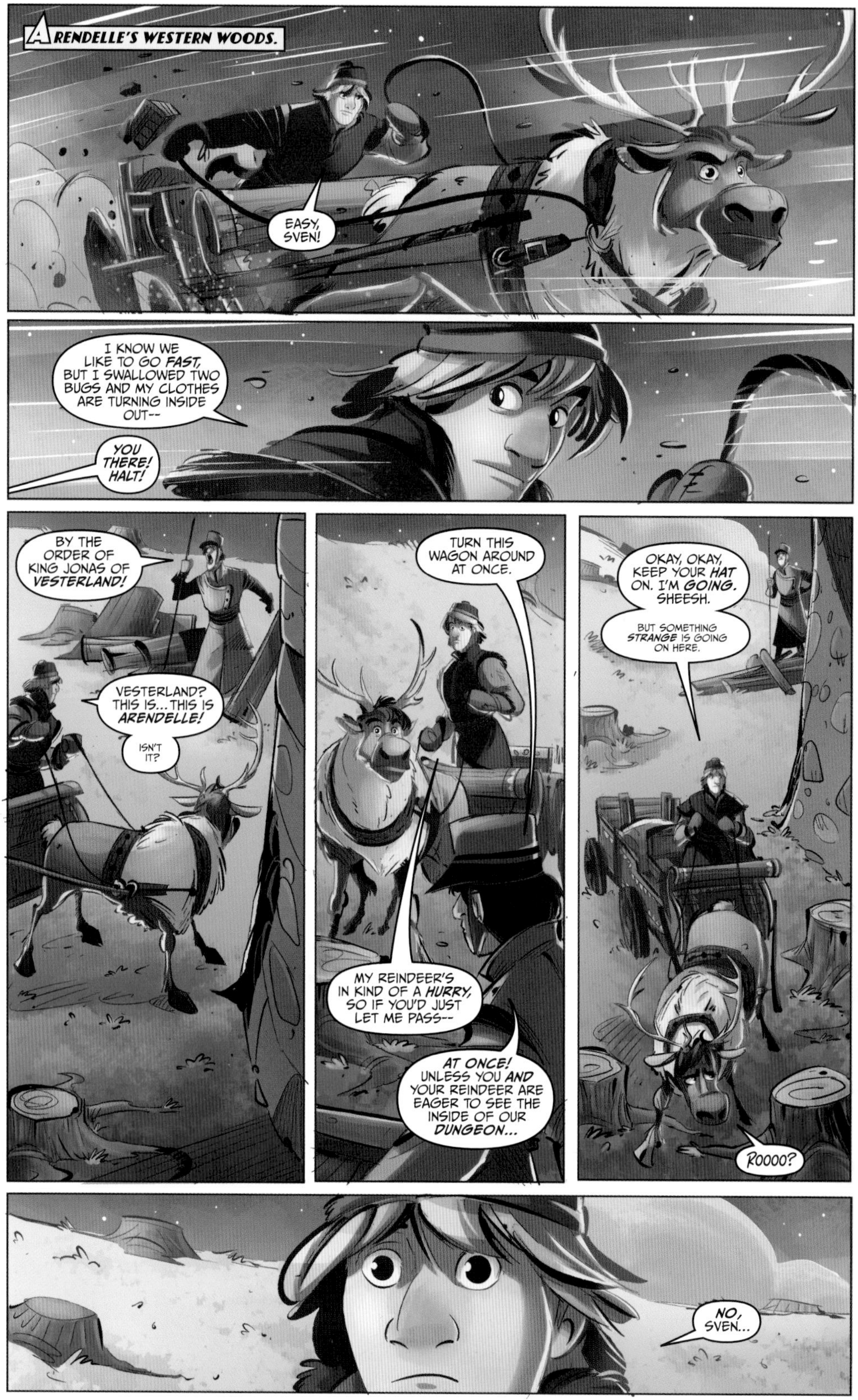
ARENDELLE'S WESTERN WOODS.
EASY, SVEN!
I KNOW WE LIKE TO GO FAST, BUT I SWALLOWED TWO BUGS AND MY CLOTHES ARE TURNING INSIDE OUT--
YOU THERE! HALT!
BY THE ORDER OF KING JONAS OF VESTERLAND!
VESTERLAND? THIS IS... THIS IS ARENDELLE!
ISN'T IT?
TURN THIS WAGON AROUND AT ONCE.
MY REINDEER'S IN KIND OF A HURRY, SO IF YOU'D JUST LET ME PASS--
AT ONCE! UNLESS YOU AND YOUR REINDEER ARE EAGER TO SEE THE INSIDE OF OUR DUNGEON...
OKAY, OKAY, KEEP YOUR HAT ON. I'M GOING. SHEESH.
BUT SOMETHING STRANGE IS GOING ON HERE.
ROOOO?
NO, SVEN...

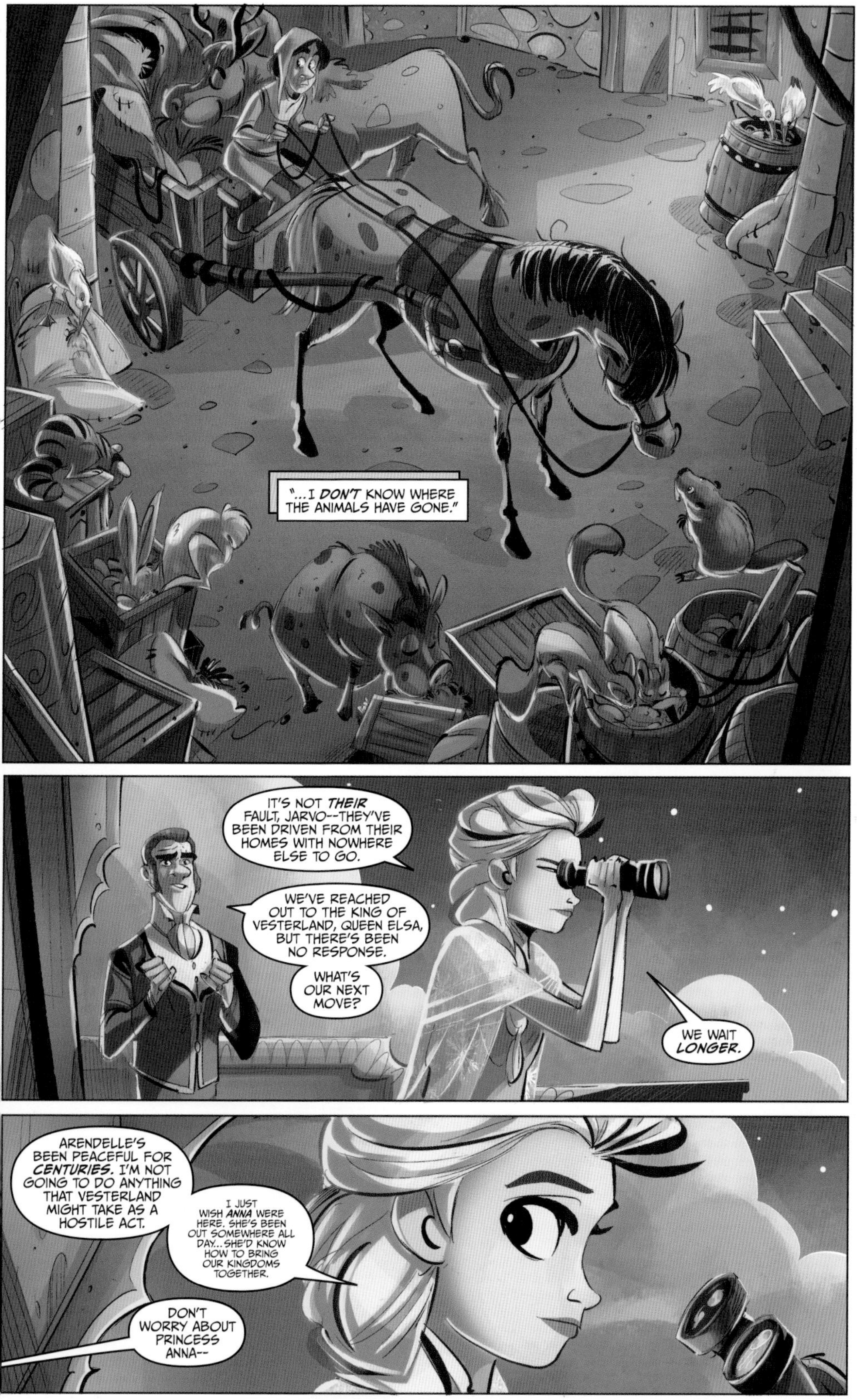
"...I DON'T KNOW WHERE THE ANIMALS HAVE GONE."
IT'S NOT THEIR FAULT, JARVO--THEY'VE BEEN DRIVEN FROM THEIR HOMES WITH NOWHERE ELSE TO GO.
WE'VE REACHED OUT TO THE KING OF VESTERLAND, QUEEN ELSA, BUT THERE'S BEEN NO RESPONSE.
WHAT'S OUR NEXT MOVE?
WE WAIT LONGER.
ARENDELLE'S BEEN PEACEFUL FOR CENTURIES. I'M NOT GOING TO DO ANYTHING THAT VESTERLAND MIGHT TAKE AS A HOSTILE ACT.
I JUST WISH ANNA WERE HERE. SHE'S BEEN OUT SOMEWHERE ALL DAY...SHE'D KNOW HOW TO BRING OUR KINGDOMS TOGETHER.
DON'T WORRY ABOUT PRINCESS ANNA--

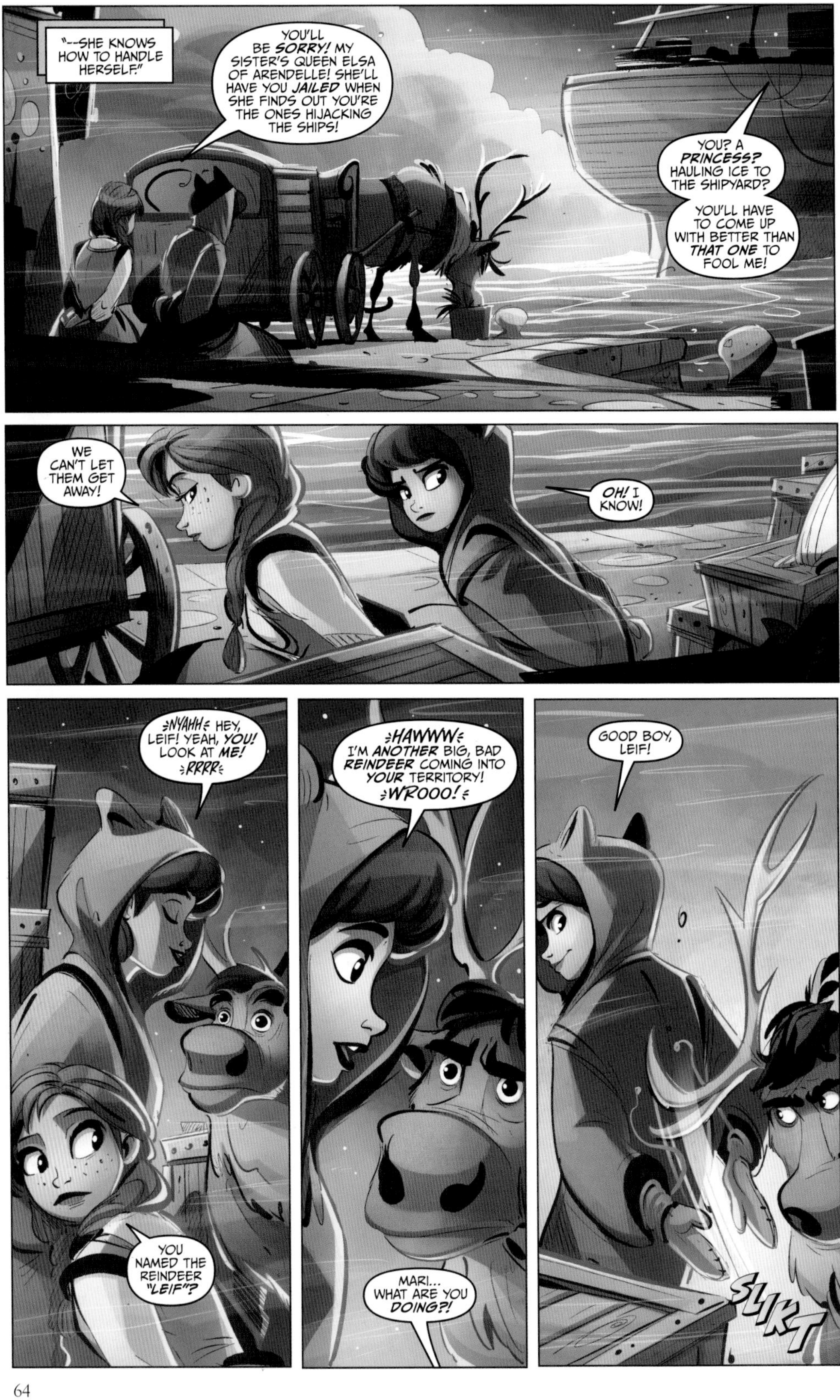
"--SHE KNOWS HOW TO HANDLE HERSELF."
YOU'LL BE SORRY! MY SISTER'S QUEEN ELSA OF ARENDELLE! SHE'LL HAVE YOU JAILED WHEN SHE FINDS OUT YOU'RE THE ONES HIJACKING THE SHIPS!
YOU? A PRINCESS? HAULING ICE TO THE SHIPYARD?
YOU'LL HAVE TO COME UP WITH BETTER THAN THAT ONE TO FOOL ME!
WE CAN'T LET THEM GET AWAY!
OH! I KNOW!
NYAHH HEY, LEIF! YEAH, YOU! LOOK AT ME! RRRR
YOU NAMED THE REINDEER "LEIF"?
HAWWW I'M ANOTHER BIG, BAD REINDEER COMING INTO YOUR TERRITORY! WROOO!
MARI... WHAT ARE YOU DOING?!
GOOD BOY, LEIF!
SLIKT

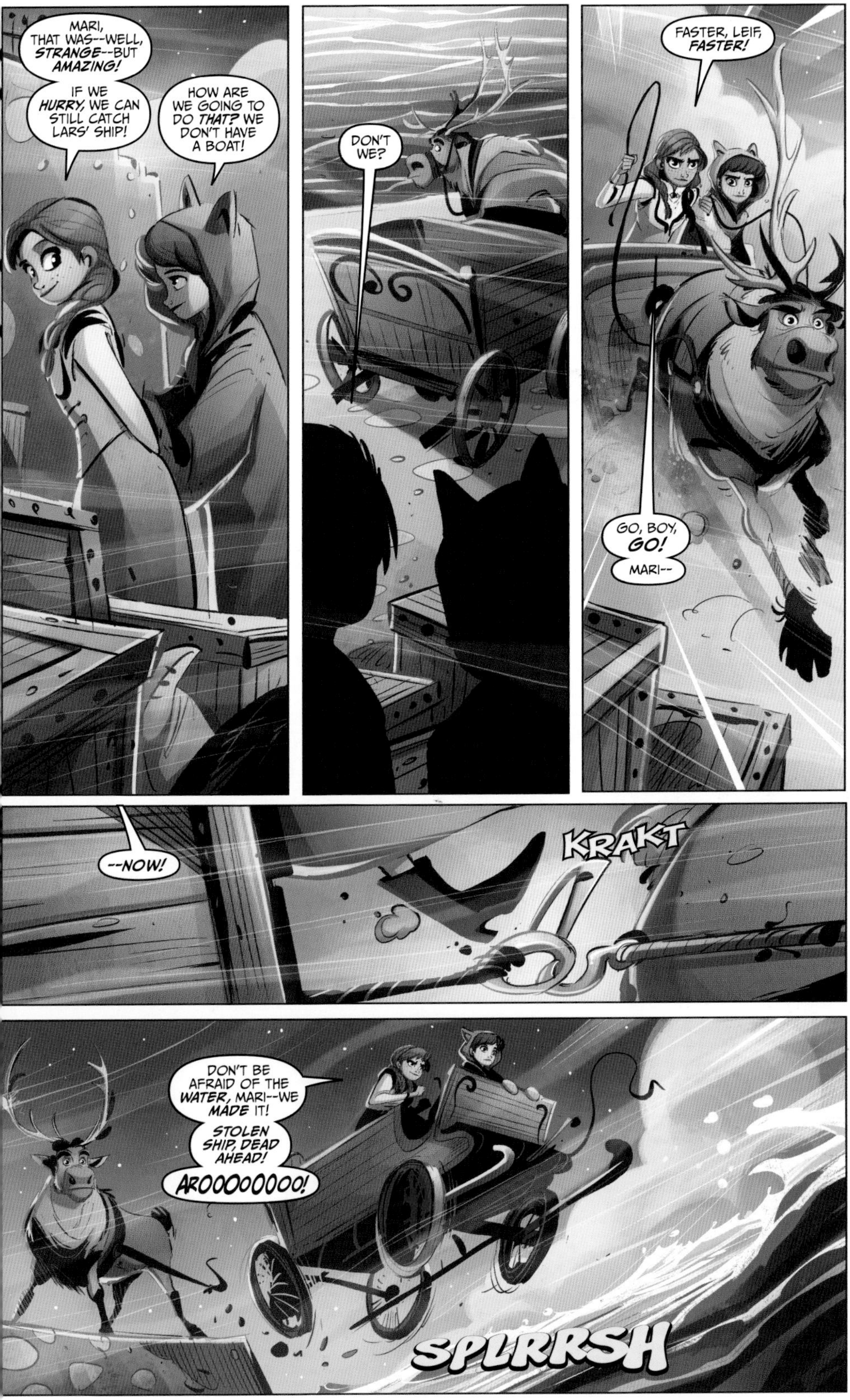
MARI, THAT WAS--WELL, STRANGE--BUT AMAZING!
IF WE HURRY, WE CAN STILL CATCH LARS' SHIP!
HOW ARE WE GOING TO DO THAT? WE DON'T HAVE A BOAT!
DON'T WE?
FASTER, LEIF, FASTER!
GO, BOY, GO!
MARI--
--NOW!
KRAKT
DON'T BE AFRAID OF THE WATER, MARI--WE MADE IT!
STOLEN SHIP, DEAD AHEAD!
AROOOOOOOO!
SPLRRSH

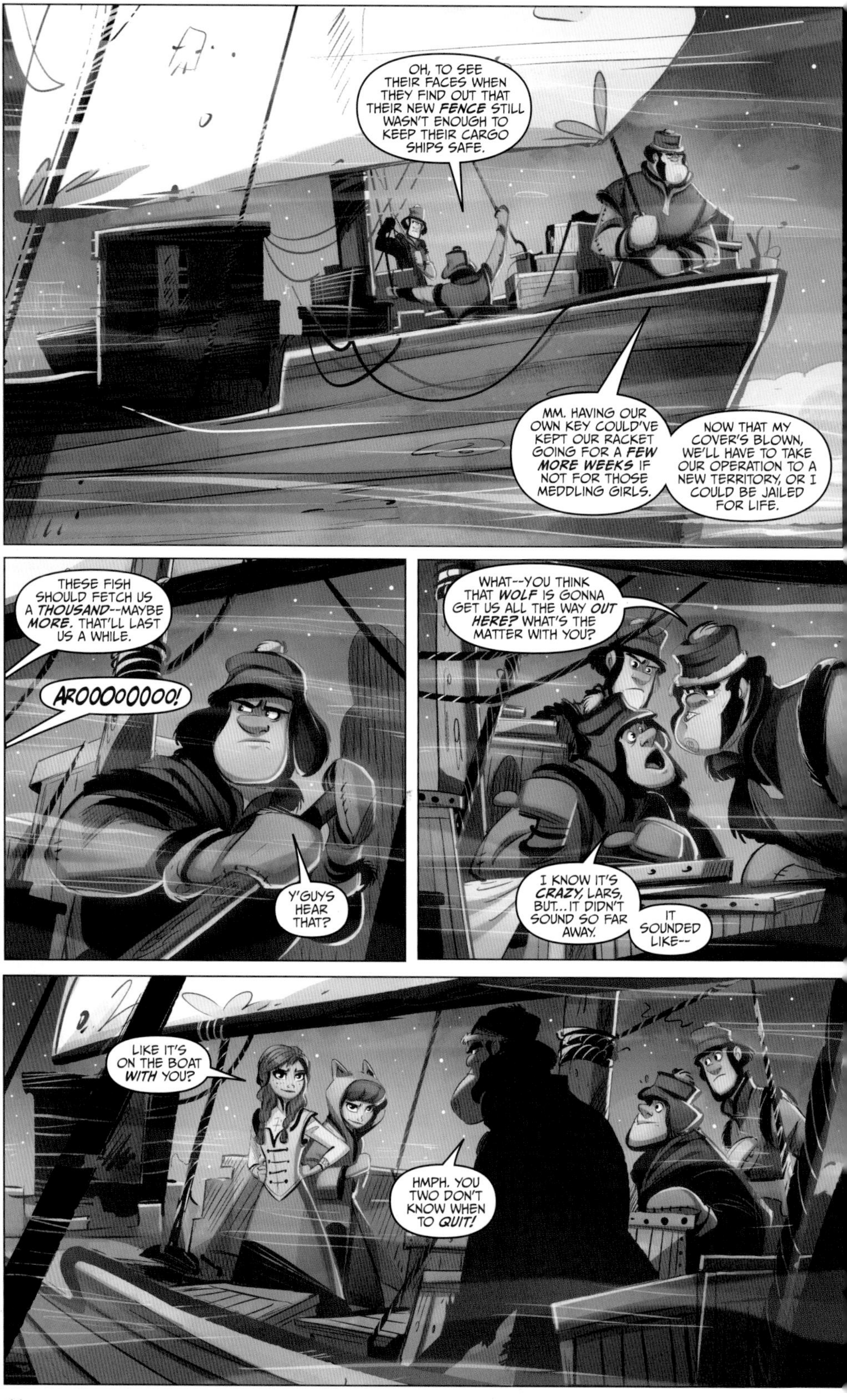
OH, TO SEE THEIR FACES WHEN THEY FIND OUT THAT THEIR NEW *FENCE* STILL WASN'T ENOUGH TO KEEP THEIR CARGO SHIPS SAFE.
MM. HAVING OUR OWN KEY COULD'VE KEPT OUR RACKET GOING FOR A *FEW MORE WEEKS* IF NOT FOR THOSE MEDDLING GIRLS.
NOW THAT MY COVER'S BLOWN, WE'LL HAVE TO TAKE OUR OPERATION TO A NEW TERRITORY, OR I COULD BE JAILED FOR LIFE.
THESE FISH SHOULD FETCH US A *THOUSAND*--MAYBE *MORE.* THAT'LL LAST US A WHILE.
AROOOOOOOO!
Y'GUYS HEAR THAT?
WHAT--YOU THINK THAT *WOLF* IS GONNA GET US ALL THE WAY *OUT HERE?* WHAT'S THE MATTER WITH YOU?
I KNOW IT'S *CRAZY,* LARS, BUT...IT DIDN'T SOUND SO FAR AWAY.
IT SOUNDED LIKE--
LIKE IT'S ON THE BOAT *WITH* YOU?
HMPH. YOU TWO DON'T KNOW WHEN TO *QUIT!*

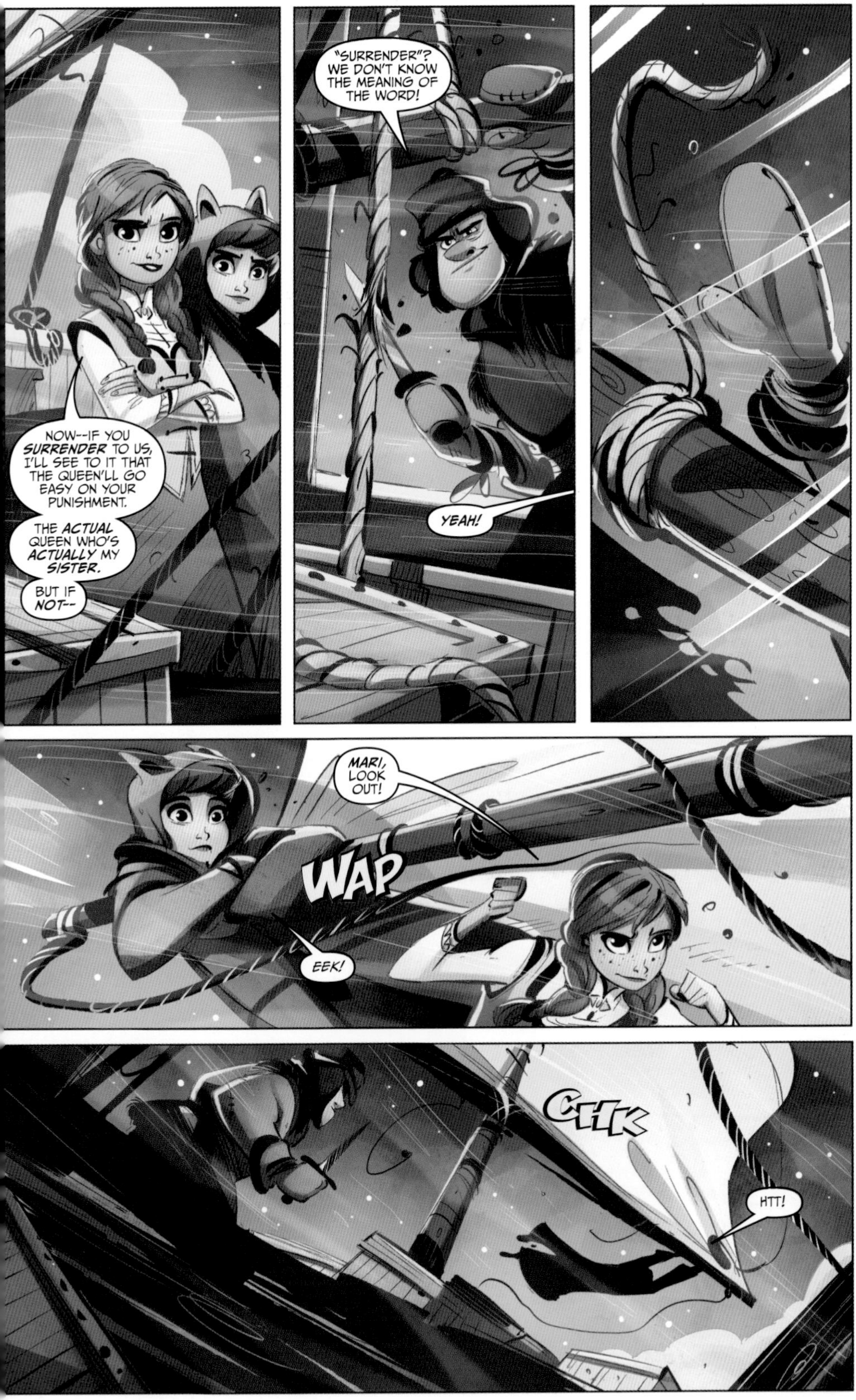
NOW--IF YOU SURRENDER TO US, I'LL SEE TO IT THAT THE QUEEN'LL GO EASY ON YOUR PUNISHMENT.
THE ACTUAL QUEEN WHO'S ACTUALLY MY SISTER.
BUT IF NOT--
"SURRENDER"? WE DON'T KNOW THE MEANING OF THE WORD!
YEAH!
MARI, LOOK OUT!
WAP
EEK!
CHK
HTT!

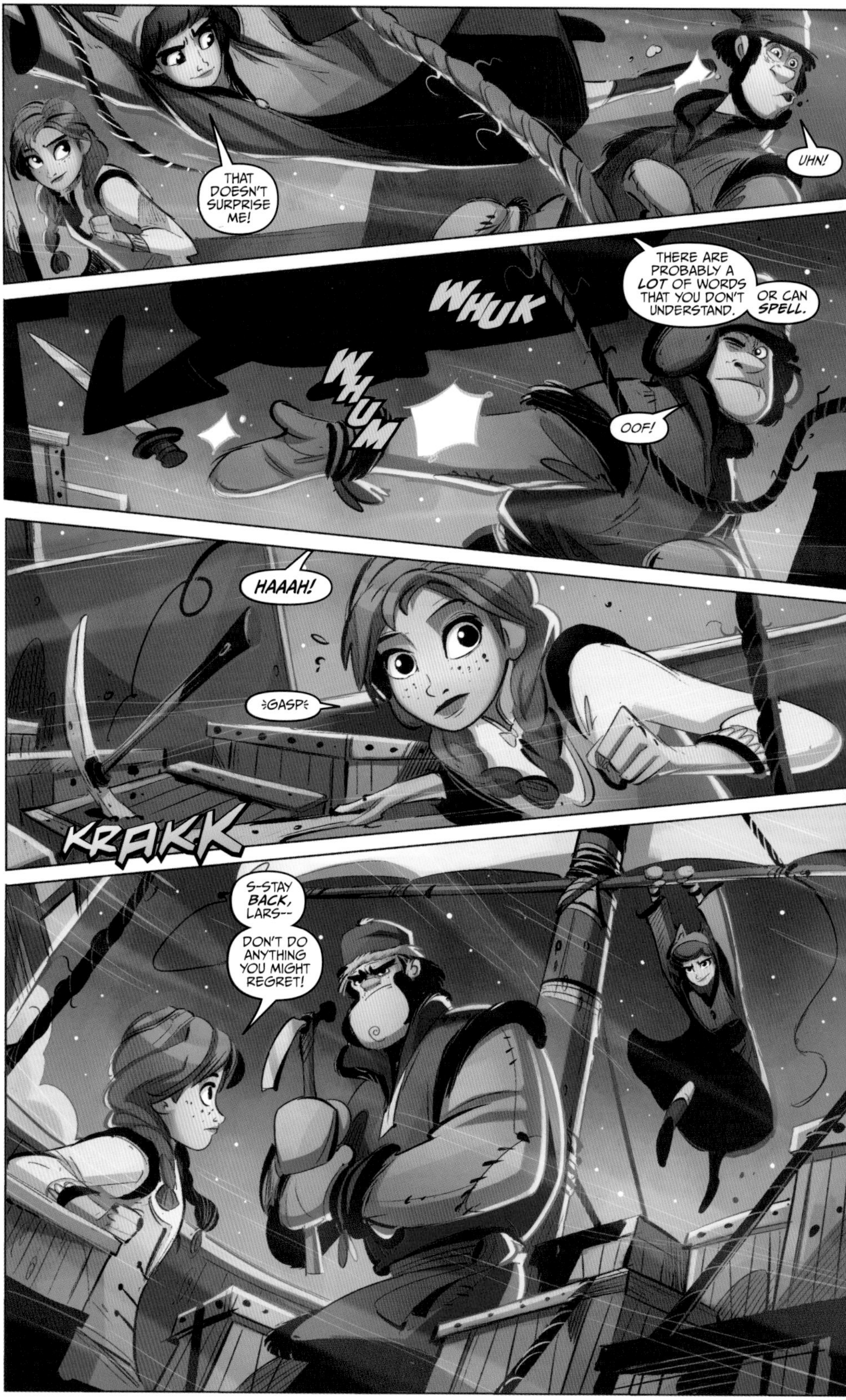
THAT DOESN'T SURPRISE ME!
UHN!
THERE ARE PROBABLY A LOT OF WORDS THAT YOU DON'T UNDERSTAND.
OR CAN SPELL.
WHUK
WHUM
OOF!
HAAAH!
GASP
KRAKK
S-STAY BACK, LARS--
DON'T DO ANYTHING YOU MIGHT REGRET!

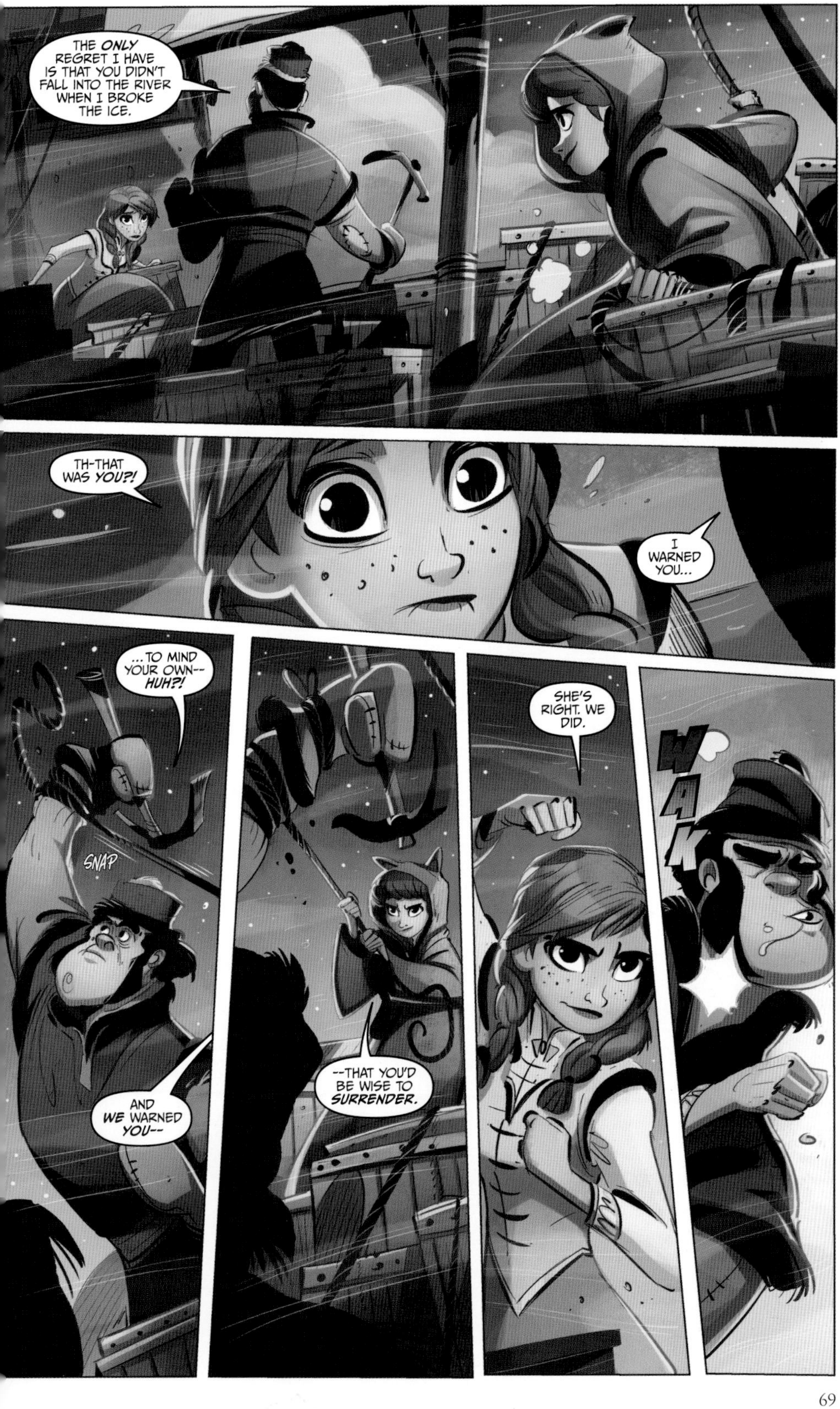
THE *ONLY* REGRET I HAVE IS THAT YOU DIDN'T FALL INTO THE RIVER WHEN I BROKE THE ICE.
TH-THAT WAS *YOU?!*
I WARNED YOU...
...TO MIND YOUR OWN-- *HUH?!*
SNAP
AND *WE* WARNED *YOU*--
--THAT YOU'D BE WISE TO *SURRENDER.*
SHE'S RIGHT. WE DID.
WAK

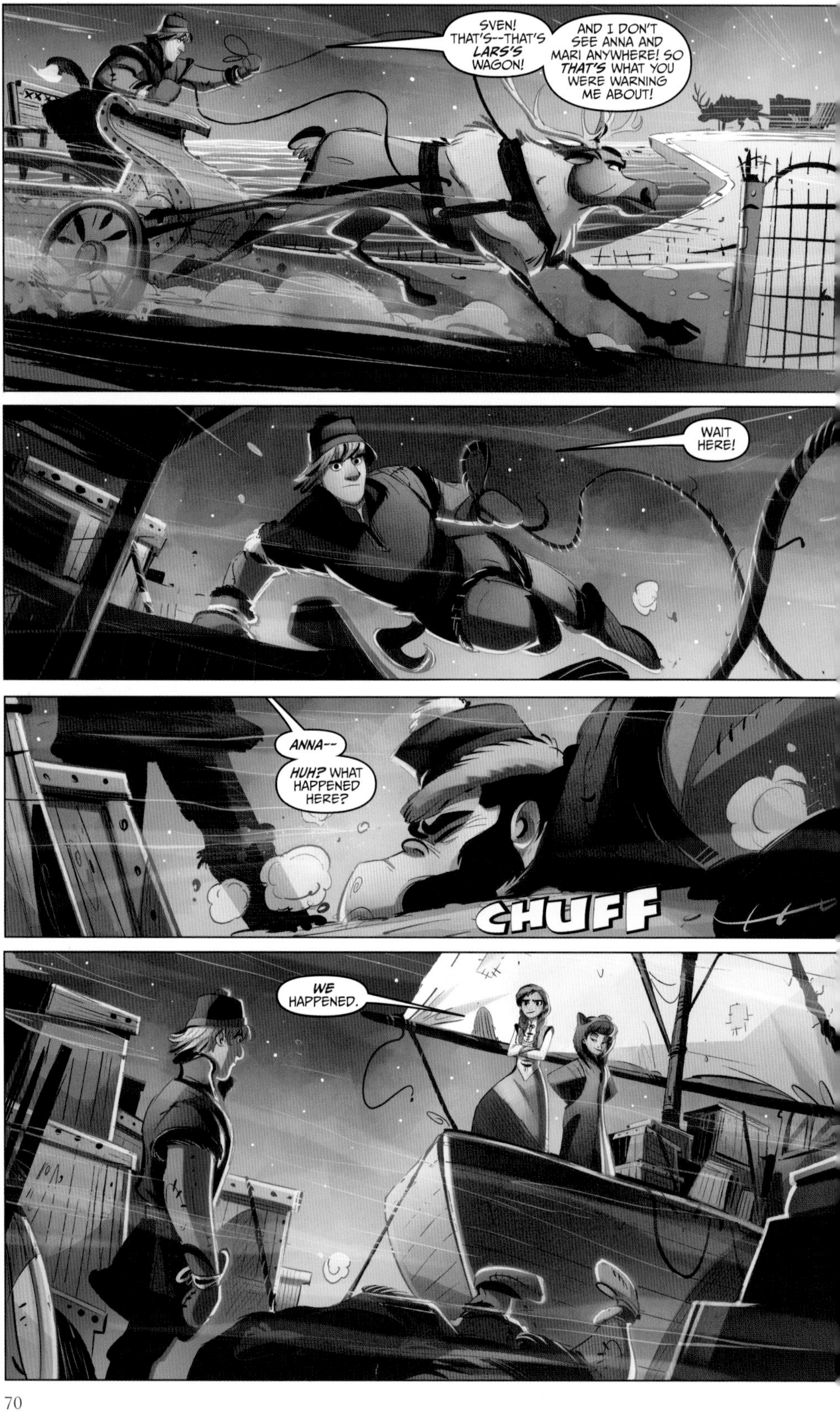
SVEN! THAT'S--THAT'S *LARS'S* WAGON!
AND I DON'T SEE ANNA AND MARI ANYWHERE! SO *THAT'S* WHAT YOU WERE WARNING ME ABOUT!
WAIT HERE!
ANNA--
HUH? WHAT HAPPENED HERE?
CHUFF
WE HAPPENED.

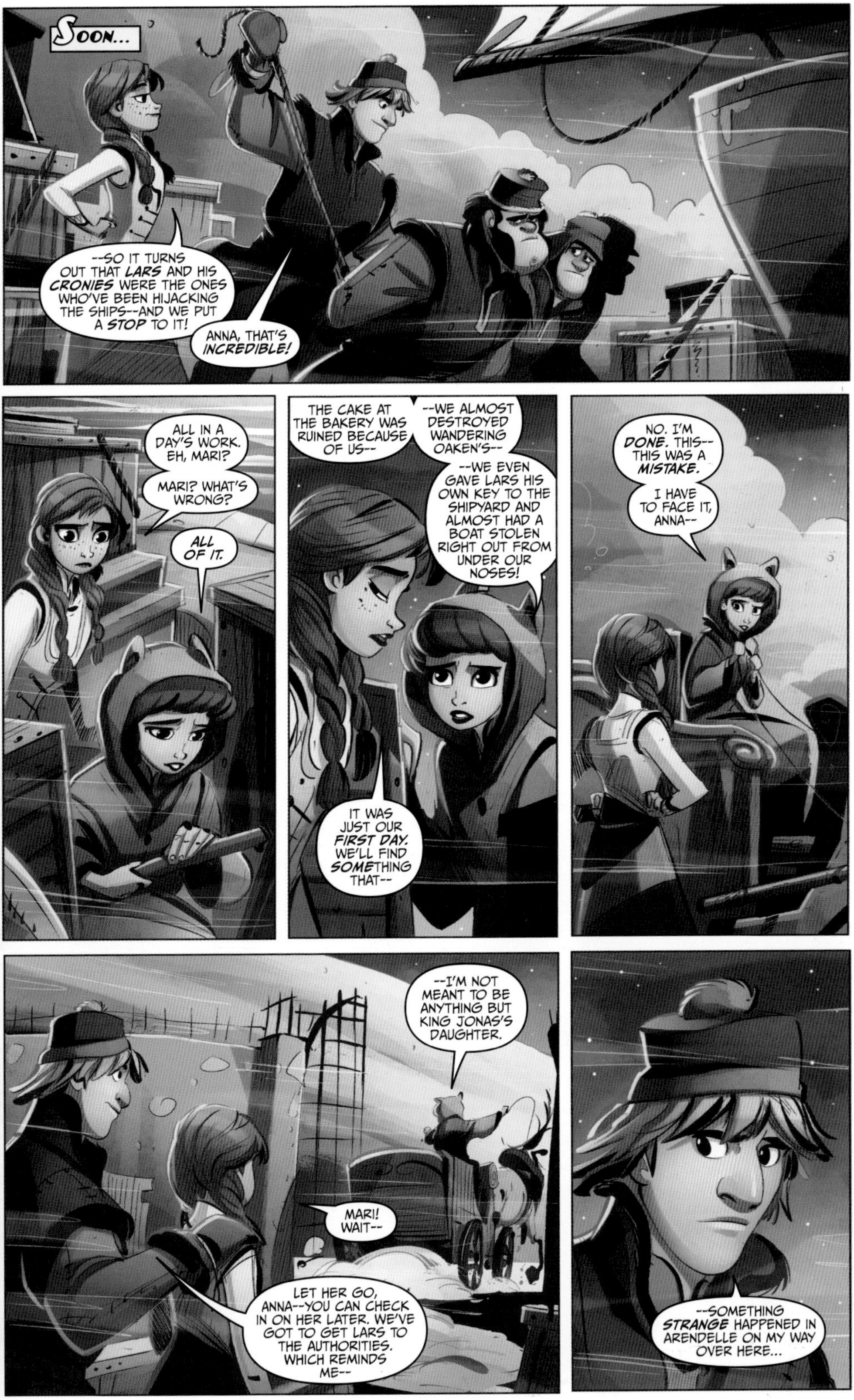

SOON...
--SO IT TURNS OUT THAT LARS AND HIS CRONIES WERE THE ONES WHO'VE BEEN HIJACKING THE SHIPS--AND WE PUT A STOP TO IT!
ANNA, THAT'S INCREDIBLE!
ALL IN A DAY'S WORK. EH, MARI?
MARI? WHAT'S WRONG?
ALL OF IT.
THE CAKE AT THE BAKERY WAS RUINED BECAUSE OF US--
--WE ALMOST DESTROYED WANDERING OAKEN'S--
--WE EVEN GAVE LARS HIS OWN KEY TO THE SHIPYARD AND ALMOST HAD A BOAT STOLEN RIGHT OUT FROM UNDER OUR NOSES!
IT WAS JUST OUR FIRST DAY. WE'LL FIND SOMETHING THAT--
NO. I'M DONE. THIS--THIS WAS A MISTAKE.
I HAVE TO FACE IT, ANNA--
--I'M NOT MEANT TO BE ANYTHING BUT KING JONAS'S DAUGHTER.
MARI! WAIT--
LET HER GO, ANNA--YOU CAN CHECK IN ON HER LATER. WE'VE GOT TO GET LARS TO THE AUTHORITIES. WHICH REMINDS ME--
--SOMETHING STRANGE HAPPENED IN ARENDELLE ON MY WAY OVER HERE...

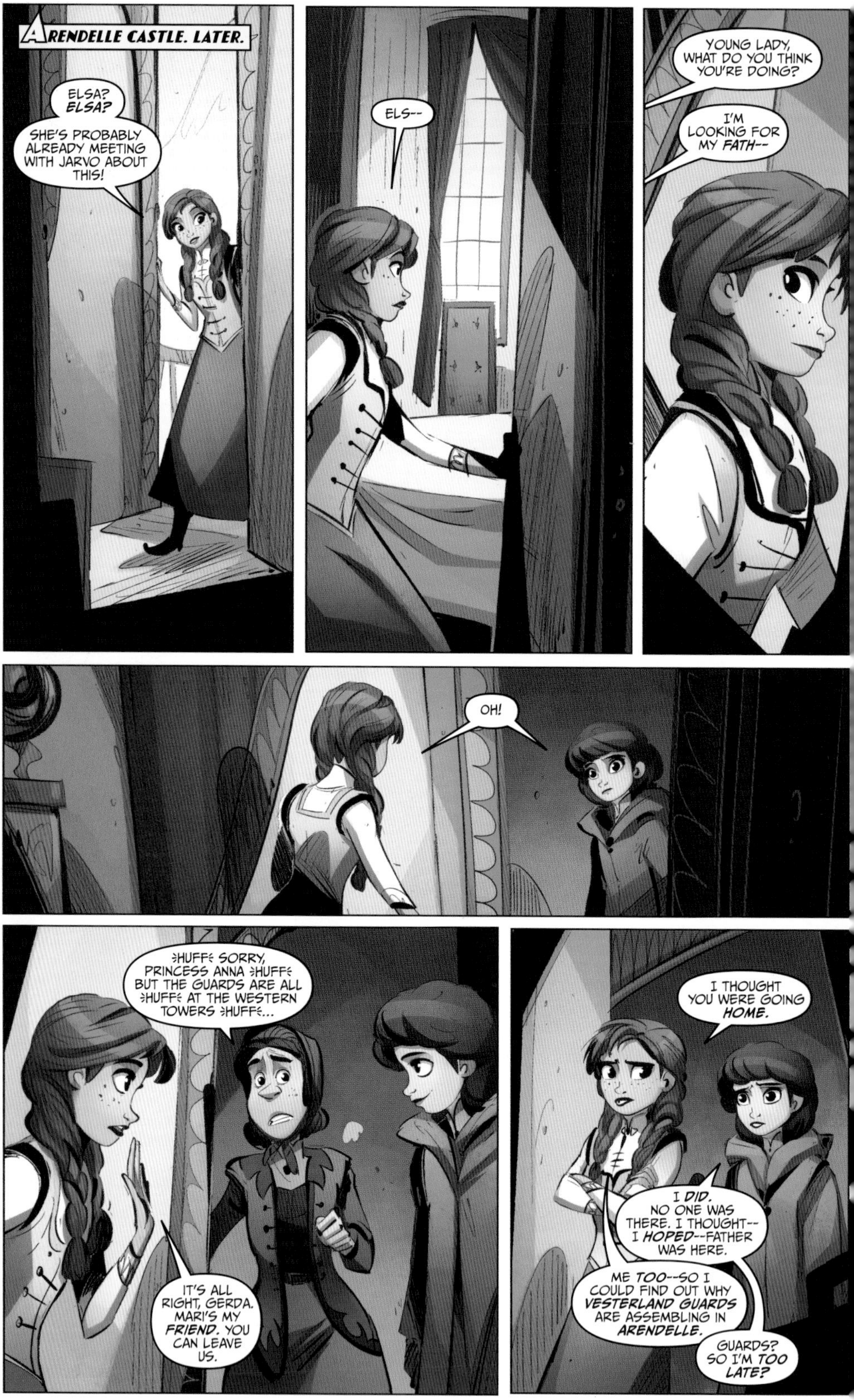
ARENDELLE CASTLE. LATER.
ELSA? ELSA?
SHE'S PROBABLY ALREADY MEETING WITH JARVO ABOUT THIS!
ELS--
YOUNG LADY, WHAT DO YOU THINK YOU'RE DOING?
I'M LOOKING FOR MY FATH--
OH!
⋟HUFF⋞ SORRY, PRINCESS ANNA ⋟HUFF⋞ BUT THE GUARDS ARE ALL ⋟HUFF⋞ AT THE WESTERN TOWERS ⋟HUFF⋞...
IT'S ALL RIGHT, GERDA. MARI'S MY FRIEND. YOU CAN LEAVE US.
I THOUGHT YOU WERE GOING HOME.
I DID. NO ONE WAS THERE. I THOUGHT-- I HOPED--FATHER WAS HERE.
ME TOO--SO I COULD FIND OUT WHY VESTERLAND GUARDS ARE ASSEMBLING IN ARENDELLE.
GUARDS? SO I'M TOO LATE?

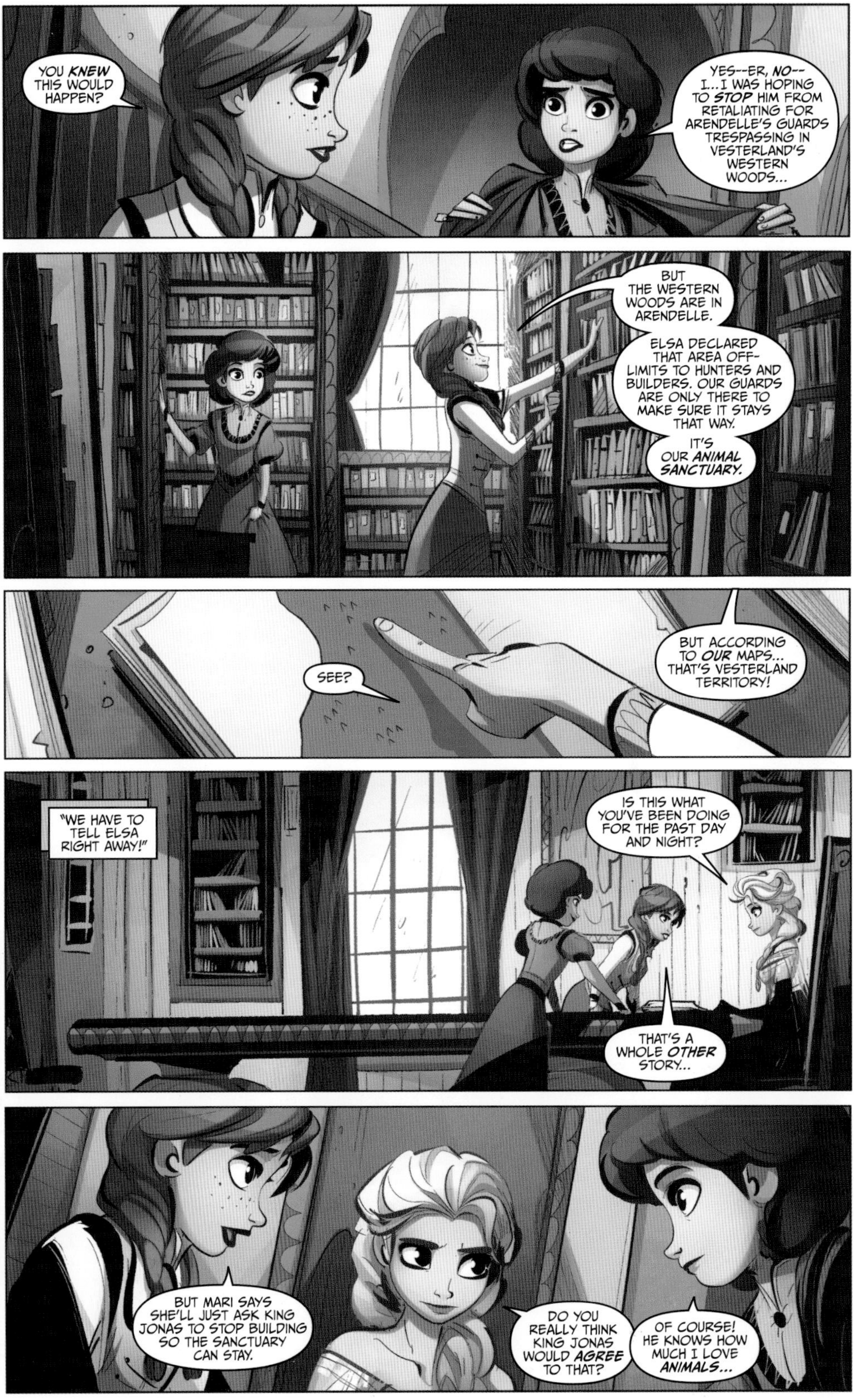
YOU *KNEW* THIS WOULD HAPPEN?
YES--ER, *NO*-- I...I WAS HOPING TO *STOP* HIM FROM RETALIATING FOR ARENDELLE'S GUARDS TRESPASSING IN VESTERLAND'S WESTERN WOODS...
BUT THE WESTERN WOODS ARE IN ARENDELLE.
ELSA DECLARED THAT AREA OFF-LIMITS TO HUNTERS AND BUILDERS. OUR GUARDS ARE ONLY THERE TO MAKE SURE IT STAYS THAT WAY.
IT'S OUR *ANIMAL SANCTUARY.*
SEE?
BUT ACCORDING TO *OUR* MAPS... THAT'S VESTERLAND TERRITORY!
"WE HAVE TO TELL ELSA RIGHT AWAY!"
IS THIS WHAT YOU'VE BEEN DOING FOR THE PAST DAY AND NIGHT?
THAT'S A WHOLE *OTHER* STORY...
BUT MARI SAYS SHE'LL JUST ASK KING JONAS TO STOP BUILDING SO THE SANCTUARY CAN STAY.
DO YOU REALLY THINK KING JONAS WOULD *AGREE* TO THAT?
OF COURSE! HE KNOWS HOW MUCH I LOVE *ANIMALS...*

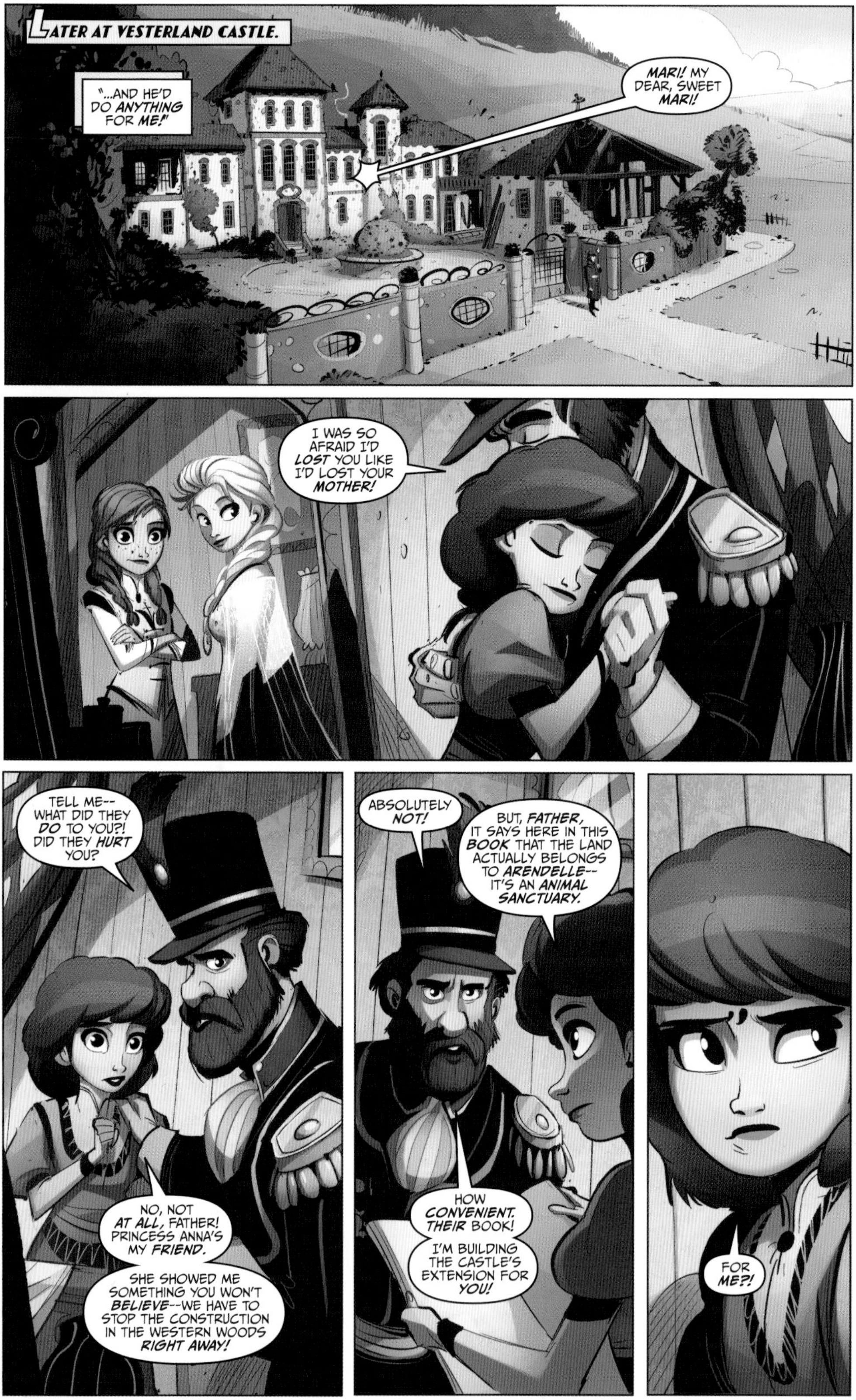
LATER AT VESTERLAND CASTLE.
"...AND HE'D DO ANYTHING FOR ME!"
MARI! MY DEAR, SWEET MARI!
I WAS SO AFRAID I'D LOST YOU LIKE I'D LOST YOUR MOTHER!
TELL ME--WHAT DID THEY DO TO YOU?! DID THEY HURT YOU?
NO, NOT AT ALL, FATHER! PRINCESS ANNA'S MY FRIEND.
SHE SHOWED ME SOMETHING YOU WON'T BELIEVE--WE HAVE TO STOP THE CONSTRUCTION IN THE WESTERN WOODS RIGHT AWAY!
ABSOLUTELY NOT!
BUT, FATHER, IT SAYS HERE IN THIS BOOK THAT THE LAND ACTUALLY BELONGS TO ARENDELLE--IT'S AN ANIMAL SANCTUARY.
HOW CONVENIENT. THEIR BOOK!
I'M BUILDING THE CASTLE'S EXTENSION FOR YOU!
FOR ME?!

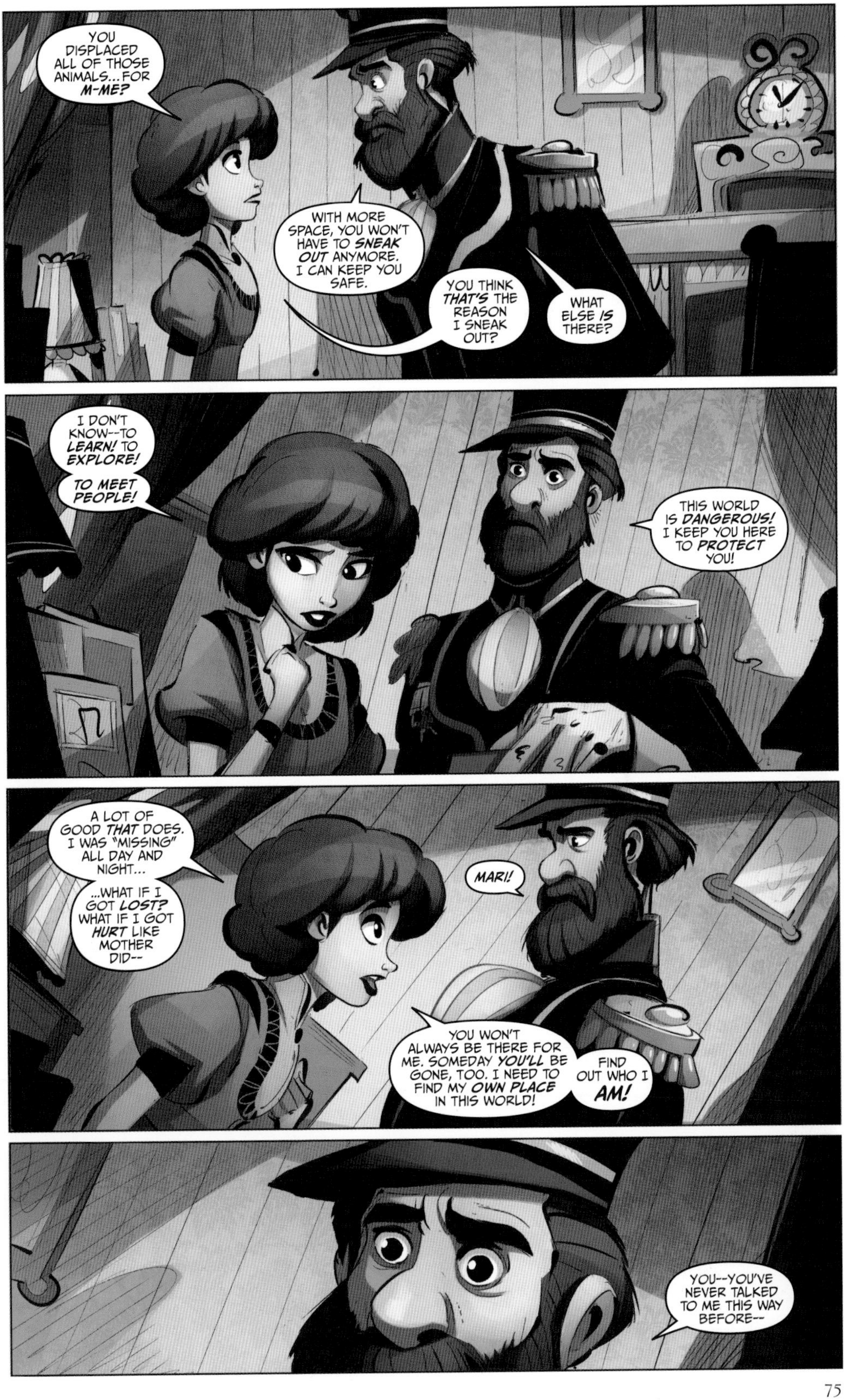
YOU DISPLACED ALL OF THOSE ANIMALS...FOR M-ME?
WITH MORE SPACE, YOU WON'T HAVE TO SNEAK OUT ANYMORE. I CAN KEEP YOU SAFE.
YOU THINK THAT'S THE REASON I SNEAK OUT?
WHAT ELSE IS THERE?
I DON'T KNOW--TO LEARN! TO EXPLORE!
TO MEET PEOPLE!
THIS WORLD IS DANGEROUS! I KEEP YOU HERE TO PROTECT YOU!
A LOT OF GOOD THAT DOES. I WAS "MISSING" ALL DAY AND NIGHT...
...WHAT IF I GOT LOST? WHAT IF I GOT HURT LIKE MOTHER DID--
MARI!
YOU WON'T ALWAYS BE THERE FOR ME. SOMEDAY YOU'LL BE GONE, TOO. I NEED TO FIND MY OWN PLACE IN THIS WORLD!
FIND OUT WHO I AM!
YOU--YOU'VE NEVER TALKED TO ME THIS WAY BEFORE--

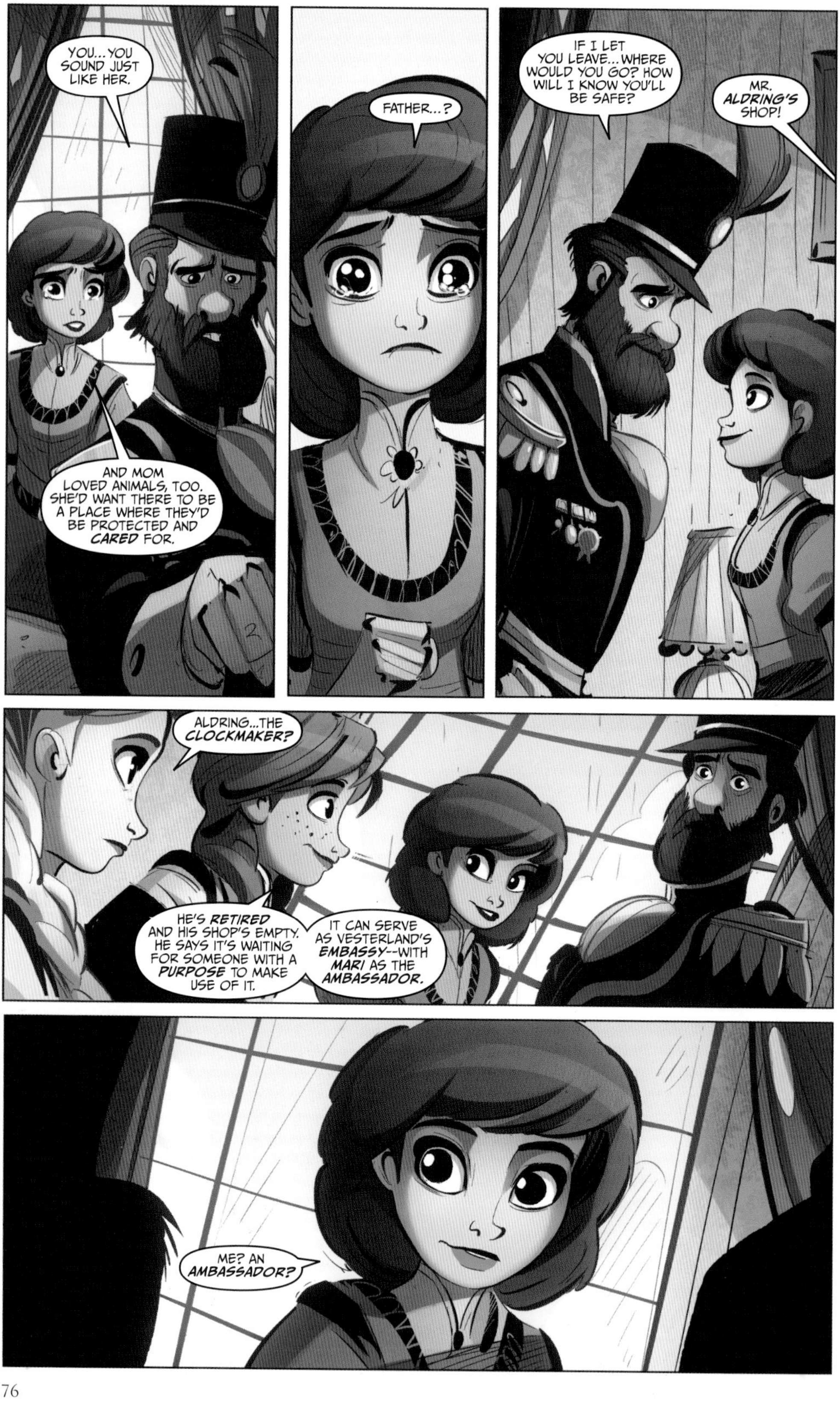
YOU...YOU SOUND JUST LIKE HER.
AND MOM LOVED ANIMALS, TOO. SHE'D WANT THERE TO BE A PLACE WHERE THEY'D BE PROTECTED AND CARED FOR.
FATHER...?
IF I LET YOU LEAVE...WHERE WOULD YOU GO? HOW WILL I KNOW YOU'LL BE SAFE?
MR. ALDRING'S SHOP!
ALDRING...THE CLOCKMAKER?
HE'S RETIRED AND HIS SHOP'S EMPTY. HE SAYS IT'S WAITING FOR SOMEONE WITH A PURPOSE TO MAKE USE OF IT.
IT CAN SERVE AS VESTERLAND'S EMBASSY--WITH MARI AS THE AMBASSADOR.
ME? AN AMBASSADOR?

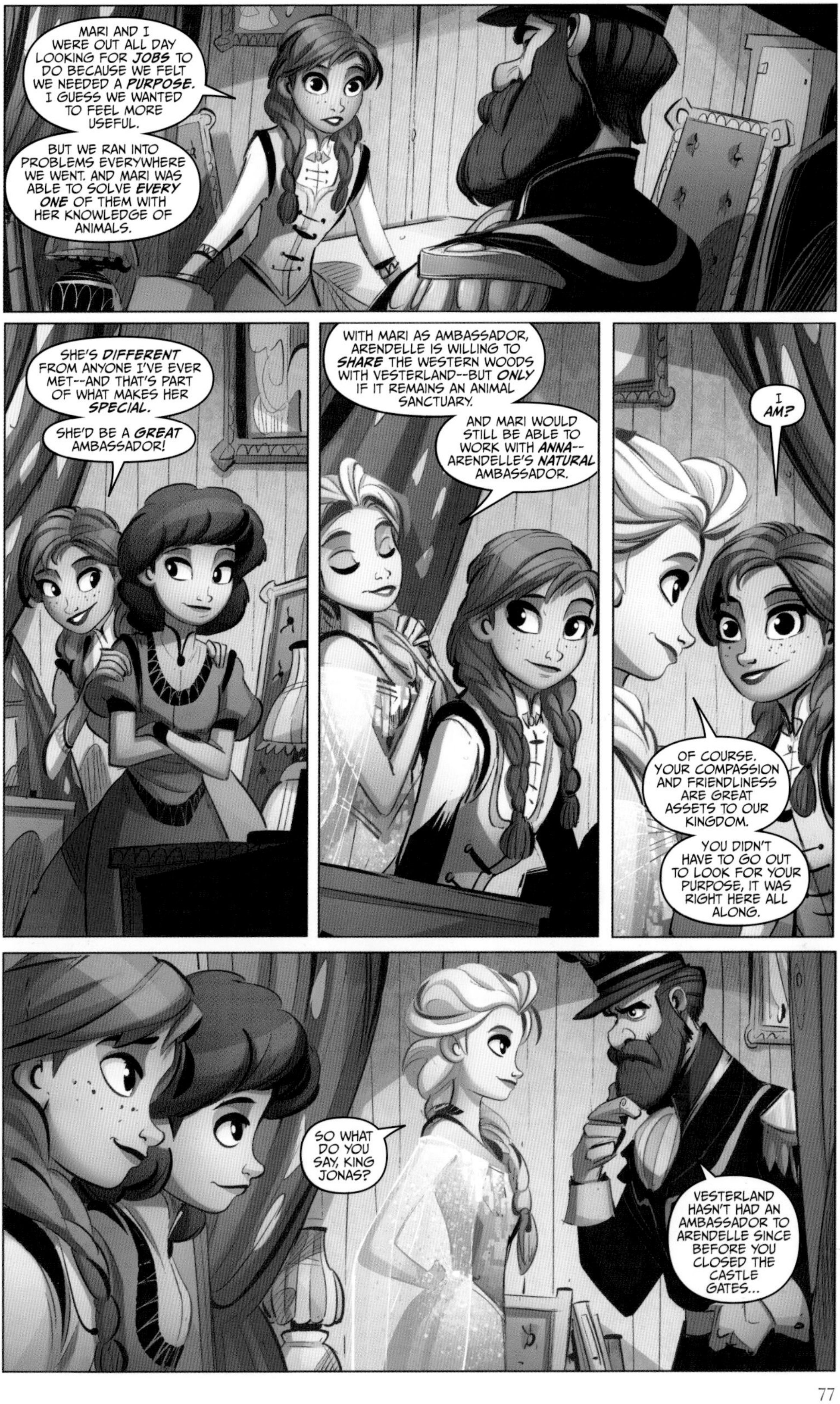
MARI AND I WERE OUT ALL DAY LOOKING FOR JOBS TO DO BECAUSE WE FELT WE NEEDED A PURPOSE. I GUESS WE WANTED TO FEEL MORE USEFUL.
BUT WE RAN INTO PROBLEMS EVERYWHERE WE WENT. AND MARI WAS ABLE TO SOLVE EVERY ONE OF THEM WITH HER KNOWLEDGE OF ANIMALS.
SHE'S DIFFERENT FROM ANYONE I'VE EVER MET--AND THAT'S PART OF WHAT MAKES HER SPECIAL.
SHE'D BE A GREAT AMBASSADOR!
WITH MARI AS AMBASSADOR, ARENDELLE IS WILLING TO SHARE THE WESTERN WOODS WITH VESTERLAND--BUT ONLY IF IT REMAINS AN ANIMAL SANCTUARY.
AND MARI WOULD STILL BE ABLE TO WORK WITH ANNA-- ARENDELLE'S NATURAL AMBASSADOR.
I AM?
OF COURSE. YOUR COMPASSION AND FRIENDLINESS ARE GREAT ASSETS TO OUR KINGDOM.
YOU DIDN'T HAVE TO LOOK FOR GO OUT TO LOOK FOR YOUR PURPOSE, IT WAS RIGHT HERE ALL ALONG.
SO WHAT DO YOU SAY, KING JONAS?
VESTERLAND HASN'T HAD AN AMBASSADOR TO ARENDELLE SINCE BEFORE YOU CLOSED THE CASTLE GATES...

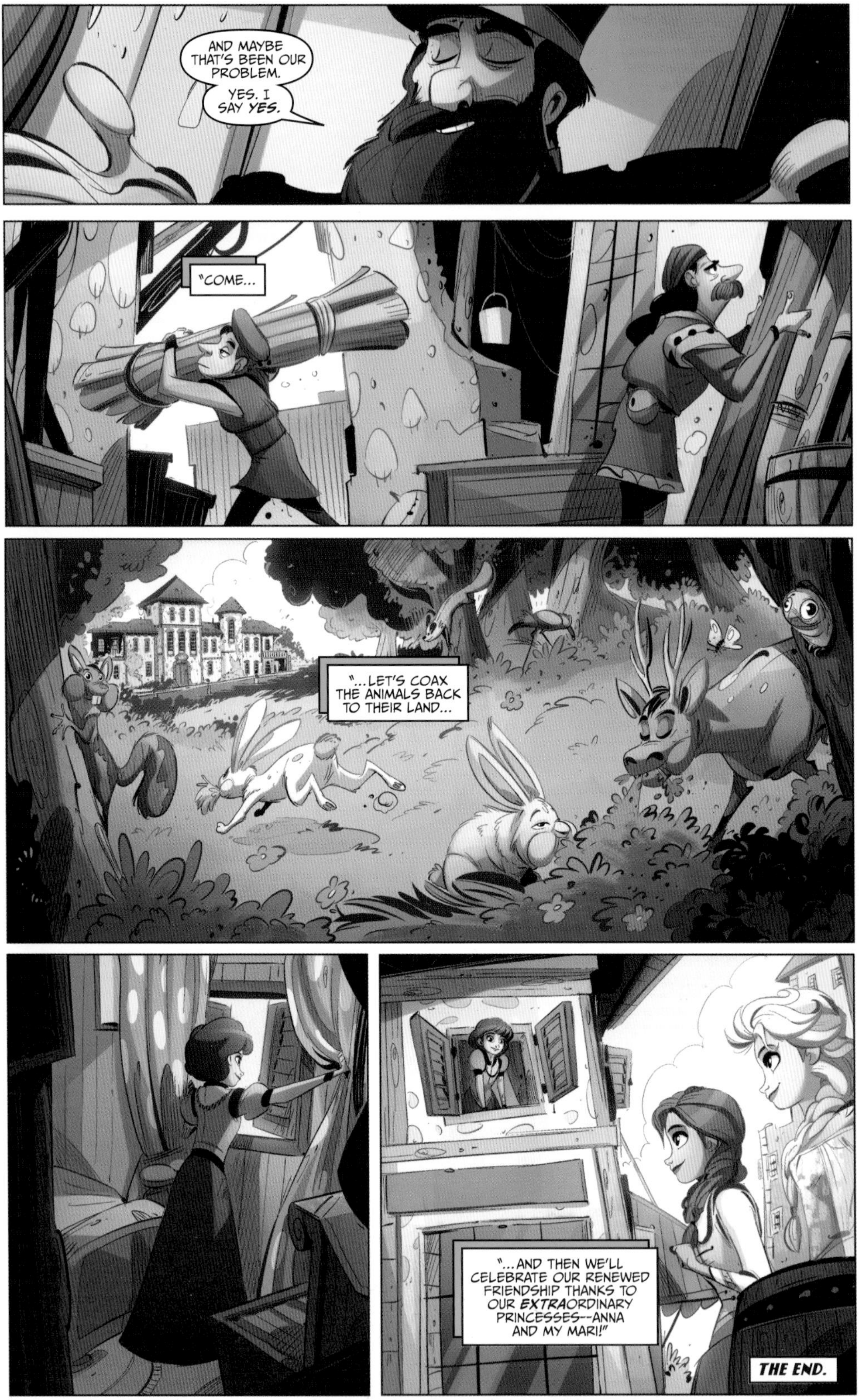
AND MAYBE THAT'S BEEN OUR PROBLEM.
YES. I SAY *YES*.
"COME...
"...LET'S COAX THE ANIMALS BACK TO THEIR LAND...
"...AND THEN WE'LL CELEBRATE OUR RENEWED FRIENDSHIP THANKS TO OUR *EXTRA*ORDINARY PRINCESSES--ANNA AND MY MARI!"
THE END.

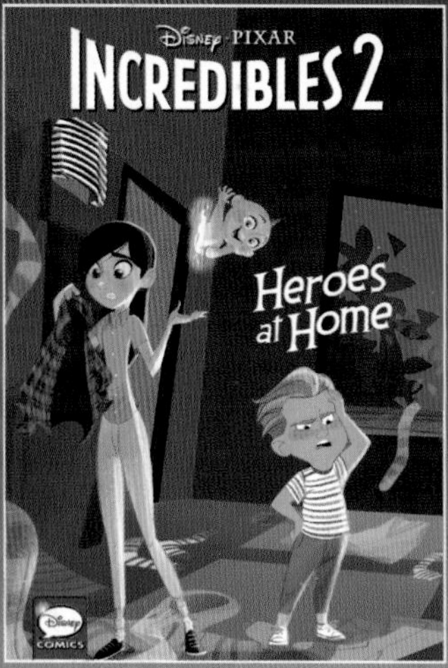
Disney·PIXAR
INCREDIBLES 2
Heroes at Home
Disney COMICS

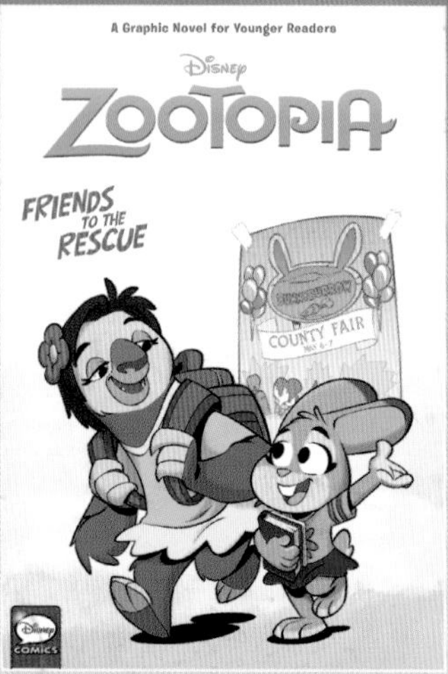
A Graphic Novel for Younger Readers
Disney
ZOOTOPIA
FRIENDS TO THE RESCUE
COUNTY FAIR
Disney COMICS

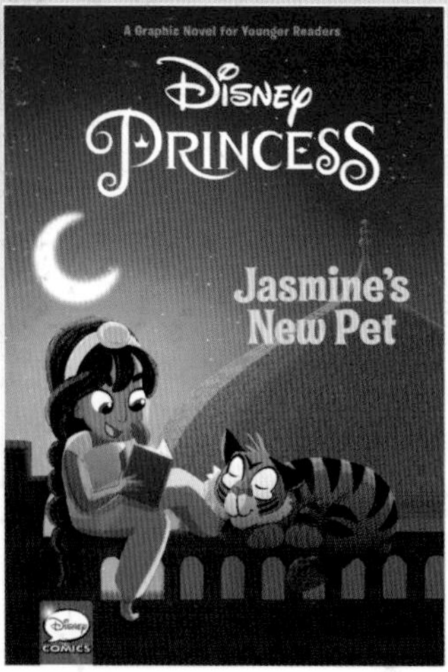
A Graphic Novel for Younger Readers
Disney
PRINCESS
Jasmine's New Pet
Disney COMICS

LOOKING FOR BOOKS FOR YOUNGER READERS?

$7.99 each!

EACH VOLUME INCLUDES A SECTION OF FUN ACTIVITIES!

DISNEY•PIXAR INCREDIBLES 2: HEROES AT HOME

Violet and Dash are part of a Super family, and they are trying to help out at home. Can they pick up groceries and secretly stop some bad guys? And then can they clean up the house while Jack-Jack is "sleeping"?

ISBN 978-1-50670-943-7 | $7.99

DISNEY ZOOTOPIA: FRIENDS TO THE RESCUE

Young Judy Hopps proves she's a brave little bunny when she helps a classmate. And can a quick-thinking young Nick Wilde liven up a birthday party? Friends save the day in these tales of Zootopia!

ISBN 978-1-50671-054-9 | $7.99

DISNEY PRINCESS: JASMINE'S NEW PET

Jasmine has a new pet tiger, Rajah, but he's not quite ready for palace life. Will she be able to train the young cub before the Sultan finds him another home?

ISBN 978-1-50671-052-5 | $7.99

AVAILABLE AT YOUR LOCAL COMICS SHOP OR BOOKSTORE! TO FIND A COMICS SHOP IN YOUR AREA, VISIT COMICSHOPLOCATOR.COM

For more information or to order direct: On the web: DarkHorse.com | Email: mailorder@darkhorse.com
Phone: 1-800-862-0052 Mon.–Fri. 9 AM to 5 PM Pacific Time